THE SMART ONE

THE SMART ONE

DREW YANNO

A PELLEGRINO PRESS Imprint
Copyright © 2016 by Drew Yanno
ISBN-13: 9780692761724
ISBN-10: 0692761721

To Suzanne

WHICH PATH

I GLANCED UP at the cinder-block wall where the ancient analog clock told me that I only had five minutes left to decide my fate. It was the kind of time piece one might have found in a public elementary or high school when I was growing up, and I smiled at how fitting that was, considering what I'd just been told minutes before. I doubt that those men had made the connection or even noticed, but if they had, then I underestimated them even more than I thought.

On the simple wooden table in front of me sat the vial containing the clear liquid; next to it was a new syringe, just out of its wrapper. I guess they had assumed that I knew how to use it. If so, they had assumed correctly. After all, anyone who's ever seen a movie or television show knows how to draw liquid from a vial into a syringe. I most certainly did. I even knew that I had to flick the side of the plastic with my fingernail a few times to make sure that there were no air bubbles trapped in there. In my mother's dying days, I was assigned the task of administering blood thinner to her every morning via an injection into a fold of skin on her stomach. When her doctor instructed me how to do it, he warned that an injected air bubble could kill her instantly. He was quite serious about it. I suppose that was a third option for me to consider, albeit not one that they offered. Perhaps they weren't aware of it. I hoped not anyway.

As it turned out, I didn't need the full ten minutes they had allotted for me to decide. In fact, I'd made up my mind before they even walked out the door, as soon as they had informed me of what was in that vial. I'm guessing that they thought that I'd spend the time weighing the pros and cons of each of the two paths they'd laid out, only to settle on the one they perceived as being in both our best interests. After all, they'd shown me quite clearly what would come my way if I didn't do as they suggested. Ultimately, it didn't matter. I simply made the decision and prepared to go forward with the rest of my life, however long or short that turned out to be.

Once that was done, I used the remainder of the time to reflect back on the entirety of that life and, in particular, the three weeks leading up to me sitting in that room. When the second hand on the clock finally reached the appointed time with an audible click, I pocketed the now-empty vial and sat back, putting a neutral expression on my face. Seconds later, there came another click, this one louder, signaling the lock turning on the heavy metal door. As it did, I placed the equally empty syringe, save a drop or two, back on the table to let them know what I had decided.

Before I tell you what that was and how I arrived at the choice, allow me to take you back to when I was living what I thought was a relatively normal life and had never heard of what was in that vial or how it might be connected to me.

Ironically, I keep mentioning life when, in fact, it was a death that started the ball rolling...

THREE WEEKS EARLIER

CHAPTER 1

THE MESSAGE

Growing up in my family, I was always referred to as the "smart" one. Not intelligent. Not learned. "Smart." Right up until my high school education ended, what that meant, at least to me, was that I was very good at taking exams and completing homework assignments. My talents showed up best on standardized tests, those educational hurdles that most students fear and often underperform on. Not me. I got 800s on my SATs, including all three of the achievement tests, without even breaking a sweat. Combined with finishing first in my class, that was enough to get me admitted to three of the Ivies and, based upon my family's very modest means, I was offered a full academic scholarship to each. I chose the one based in southern Connecticut, an institution full of high achievers like I was then. Much to my surprise, I soon came to discover that I was head and shoulders above even the most elite students there, and I managed to complete my undergraduate degree in just three years. Then, with the assistance of a famous and well-regarded professor who had taken quite a shine to me, I was admitted to a graduate program there and earned my PhD. in even less time.

Armed with a strong endorsement from that same teacher, my dissertation was quickly published and transformed into a best-selling non-fiction book that changed the way many people thought about and approached certain aspects of their day-to-day personal and business lives. Basically, a new way of thinking and problem solving. Part psychology, part sociology. Neuroscience. A witch's brew that included various forms of radical risk assessment, event probability analysis and advanced level contingency planning. I won't bore you with all the details, and trust me you would be bored, unless you went to someplace like Stanford or MIT and studied that kind of thing. Fresh off of that success, I was pursued by all of those same Ivies to become a member of their faculty at the tender age of twenty-seven. Instead, I chose a position at a smaller school that had a solid but lesser academic reputation, in part because I liked the downtown area in that particular college town.

Two more books followed, along with numerous high-paying consulting jobs and some rather lucrative research grants. Fortunately for me, my area of study was just academic enough to attract those endowments, while at the same time commercial enough in its application to earn the attention of many in the business world. In the ensuing years, I made lots of money. I also got married. And divorced not long after. Unfortunately, I didn't use my own theories and analysis when it came to selecting a wife, relying instead on the romantic notion of true love. I thus proceeded to lose half of that money in the bargain. I then went on to make and spend even more dollars, while still managing somehow to avoid further commitment. All while remaining in the same college town.

I left that professorship almost three years ago. I didn't make the decision as much as it was made for me. That's not to suggest that I was fired or forced out. In the end, I simply found that I didn't want to teach anymore and resigned my post. To be completely candid, in my last two years on the faculty, I began to take my duties rather lightly. I stopped preparing for lectures, and I sometimes lost my train of thought when speaking to students. I failed to correct exams on time or to even update them to reflect changes in my field, and instead relied on my teaching assistant to do both. At one point I remember looking at one of those exams he came up with and wondering whether I could earn a passing grade on it.

With royalties still coming in from my books, along with the growth of the shares of stock that I had received as compensation from many of those consulting jobs, I was able to "retire" comfortably, although I never used that word when people asked what I was going to do after announcing that I was leaving. Instead, I paid cash for a lovely little brick building on the main street of that same downtown and turned it into my office, fully intending to do more research and write again. I was still regarded as an important voice in my field, so no one questioned why I left the university at an age when most professors are still considered to be in their prime. I even continued to employ the ever-faithful Gloria, the secretary who came to work for me in the same capacity in my first year as a professor at the college.

Instead of questioning my early departure, everyone just assumed that I was working on something new and even more advanced than anything I had done previously, the secrecy only making the move that much more intriguing to friends and colleagues. Of course, I did nothing to dissuade that line of thinking and continued to show up at my office every day as if what they believed was actually true.

What no one knew was that I wasn't working at all. Not a lick. Instead, I read newspapers and magazines and followed my favorite sports teams to the point of near obsession. Gloria never once questioned what I was doing behind my closed door every day, nor did she ever wonder where I went for hours at a time during many of those so-called workdays. She has claimed not to understand a word of what is in those books I wrote, so I'm guessing that she didn't ask simply because she didn't want to receive a response that was beyond her ability to comprehend. It was like that with some people. They were almost afraid to ask me anything for fear that I would then try to explain something that they had no chance of understanding.

As I said, I'm still considered an important voice in my field, and so I am sometimes invited to conferences where I give talks culled from the pages of those books. It's easy money and even easier work. Everyone seems pretty pleased by the effort. Everyone except me, that is. And so, feeling that I needed a push to do something, last year I managed to convince my publisher to pay me an advance on a new book, providing them with only the barest of proposals. Because of my insistence on not being more specific, the advance wasn't nearly as large as those I had received from my other books, but together with what I've amassed over the years, it's plenty to sustain both me and the office for the foreseeable future. What the publisher didn't know is that I had no more of an idea of what I was going to write than they did. It wasn't that I was bored. It wasn't that I was tired of what I was doing and wanted a change. It was worse than that. I was afraid. Afraid that I could no longer do it. Afraid that I had hit a wall.

That's how life was for me until that Thursday in late March when I returned from a two-hour lunch with an older colleague who had formally retired from the university and who liked watching college basketball as much as I did. It was the first day of the first round of the NCAA men's tournament, a day when sixteen games are played in about twelve hours at various arenas around the country. (For the record, I don't consider the so-called "play-in games" to be the "first" round and still stick to the old-school nomenclature.) Four television networks cover every one of those games, and it's like a holiday for the dedicated fans of the sport like me. That day, we watched the first of those games in a restaurant we frequently patronized, and I bade him farewell and hurried back to my office so that I could get comfortable in my leather chair and turn on my large flat screen TV in time for the tip off for the next game. As fate would have it, I never got the chance.

I knew something was amiss as soon as I walked in the door and saw Gloria's face. She wore a somber expression, not that she's ever bubbly or ebullient. It's funny how knowing someone so well can cause such a reaction without a word spoken. I stood stock still with the door open behind me. Rather than wait for me to inquire, she simply handed me a pink phone message slip and said, "I'm sorry."

I assumed right away that it must have something to do with my brother, my closest living blood relative. I was both relieved and confused when I saw that the name on the message slip wasn't his. In fact, for an instant, I thought it had to belong to a stranger and must be some sort of mistake. That was before I realized that it was only the first name that was unfamiliar to me. I knew the last. The note from Gloria in the message line under the caller's name read: "Dr. Condon - Funeral Saturday at 10 am."

When I finished reading it, I looked up and asked her what it was all about. That's when she told me that she was sorry once more.

"He died yesterday," she informed me. "She said she thought you would want to be there."

For the second time in a matter of seconds, I was utterly confused. "She?"

"Yes," she told me. "His wife. That's her name isn't it?"

In truth, I didn't know. I seemed to recall that he was married when I knew him. I didn't remember any children. "You must have been close," Gloria said. "Was he a relative?"

I shook my head. "No," I told her, still not quite sure what was going on. "He was my doctor. Growing up. I haven't seen him in at least thirty years."

Now she was the one looking confused. "Oh," was all she said.

"Are you sure that's what she said?" I asked. "That I would want to be there?"

She nodded. "She was pretty clear about it. You mean you don't?"

I wasn't quite sure how to respond to that. In point of fact, I didn't. Not that I didn't like or respect Doctor Condon. He was always nice to me. Like in that Norman Rockwell painting, he was the very picture of the friendly family doctor. But it wasn't like we spent holidays together. I don't think he ever set foot in our house other than for a purely professional reason. I know I was never inside his and, as I said, I didn't even know his wife's name. It was just plain weird. I looked down at the message slip again.

"There's no phone number on here," I said. "Didn't she give you one?"

She shook her head. "I asked. But she said there was no need for you to call her back and that she would see you at the church. She said her husband left very specific instructions to have you notified when he died."

That did it. I couldn't think of a single reason why my former family doctor would want me to be notified when he left this earth. It almost seemed like a practical joke, except that it wasn't funny, nor could I imagine why someone would make light of such a thing.

"I looked at your schedule and you're free for the next three days," Gloria said.

We both knew what a farce that was. I was almost always "free for the next three days." Why she even bothered to look, if she actually did, was a puzzle to me.

"Well, it doesn't matter," I told her. "I'm not going."

She looked surprised and, if I read it correctly, disappointed.

"It has to be some sort of mistake," I explained. "We weren't close. I haven't seen him since I was eighteen years old. Maybe she confused me with my father, although I can't imagine why she would think that her husband would want him to be there either. Which wouldn't matter since my father died ten years ago. And she would had to have known that, too, if she still lives there."

Gloria nodded as if that might explain everything when, in fact, it did no such thing.

"Did she say what he died of?" I asked.

She said she didn't mention it.

"I'm only asking because he might have had dementia or something," I said. "That's about the only thing that would explain this." I held up the message slip.

"So you're not going?" she asked, as if confirming what I said before.

"No," I told her. "Maybe you could call a florist and send some flowers. If you Google the town I'm sure you can track down a flower shop there. They'll know where the funeral is being held."

I didn't bother to tell her the name of the town. She knew. Anyone who knew anything about me knew where I came from. It was a big part of my biography, everyone being so impressed that I could come from such a small, nondescript community with only a public high school education and change the way folks thought about things in a field dominated by people whose backgrounds provided them with considerably more in the way of advantages.

That was the extent of our conversation and I was prepared to write off the whole thing as one of those inexplicable occurrences that we all experience from time to time. Rather than risk getting into more of a discussion with Gloria about it, I left for the day and went home to catch the rest of the basketball games, which I watched straight through until after midnight, when I went to bed without giving the matter another thought.

Since I'm not accustomed to staying up so late, I allowed myself to sleep in the next morning and arrived at the office at about ten thirty, at which point Gloria greeted me with the same expression she had worn nearly twenty-four hours before. To complete the sense of déjà vu, she held out another pink message slip.

"She called again?" I asked.

She nodded. "First thing. The phone was ringing as I unlocked the door."

I plucked the message from her hand. This time it read: "You have to come. It's urgent. I'll explain when you get here."

I looked up from the message. Gloria seemed to be waiting for some further explanation from me. "This is crazy," I said. "Did she sound nuts?"

She shook her head. "As sane as you or me. And quite insistent."

"Why would she think I wasn't coming?" I asked. "You didn't say anything to her did you?"

Her face gave her away. "She asked me first if you got the message yesterday. She wanted to make sure. I told her you couldn't make it and that we were sending flowers instead."

I don't know why, but I felt a sharp pang of guilt just then. "And that's when she said I had to go?"

"She didn't say anything at all at first," Gloria said. "Then she told me it probably wasn't a good idea to talk anymore about it over the phone. That's when she told me that it was very important that she see you."

I couldn't quite grasp what was going on or why, but something in the back of my mind was telling me I should listen. "I don't suppose she gave you a number for me to call," I said.

"That was the other thing," she said. "I think she was calling from a phone booth."

It took me a second to process that. "A phone booth?" I asked. "In this day and age?"

She nodded. "I could hear the sound of traffic in the background. I thought at first it must be her cell phone. But then a recorded voice came on the line asking her to put in more money. Not much doubt there."

I didn't know what else to say, so I told her thanks and went into my office and closed the door. Then I turned on my laptop and went on-line where I searched and quickly found the doctor's obituary on the town newspaper's web site. It was rather brief and said that he died at the age of eighty-one after a long struggle with cancer. It didn't specify what kind. The write-up confirmed my memory that there were no children and that only his wife survived him. There was but one paragraph about his long years in family practice. Nothing about the article was noteworthy or informative. For a brief moment I thought of how sad it was that an entire life was lived for eighty-one years in service to others and all that it earned was a few sentences in his obituary. I knew mine would be much more extensive, not that longer meant that I had contributed more to the world than he did. In fact, despite the disparity in our respective levels of success, I was quite sure that it didn't.

Using one of those find-a-person web sites, I then looked up the family's phone number. It was surprisingly easy to find, and I dialed it without giving much thought to what I would say when the widow answered. I guess I just wanted to hear for myself if she sounded unbalanced. There was no answer after four rings, and I chose to hang up before the machine picked up. I didn't want to leave a message. Gloria's assumption about the previous call sounding as if it came from a pay phone probably had something to do with it, I suppose, although I didn't really explore why that was.

When I came out of my office an hour later to go to lunch, Gloria looked up at me expectantly. How she knew that I had changed my mind, I'll never know.

"Do you want me to try to book a flight?" she asked.

"No," I told her. "I'm going to drive."

She looked at me skeptically and with good reason. I have a spotty driving record at best. Three relatively minor accidents in the past three years, but only that few because I've chosen not to get into my car very often. I walk to the office from my nearby condominium, and I fly or take trains on those occasions when I have to leave town. Truth is, I've never been a very good driver and have only gotten worse since "retiring." I think I become too easily distracted behind the wheel, something I've attributed to my no longer working on a daily basis and struggling with trying to come up with a topic to write about for that book.

"Are you leaving now?" she asked.

I shook my head. "First thing in the morning," I told her.

Again she looked skeptical.

"It's only a four hour drive," I said, defensively. "I'll wake up early and be on the road by five."

For whatever reason, she chose not to elevate it to the level of a debate. Instead, she offered graciously to call me at four thirty the next morning to make sure that I'd be up and out the door on time. I thanked her and then went off to grab lunch and watch the second day of the first round of the basketball tournament.

I didn't tell her I would be up at least until midnight watching the full slate of games, meaning that I'd be lucky to get about four hours of sleep. I also didn't tell her that the reason I chose to leave as late as possible was that I wanted to put off seeing the doctor's widow for as long as I could. My motivation for going there in the first place was simple: I was curious and wanted to find out what the hell it was all about. Plus, I hadn't been back to my hometown in almost ten years, and a funeral for my family doctor seemed about as good a reason as any.

CHAPTER 2

THE FUNERAL

SURPRISINGLY, I WAS awake before Gloria's call, and I was on the road with a large cup of coffee resting between my thighs at five minutes before five. Thankfully, the majority of the drive was on the interstate, and I was able to make the journey in just over four hours, even with a stop to empty my bladder and swallow a couple of Tylenols. I listened to some national sports talk radio program that allowed me to rehash the games of the previous day and consider the ones to be played later on, beginning at noon. Rather than a distraction, the talk kept my mind from wandering, and I managed to avoid crashing into anything. It was my plan to attend the funeral, see what the widow had to say, if anything, and then check into a hotel somewhere in the first town I came to on the ride back, where I would order a generous amount of takeout food and watch all of the remaining games before driving back the next morning. It didn't exactly work out according to plan.

I got to the church a good twenty minutes before the funeral mass started and took a seat in the back. There were only about thirty people in the cool cavernous space, but by taking a spot in one of the last pews I avoided having to make contact with any of the others in attendance. A brief look around told me that not much had changed about the church since I was a boy. Same stained glass windows. Same pews. Same smell that was an unnatural combination of furniture polish and incense. The only difference was the sound system up at the altar, causing me to wonder if the priests of my youth had to shout or if we just didn't bother to listen when we sat in the back.

When the casket finally came in, ushered by six bearers who all looked to be employees of the funeral parlor, it was trailed by an older woman I assumed to be the widow. I couldn't recall if I had ever seen her before, which would be surprising given the size of the community. She didn't look in my direction as she passed by. There were no other apparent family members with her, and she took a seat by herself up in the very first pew.

I stayed for the entire mass, going along with all of the sitting, standing and kneeling that I had drilled into my brain as a child. I couldn't remember the last time I had attended a Catholic service, but the routine was as ingrained in my memory as throwing a football or swinging a bat. When it came time for communion, I remained seated. There was only so far I was willing to go. Part of me simply wanted to make sure that she knew I had come, if only to satisfy whatever perceived need she or her husband might have had, and I was certain that she would see me when they brought the casket back out. Truthfully, I was hoping to avoid talking to her at all, for fear that she might turn out to be as crazy as I suspected when Gloria first told me about her call.

In the end, it was me who was anxious to talk to her. When the bearers led the coffin out of the church after the mass ended, the widow looked up at me for just the briefest of moments and her expression informed me immediately that she was of sound mind. I'm not sure what it was that I read in her face, but whatever it was, I was certain that she was not unbalanced. I knew then I had to stick around and find out what was going on, so I joined the small group of cars that headed from the church out to the graveyard at the far eastern end of town.

The ceremony there was brief, and those who came to pay their final respects formed a short line to extend their condolences to the widow. Although I didn't recognize any of them, one or two seemed to look at me as if they had some idea of who I might be. I'm guessing that my picture has probably appeared in the local newspaper a number of times over the years, what with my notoriety. However, no one came up to greet me, and I stayed far away from them and waited to join the line until I was certain that no one else would be coming up after me. By then, the only people remaining in the area of the gravesite were the workers from the cemetery waiting to cover the casket after everyone left, and they weren't close enough to hear a conversation. When the last person in front of me finished speaking to the widow, I approached her and was struck with how beautiful she looked even at her advanced age.

I started to introduce myself, but she cut me off.

"I know who you are," she said in a low voice. "Thank you for coming. But we shouldn't talk here. Please come to my house in an hour. I should be back home by then."

If I was confused before, it was nothing compared to what I felt at that moment, and so I simply nodded and returned to my car and headed back into town. I briefly considered just leaving and putting all the mystery behind me, but there was something in her voice that told me it was important that we speak. With some time to kill, I thought about doing what most people probably do when returning to their hometown after a long absence. That is, looking up an old friend or acquaintance. However, when I considered the possibilities, I realized that there wasn't anyone I was particularly anxious to see. Not because I never had any friends growing up, but because I had done such a poor job of keeping in touch with them that I was certain that anyone I contacted would be stunned to hear from me. Besides, I would have to explain my reason for being there and I didn't even understand that myself. So instead, I found a tavern down on Main Street, one that wasn't there when I grew up, and I ate some lunch and watched the first ten minutes of the first of the afternoon slate of tournament games. When an hour had passed, I paid the check and got back in the car and headed for her house.

Looking back, I never even gave much thought to asking where that house was. I guess I simply assumed that she and the good doctor still lived where they did when I was growing up. He had his office in the rear back then, in what was probably a stable a hundred years before that, and I had been there often enough to recall where it was located. That's how it is in my old hometown. People stay in their houses. When they get to retirement age, they don't "downsize." First of all, there isn't anywhere to downsize to, except for the assisted living floor of the local hospital, and that's a last resort. Literally. Retirement communities with spacious, one level apartments and resident health clubs haven't found a market there.

Nowhere in town takes more than five minutes to get to, so I was parked in front of her large Victorian home before I even had time to start digesting my cheeseburger. I looked around after I got out, but no one was on the street. Being late March in the northeast, it was still quite cold, and I buttoned my coat reflexively as I walked up to the front door and knocked. It opened immediately, as if the widow had been watching out the window for me. She gave me a nervous smile, told me to come in, and quickly shut the door behind her. I noticed that she had already changed out of her black mourning clothes and wore a smart pink sweater and grey wool skirt. It almost appeared as if she might be going somewhere. I didn't have time to inquire.

Instead, she told me to follow her, which I did, ending up in what she described as her husband's "study." Long before the "home office," people like the good doctor had a study, and this one was the real deal. Carved wood walls. Shutters. Books everywhere, along with a mammoth mahogany desk. She offered me the worn but comfortable brown leather chair in front of it, while she went behind and fiddled with some keys and the top drawer. After she managed to get it open, she pulled out a simple manila envelope, with the flap unclasped, allowing me to see several sheets of paper inside. Then she laid the whole thing atop the ancient green blotter on the desk.

"I found this in Wallace's safety deposit box down at the bank the morning after he died," she told me. "One of the last things he told me before the morphine put him under for good was about the box and where I could find the key. I had no idea we even had one."

I didn't have a response to that, so I just nodded and waited for her to go on. She pulled out the top sheet and handed it to me. Written at the top were the words: "Instructions After I'm Gone." In addition to the usual matters such as which funeral home he preferred and his favorite charities for those wishing to contribute a memorial, there was a simple sentence at the bottom. It said to contact me and to give me the "attached."

I looked up after reading that and she was already holding out the next page. Which was a list. Of names. A dozen of them. I read it over and looked back at the widow.

"I'm sorry Mrs. Condon, but I'm confused. I have no idea what any of this means. Perhaps you can explain."

She shook her head solemnly. "I'm afraid I don't know any more than you do."

I let that sink in before looking at the list again. "I don't recognize any of the names on here," I said. "And I don't know why your husband would want you to contact me when he passed."

She stared at me with what I can only describe as exasperation. I thought long about what I was going to say next, but ultimately decided that it needed to be said.

"Did your husband suffer any cognitive issues in the last year or so of his life?"

Part of me feared that she would be offended at the suggestion, so I was surprised when she smiled.

"He was as sharp as ever right up until the end," she said.

I nodded and looked back at the envelope on the desk. The edge of one more piece of paper was peeking out. "What does that one say?" I asked, nodding at it.

She picked up the envelope and pulled out the last sheet of paper and handed it to me. There was a simple note addressed to me. It stated simply: "Take all of these with you and look into it. You'll know what to do after you discover what those people on that list have in common. Under no circumstances should you tell anyone where you got this, especially the police. My wife has no knowledge of this and is not connected with it in any way. It is my dying wish that it remain that way."

I looked up to find her staring at me. "You obviously read these before you gave them to me," I said. She nodded. I paused to give it some thought before proceeding. "Did you ever know your husband to be involved in something illegal?" I asked.

She laughed. It was a bitter one, but a laugh nonetheless. "Hardly," she said.

I nodded and put all three sheets back in the envelope and clasped it. "Well," I said, "I have no idea what any of this means, but I'll be glad to take these with me and honor your husband's wishes. Although why he chose me to do this is still unclear."

"I wondered the same thing myself," she said. "But when I gave it some thought, it seemed rather obvious."

"And how is that?" I asked.

She blushed and lowered her eyes. "You're quite famous around here. Probably our most distinguished former resident."

For whatever reason, I hadn't considered that. Given what I have done professionally, it wasn't hard to imagine that the doctor might presume that I could solve his riddle. It certainly made sense, or at least I thought it might to him or anyone else in my hometown.

"And you believe he thought that I'd be able to find out what he wanted me to learn about this without him having to write it out explicitly, is that it?"

"Yes, that's exactly what I think," she said. "If he wrote it out, then I would also know. And he was quite clear in stating his wish that I not have that knowledge."

What she laid out sounded like a rather clever plan on the doctor's part, except that he could have simply mailed me the list and his instructions anytime before he died. Of course, then I would have called and bombarded him with questions. Being assigned the task only upon his death, and by his widow no less, made it all the more difficult to turn down. Nevertheless, what I really thought was that her husband had probably declined mentally, but not so much as to warrant any concern or acknowledgement from his wife. Or maybe she was just protecting him, although I didn't think that was very likely.

"I'm not as confident as your husband was about my ability to unravel this," I told her. "But I'll check on these names when I get home and let you know if I discover anything."

"Please don't," she said, more forcefully than probably either of us expected.

18

"Right," I told her, looking down at her husband's admonition to me right there in my hand. "Not a problem." And it wasn't. At the time, I was pretty certain that a Google search would yield nothing of note about those names. There wasn't a single surname matching any from the people I had known when I was younger and living in that town, meaning that there was little likelihood of a connection there. The doctor may have known those people on the list at various points in his life. Or maybe he had read about them somewhere. Or maybe he just made them all up. At the time, it really didn't matter to me. As soon as I ran the search on each, I planned to shred the pages and put it all behind me. After all, the doctor was dead, and the widow had made it clear that she had no further interest in the matter. Who would care or even know if I did nothing more than that?

I got up then and tucked the envelope under my arm. "I guess I'll get going," I told her. She didn't object. In fact, she didn't say a word. Instead, she led me through the house to the front where I opened the door and turned back to her.

"Your husband was a fine man," I told her. "And a good doctor. I always liked him."

"So did I," she said, without a hint of humor. And that was it. I walked out and got in my car and headed out of town in the direction of the interstate.

CHAPTER 3

MEN IN SUITS

I HAD JUST about reached the ramp that would take me onto the highway when my cell phone rang and I hit the "talk" button. It was the widow. Again.

"You need to come back," she said. "I've found something else." There was urgency to her voice that wasn't there when we spoke just a few minutes earlier, causing me to pull over to the side of the road.

"What is it?" I asked.

She paused for just a beat. "I'd rather not say over the phone," she told me. "You need to see for yourself."

"With all due respect, Mrs. Condon, I think I have--"

The line went dead before I could finish, so I hit "call back." The phone rang four times and then went to voicemail. Only it wasn't her on the recording. It was her husband, which was jarring. I hadn't heard the man's voice in almost thirty years, and to do so right after attending his funeral seemed slightly surreal. Of course, she wouldn't have thought of changing it yet. I imagined that she wasn't picking up because she thought that avoiding me would make it more likely that I'd go along with her request. If so, she was right. I couldn't help but think that she had just lost her husband who had left her with some strange kind of task, after most likely suffering the beginning stages of dementia. As much as I didn't want to go back, I felt no small degree of sympathy for her and decided that I would go see what she had to show me. Then I'd tell her that I really needed to get back home to attend to my own affairs, and I would turn off my phone as soon as I left to avoid any further manipulation. It was only as I pulled onto her street that I wondered how she got my cell phone number.

I parked in the same space as I did earlier. Like then, the street was empty. I walked onto the porch and knocked on the door, just as I did before. However, unlike the last time, it didn't open immediately. I waited there for about twenty seconds more and then knocked again, only louder this time. Once more, I waited and no one came, so I walked down the wrap-around porch to where the living room window was and shaded my eyes to look in. The house appeared to be empty. I tapped on the window, hoping that maybe a different sound would cause her to come to the front. When it didn't, I took out my phone and dialed her number.

I could hear it ring inside. I could also see the old-fashioned wall phone hanging in the kitchen near the doorway to the living room. No one approached it. I let it ring until the recording came on again and then I hung up. My heart started beating a little faster as the thought entered my mind that something might not be right. I went back and tried the door, and I found it locked. When I lived in that town, no one locked their doors when they were home. Most never locked them at all, even when they were away on vacation. Crime was never much of an issue back then, and I wondered if things might have changed since I left.

I stepped off the porch and hurried up the driveway and around to the small landing at the back. I knocked on the door there and didn't have any more luck in getting a response. I tried the handle then and, to my surprise, the door clicked opened. After taking a few seconds to decide whether to enter, I took a couple of cautious steps inside, leaving the door open behind me. I called out the widow's name. All I heard in response was the loud ticking of the grandfather clock I'd seen when I was in there before. I looked around to get my bearings and then proceeded down the hallway that I thought might lead me to the doctor's study. I was right. From a few feet away, I could see that the door to the room was slightly ajar. I approached it slowly, cringing at the squeaks from the hardwood floor. When I got there, I pushed it all the way open and peered in.

The widow was laying there on the floor, arms splayed out, and her eyes open but lifeless. I took a step toward her to see if there was any chance that she might still be breathing. When I did, I caught sight of two men standing stiffly against the wall to my left, some eight feet away. One was tall and slim and looked to be in his late fifties or early sixties. Older than me anyway. The other was of medium height and weight and considerably younger. No more than thirty. Both wore dark suits. And latex gloves, the kind dentists wear when they don't want to risk an infection. Or criminals when they don't want to leave fingerprints.

The taller one said my name in a soft and calm voice, almost as if we were old friends. I froze there in the doorway.

"If you'll just give us those papers she gave you, we'll let you leave and forget all about this," he said.

Neither he nor the other man made a move toward me. Given the widow's dead body on the floor, I didn't exactly believe him.

"What happened to her?" I asked.

"Looks like a heart attack," the younger one said with a slight smile. "Probably from the grief. You'd be surprised at how often it happens."

The gloves alone revealed the absurdity of that statement, but I chose not to respond.

"That list?" the older one said.

"Sure," I said. For about three seconds, I didn't make a move, and neither did they. Then the younger one took a step toward me and I reacted, backing through the door and pulling it shut as I did. Then I turned and ran through the kitchen. As I did, I heard the sound of them coming out behind me.

I was out the open back door, slamming it shut, and around to the front of the house in no time. I didn't bother looking back until I was at my car and pulled open the door on the driver's side. When I did, there was no one in the driveway. However, as I got in and closed the door, I could see a face in the living room window I had peeked into just moments before. It was the older of the two men. He shook his head as if he were disappointed about something.

I pulled the car out of the parking spot and punched it. As I did, I saw a boy who appeared to be about ten or eleven years old standing astride a bicycle on the sidewalk across the street from the widow's home. We made eye contact for about a second and then I looked away. As I turned the corner at the end of the street, I wondered if someone that young would be capable of memorizing a license plate. By the time I had made it onto the interstate, I had convinced myself that, even if he could, he would have had no reason to log my plate number since he had no way of knowing that the widow was dead when he saw me. There was nothing suspicious about me getting into my car and driving away, even at that speed. He would probably find out about the widow soon enough, but it was unlikely that he'd be able to think back and recall my plate. Under that scenario, no one would, regardless of how old they were.

Nevertheless, I continued to check the rear view mirror all the way back to Connecticut and what I hoped was the relative safety of my condominium.

CHAPTER 4

THOSE THINGS ARE NOT TRUE

I GOT HOME late in the afternoon and tried to watch the rest of the basketball games until they ended at nearly eleven o'clock, but my mind kept going back to the doctor's house and those two men. I double-locked my door, something I never do, and lowered the volume every so often to listen for any sounds out in the hallway. I live in a modern building containing over forty units on six floors. There's a doorman on duty in the lobby twenty-four hours a day, but that doesn't mean that the place is crime-proof. Sneaking in wouldn't be that difficult for professionals, something I assumed those two men to be, but committing a violent crime – murder, for instance – would be considerably more difficult to pull off without being noticed by someone. The insulation between the adjoining walls and floors is meant to muffle noise and works quite well. It's one of the selling points of the place. But a neighbor would probably hear a scream for help and the sounds of a struggle. Plus, there are alarms on all the windows, so that a chair hurled through one would trigger a response from both the building's management company and the local police, giving me at least some sense of security. Still, I knew I couldn't stay inside forever.

Not that I wasn't motivated to. I had enough coffee and food in the refrigerator to make Sunday a tolerable day to hole up while I thought about what to do. With the last of the weekend's basketball games starting at noon and running all the way up to midnight, it wasn't much of a hardship. It was only when I let my mind drift from the games and saw the vision of the widow on the floor of her husband's study that I wondered just how they managed to pull off the killing. I checked the news on-line for the town and the surrounding area and there was no mention of her death. From that I had to assume that her body had been left there and hadn't yet been discovered.

When the games finally ended, I went into my home office to retrieve the list the widow gave me and started my search of the names. I probably should have done it the minute I got home, but frankly I was spooked and wanted to avoid having to deal with it. As I said, I didn't recognize any of the names as being from the town, and I couldn't recall ever hearing of them before. They were just names to me, no different than if the doctor had selected them at random from the phonebook, if they even have phonebooks any more. On the surface, there was nothing about any of them that would lead me to think that they could be mixed up in anything criminal. But given the appearance of those two men and whatever they did to the widow, I was forced to reassess my original take that the good doctor had lost his mind. There had to be something significant about those names for those men to want to get the list back and out of my hands.

The search results on the first name showed him to be a couple of years older than me, and a professional musician. Not a rock star. A real musician. He played first chair violin in the Chicago Symphony for twenty years. He grew up in a small town in Pennsylvania and attended Columbia on a full scholarship. He was married but with no children that I could find, although information about his personal life was light on the details. He was retired from the symphony, and it didn't say what he was doing now or where he might be living.

I paid for one of those on-line "person searches" that promises to deliver address, phone number and criminal records, and the last known residence for him was a suburb of Chicago. He had no criminal past. I read every word of every article written about him and all of the available information that came up in the search and still couldn't figure out how he could possibly be connected to Doctor Condon in upstate New York. Nor could I imagine how he might be of any interest to the two men I had encountered in the good doctor's home. Would anyone have reason to kill someone – an eighty something year old widow no less - over a retired violinist?

I closed out of that search and tried the next name on the list. This was a woman two years younger than me, according to what I found on Google. She was a senior partner in a large New York City law firm, the highest-ranking woman in the firm. Her picture showed her to be moderately attractive, with a professional demeanor, at least as much as that can be judged from a mere photograph. The accompanying bio stated her specialty to be anti-trust law and noted that she was involved in several notable cases over the past twenty years, nearly all of which resulted in verdicts for her clients. She was born in Miami, lived in the Seattle area during her high school years, and attended Antioch and Georgetown Law School. Again, there was nothing in the search results that would even remotely connect her with a doctor practicing family medicine in upstate New York. Given her position and standing in the firm, it was no surprise to learn that she likewise had no known criminal past. There was also nothing to indicate that she played a musical instrument or had even a remote connection to the retired violinist.

I was beginning to think that I should have just given those men the list and trusted that I wouldn't end up like the widow, as foolish as that might have been. After all, what could the doctor have intended by

creating that list? Why all the secrecy? Why not at least give me a hint? His wife seemed to think that my intellect was the reason behind her husband wanting me to investigate it. Flattering as that might seem, I didn't think my intelligence, if that's truly what he was relying on, gave me any special advantage for solving the mystery. True, many people had claimed that I offered a new way of looking at things, a unique approach to problem solving and critical thinking, but I always looked at it as mostly academic and something only academics would care about.

I never thought of the doctor as an academic. I tried to picture the diplomas in his office to see if I could recall where he went to school and if that might have been a connection to either of the first two names. Then I remembered the obituary and returned to that page on the local paper's website and learned that he had attended a small college in the mid-west and state medical school in Buffalo. There was no indication that he had an academic view of the world. It was just another dead end.

I went back to the list and ran a search on two more names before bed. Both were as mystifying as the first two. Except that one was dead. Forty-six when he passed. Cancer. Prior to that he seemed to have lived a full life. I don't know much about the world of finance. I leave that to my own investment advisor who has done an admirable job keeping my savings safe and even on somewhat of a growth curve through all the recent ups and downs of the economy. This fellow on the list had something to do with commodities trading and had relied upon a formula that he devised for both himself and the paid subscribers to his fund. There wasn't anything in any of the stories to suggest that he had acted inappropriately at any time. Certainly nothing to imply that he was on the wrong side of the law.

At the same time, I could envision the two men in suits having an interest in someone who seemed to have a knack for making money. Lots of money apparently. Except that he had died two years before the good doctor did and there didn't appear to be any connection between him and the first two I researched. Perhaps they were all investors. That wouldn't be hard to imagine. Or maybe they were all somehow tied together financially, including the two men in suits. But my gut told me that wasn't it. On paper it might make some sense, but then why would my former family physician have that list? If he were an investor and had some concern for himself and other investors, why wouldn't he just call the SEC or the Justice Department? Why notify me? And why only upon his death?

The fourth name gave me even less reason to think that this had anything to do with investments or money. This person barely showed up in Google. There was nothing to indicate what he did for a living or even if he was still alive. I went to one of those death notice sites to see if maybe he too had passed away, but there was no listing for him. The only results that came up were something about his graduating from a high school in a suburb of Little Rock, Arkansas and winning a scholarship to the local state university. That got my interest. Two of the four I looked at had attended college on a scholarship. That seemed to exceed the statistical norm. I wasn't sure what that norm was exactly, but I was fairly certain from having worked in academia for fifteen years that, while financial aid is given to a fairly high percentage of incoming students, full scholarships are awarded to only a small group of them.

However, given that they lived in different parts of the country and there was nothing to indicate that the doctor knew either of them, I had to believe it was a statistical anomaly. Once again, I went to the paid "people search" site and discovered that this fourth person's last known job was as a bank teller and that he had a felony drug conviction at age eighteen that resulted in a two year prison sentence. Moreover, the university website did not show him as having graduated, so achievement didn't seem to be a connection tying them all together either.

I quit looking after that and decided to turn in for the night, but not before I unlocked the door and checked the hallway outside my condo. As before, it was empty and quiet. I went back inside and locked it once again, using both locks. Then I peered out my bathroom window to the street below and, thankfully, saw nothing to cause me to think that those two men were watching me. Of course, they could be doing so from some other vantage point, but at least they weren't out on there in some dark sedan like in some 1940s noir film. I poured myself a glass of Bushmills and downed it before turning out the lights. I thought I might have trouble sleeping, but I dozed off quickly and slept straight through until seven the next morning.

When I awoke, it took a minute or so for my head to clear and for the situation to permeate my murky thoughts. I immediately went to the window to look for any indication that the men might be out there waiting for me. I did the same with the peephole in my door. Neither the outside nor the hallway showed any sign of anything suspicious, so I showered and dressed and sat down at the computer to go through the rest of the names.

Like the first four, there was nothing about any of them that stood out as providing a possible link between the doctor and the others on the list. For the most part, they all seemed to be living normal lives, that is, except for two others who had also died. I didn't look it up or do the math, but three out of twelve seemed just above the statistical norm, given the ages of the people on the list. One died of cancer, just like the person I read about the night before, although his was of a different variety. The third had perished in an automobile accident in his early twenties. Of the twelve, all but two had attended college. Four of the ten had obtained a graduate degree of some sort. In the case of two of the twelve, they were apparently financially secure from birth. Three seemed to come from humble beginnings, even more humble than my own. The remaining seven appeared to be the product of middle-class homes. None of them shared the same occupation. I wrote down all those thoughts, along with some others I found interesting, even though I was no closer to learning what the doctor had intended for me to find. When I finished, I realized that I had done more work in researching the doctor's list than I had on the book for which I had already been paid. In an odd way, it felt good, almost like I was embarking on a new line of work.

I looked up when I was done and saw that it was just after nine o'clock, and I knew that the ever-reliable Gloria would already be seated at her desk and nursing her first cup of green tea. I had decided the night before that I wasn't going into the office. Not right away at least. So I picked up the phone to call.

"Oh good," she said, when she heard it was me. "I was just about to call you."

Gloria almost never called me outside of work. She had both my home and cell phone numbers, of course, but had only used them on rare occasions. I got the same feeling then as I did when she handed me the telephone message a few days before, and so, with no small amount of trepidation, I asked her why she was about to do so.

She said that "my friends" had just been at the office looking for me. She actually sounded quite cheery in delivering this news, and I couldn't help but picture the two men in suits showing up at my door and making Gloria feel like they were anything but killers.

I took a moment to think about what I wanted to say next and how to do it without alarming her or, worse, causing her to be suspicious of me. After all, no one who I didn't already know had ever shown up at my office unannounced, something I'm sure Gloria was aware of. She knew everyone I knew, and so I had little doubt about who these visitors might be.

"Which friends?" I asked, trying not to give anything away with my tone of voice. Given that it had never happened before, I felt that it would be something she would expect me to say.

"Mister Botticelli and Mister Klee," she said. "From the funeral."

"Ah," I said, trying to sound as neutral as I could. The use of the names of two famous painters was curious and told me that I wasn't dealing with the usual criminal types. It also told me that Gloria had never taken an art history course at the local community college she had attended. "They must have wanted to surprise me. Did you say they're gone now?"

"Yeah," she said. "I told them you didn't have a regular time when you came in and they just said they'd go ahead and grab some breakfast in town."

"Did they tell you where they were going?"

"I told them about the diner," she said. "They told me to tell you to meet them there when you came in."

"How long ago was this?" I asked.

"Just a few minutes," she said. "Maybe ten."

"They didn't say anything else?"

"No," she said. "Why?" The way she asked me that was the first indication that she might be thinking that there was something more going on than I was telling her.

"No reason," I said. "I'll catch up to them."

I was about to say goodbye when she asked me how I knew them. I realized then that I had a decision to make. The fact that they were there, in my town, told me that they weren't going to let me just walk away, while at the same time making it clear that they could not only find me but cause considerable trouble in my sheltered little world. I made up my mind faster than I would have thought had someone posed the hypothetical the night before.

"They're not my friends, Gloria," I said. "You need to listen carefully. If they come back, they are likely to tell you things. Those things are not true. Something happened after the funeral but I'm not going to tell you what it was. That way you can't be put in a position of having to try to keep a secret."

"What are you talking about?" she asked. "You're scaring me." From her tone, it certainly sounded like it.

"Don't ask me anything else," I said. "I'm not going to be coming to the office for awhile. But if they should come back, don't tell them that. Just tell them you haven't heard from me and you have no idea where I am."

There was a pause at the other end. "OK," she said. "But it sounds like you should be calling the police."

Lord knows, I had already considered that option and dismissed it. Twice, in fact. The first time was shortly after I left the widow's house for the second time, trying to get away from the two men I was now attempting to elude once more. As I was driving toward the interstate, I'd thought of turning around and going to the local police and telling them what had just happened. But I didn't. I was too shaken, and I simply wanted to get away from those men and that town as quickly as possible. Needless to say, nothing like that had ever happened to me. I let emotion take over for reason, although I didn't completely cast aside the latter.

In fact, I ran through in my mind what I would have to say if I did go to the police. I would no doubt be questioned thoroughly and have to tell them the whole story, especially the part about the widow's phone calls and the list. Then after telling them I returned to her home after she had given me those papers, I would have to try to explain what happened with those two men who I had never seen before and who would no doubt be long gone, those gloves they'd been wearing allowing them to leave no trace of ever having been there. Assuming they had been successful in making her death appear to be a heart attack or something else that suggested a natural cause, the police would have to wonder why I was telling such a story. There would be no evidence of a crime. There would only be the crazy tale I just told them. And the envelope with the three pieces of paper inside. Worse than that, if the cause of death later turned out to be something more sinister than a heart attack, I might be the only person they could look to in an effort to find an answer to what happened.

The second time I considered calling in the authorities was the night before, after splitting my time searching all the names on the list and watching out the window to see if those men had followed me back to Connecticut. I was certainly spooked enough to want the protection that law enforcement would presumably provide. But my story would only seem crazier being told a day later and in a different state, especially with the widow's death not having yet been discovered. For all those reasons, it was even easier to dismiss the notion the second time.

However, an even more important factor had contributed to my decision: if I brought in the police, I would no doubt have to give them the papers that I had in my possession. And I didn't want to do that. After all, the doctor had specifically instructed me not to tell the police and, for some reason, did not trust them. When I first read that warning, I dismissed it as just another indication of his mental decline. But that all changed after seeing those men in his house.

Clearly, he wanted me to figure it out. On my own. Of course, he also wanted me to keep his wife safe from any possible danger, and I had already failed on that count. But that only made me feel more obligated to pursue it.

So I told Gloria that she was not to call the police, at least not until I asked her to. Thankfully, she didn't question me. Instead, I told her what to do and what to say if I ever called the office again and those two men were there. A sort of secret code, I guess. After assuring her that I wouldn't be away too long and was truly going to be okay, we hung up.

Then I went into my bedroom and packed two bags and went down to the garage to retrieve my car. Before pulling out, I locked my things in the trunk and exited the side door of the garage to take another look at the street, careful to keep myself as hidden as possible. Once I was convinced that there was no one out there waiting for me, I went back for the car and pulled out, heading for the interstate and New York City. And maybe somewhere far beyond.

CHAPTER 5

ARCHER

WHEN I GOT on the highway, I had no idea where I wanted to go or where I might be safe. That is, until I realized that the one thing I had that those men didn't was the list. It seemed reasonable for me to conclude that they couldn't know who was on it or where they lived or they wouldn't be so desperate to get it back from me. Combined with the notion that I should do more than a simple Google search to try to discover the list's importance and why it was entrusted to me, I decided to go to see the person who lived nearest to me, which is how I ended up in southern New Jersey.

That was the last known location of name number nine of the list. He was a year older than me and a mechanical engineer who had a successful but fairly unremarkable career working for a few different parts manufacturers until he patented a process for making the vital components for some of the U.S. Army's most heavily used road equipment, the kind they transport in large numbers to all of those foreign countries where they set up temporary bases and command posts. From what I was able to gather from the various newspaper articles and technical journals he was profiled in, he became somewhat well known in that industry and had amassed a small fortune. He also traveled the world for his work, and I was concerned that he might be in some remote part of the globe rather than at the sprawling country estate that I found featured in Architectural Digest.

I arrived in the town with only a vague notion of what I might say or how I might approach him, assuming he was there. It wasn't difficult to find out where he lived and worked, not with all the tools available these days with the tap of a few keys on the computer. Once I had that information in hand, I checked into a motel and rounded up some food and returned to my room to plan what I would say if and when I was able to get a meeting with the man whose name was Alden Archer.

One of the benefits of having some renown is that people whom you have never met are more likely to welcome a strange phone call and an out-of-the-blue request to meet. Such was the case with Archer. When I gave my name to his highly efficient gatekeeper of an assistant, I only had to wait about twenty seconds before I was put through to him. I quickly learned that Archer had read two of my books and was a self-described "fan." We talked briefly about current economic conditions, along with the presidential race coming up in the next year, before he asked me the million-dollar question - why was I calling? For the better part of the morning, I had rehearsed what I was going to say, going over how best to introduce the idea of the list without giving away too much. However, when the time came, I acted purely on instinct. I lied.

I told him that I was involved in a commercial venture, the nature of which I didn't want to discuss over the phone, but one that had a connection to the business of his company and that might prove to be a good investment for him. I told him that I would be happy to explain more when we met. If he suspected that I was making it all up, he didn't let on. Instead, he asked his assistant to give me the directions to his country club and said to meet him there at seven o'clock that evening. That was the end of the conversation, and so I hung up and went about planning how much and what exactly I should say to him when we sat down together.

Though I had packed clothes for a variety of possible scenarios, I still felt slightly out of place when I pulled up to the club's entrance and walked in. I was wearing the obligatory blazer and tie, having both belonged to and been a guest at enough establishments like that to be aware of the dress requirements. I didn't stand out in appearance. It was more internal, a vestige of having grown up as I did, where my parents would never have belonged to the local country club even if they'd had the wherewithal and requisite references to join.

As I was told he would be, Archer was waiting in the bar and easily recognizable, despite being a good twenty pounds heavier than in the photo on his company's website. We shook hands and sat at a table in the back, and I ordered my usual Irish whiskey neat while he refreshed his bourbon and soda. The room was dark, with oak paneling, in the same fashion of every other country club I had ever set foot in, and it smelled strongly of some sort of spice, like the most common of men's cologne. Other than the bartender, there were only four other people in the place, all seated far away, as if pre-arranged. This time Archer didn't waste any time with small talk. He wanted to know the nature of my business and how it might be of any benefit to him.

I took a large swallow of my drink and then told him that I hadn't been entirely forthcoming with him on the phone earlier. His reaction was to sit back and look around, almost as if to see if there was anyone near enough to come to his rescue if whatever I had in mind should turn out badly. It seemed rather theatrical, given that the other four souls in the place were watching a hockey game and showed no interest in us. I held up my hand and assured him that I wasn't there to cause any trouble but that I had recently been assigned a task that involved him in at least a tangential way and was merely there to try to clear it up.

He asked me who had assigned the task and I told him I wasn't at liberty to say. He didn't press the matter and instead asked about the nature of the task.

Without referring in any specific way to the doctor or his widow, or the circumstances surrounding what happened after the funeral, I told him that someone I trusted very much had given me a list of names and had asked me to determine who the people were and how they might be connected. I informed him that his name was on that list. He sat there quietly for a moment and then asked if he could see it. I told him that I didn't have it with me but that I had memorized all the names and would be happy to go over them with him, including sharing what few details I had gathered about them, if he wished.

He seemed to be taking his measure of me and, in particular, my sanity before he spoke next. "This seems a bit far afield for you, isn't it?"

I asked him what he meant, and he said that it seemed more like the job of a private detective than a college professor with a PhD in cognitive theory and a reputation for consulting on matters of far greater importance than missing persons.

I told him that he was right, in part. It was not something that had come up in the course of my normal affairs, but that the invitation to investigate had come from someone I had known for a long time and that it was a bit more personal, leaving me to feel obligated to at least inquire superficially. I also told him that, to my knowledge, no one on the list was missing, as proven by the fact that I found him quite easily. He studied me once again before he spoke.

"OK," he said, "I'll play along. Why don't you give me a couple of the names?"

So I did. Beginning with the violinist, for no other reason than the fact that he was first on the list. There was no response or any sign of recognition from Archer. Instead, he just waited for me to continue, and so I did, one by one, each time giving the name and what little I had been able to gather about them. Of course, I skipped his. Each time I finished with one of the names, he simply sat there stone-faced and waited for me to continue until I finished with all eleven.

"Where was I on that list?" he asked.

I told him.

"So it wasn't alphabetical," he noted. "Any reason that you could come up with why I was ninth and not first or third or fifth?"

I told him I hadn't yet been able to determine what he and the others had in common, let alone why their names appeared in the order they did. I then asked if any of them sounded familiar.

He shook his head. "Never heard of any of them," he said. "No idea."

And just like that, the conversation was over. The clink of glasses at the bar and the drone of the play-by-play on the television were the only sounds to be heard for minute or so. I used the opportunity to sip more of my drink. He didn't move.

"Why don't you tell me what you really came to see me for?" he asked finally.

I can admit now to being surprised that he was so suspicious of me. Other than to say that the list was my sole reason for my visit, I couldn't think of any other possible answer, even if I wanted to lie to him. I'm not a particularly good liar anyway, although having been unhappily married, I had a good deal of practice. So I told him just that. It was the list. Nothing more.

"Well then," he said, "I think your friend has sent you on a wild goose chase. Some sort of human scavenger hunt. Hell, he may have just picked our names out of a hat. Personally, I wouldn't waste another moment on it."

The part about picking the names out of a hat resonated somewhat only because I had thought the very same thing when the widow first handed me the list. Of course, seeing her sprawled out on the floor and encountering those two suited men caused me to quickly discard the notion, but I wasn't about to disclose that to Archer. He already thought I was nuts. Plus, if the widow's death were to be ruled a homicide, the cops would no doubt check her phone records and discover my name there. And if that happened, I might become a suspect and Archer would quickly replace his belief that I was crazy with a more plausible one that I was a possible killer.

I thought of all this as he waited for my answer and made up my mind rather quickly.

"I think you're probably right," I said, standing up and pulling my chair aside. "I told myself I would take one shot at it and you were the closest to me geographically. Now that we've talked and I have my answer, I think I'll probably take your advice."

If he was surprised, he didn't show it. Instead, he stood up and offered his hand and wished me luck. He didn't invite me to dinner, even though there were two menus in front of him on the table. So I just shook his hand and thanked him and, in a matter of minutes, I found myself outside the club handing my parking ticket to the valet.

I passed the rest of that night eating greasy Chinese food in the Holiday Inn Express and considering my options. Going back home was at the top of my list, except for the fact that those men knew where I lived and would no doubt return if they had even left yet. And, of course, there was the matter of the widow. If I was home and easy to locate, I might soon find myself answering questions from the New York state police, even if it wasn't ruled a homicide. After all, there was the possibility that they would check her phone records as a matter of routine, and then look at my own as a consequence, particularly if the others who attended the funeral and burial had spread the word that I had been in attendance. On top of that, the little boy might tell his parents about the man who drove away from the widow's house like it was on fire. In light of all that, I decided I couldn't go home, not unless I was willing to throw myself upon the mercy of the police, a prospect that held little appeal to me.

Instead, I decided to seek out the next closest person on the list, geographically, and try once more. This time, I vowed, I would concoct a better story for why I was inquiring. Before retiring for the night, I checked the website for my hometown's newspaper and, immediately, my breath caught. On the home page there was a notice of the widow's death. It was the headline. My heart began to race as I gave the story a quick read. To my great relief, it focused more on the timing of her death, coming on the heels of her husband's recent demise, than on the cause, which had yet to be determined. It was reported that a friend had become concerned when she couldn't reach her by phone the day after the funeral and went over to check on her and found her on the floor of the doctor's study. No foul play was hinted at. When I finished reading, I breathed another sigh of relief, even though I knew it might only be temporary. Despite the events of the day, I managed to fall asleep rather quickly and slept through the night.

The next morning found me down in the dining room of the hotel enjoying my complimentary continental breakfast and reading the latest about the basketball tournament. My bags were packed and on the floor next to me, in anticipation of the journey ahead. I had just finished eating and was reaching for my suitcase when my cell phone rang. It was Archer. Not his assistant, but Archer himself.

He asked me if I had left yet. I told him that I was just about to.

"Glad I caught you, then," he said. "I gave some more thought to what you told me last night. It turns out that one of those names did ring a bell. It didn't come to me until later, after I got home and looked through my contacts."

"Which one," I asked. I wasn't testing him. I was simply curious. It was a reflexive question.

"I think it would be better if we talked in person," he said. His tone was suddenly more serious and somber than the night before.

I told him that was fine and suggested that we meet at my hotel.

"No," he said. "Come out to my house. I don't want to risk having someone overhear us talking about this."

I took that last statement to be somewhat encouraging, as it might mean that there could be some useful information forthcoming regarding those names. So I agreed, and he gave me directions.

CHAPTER 6

A MAN OF ACTION

I THREW MY bags in the car and headed straight for his house, which turned out to be somewhere out in horse country, where neighbors are few and far between, the complete opposite of my living situation.

It took some backtracking and nosing about, but I finally found the entrance for his home. It looked like what you might expect in an area zoned for exclusion and, predictably, an eight-foot wrought iron fence guarded it. I pressed the button on the intercom outside the gate and, once again, Archer answered himself. I told him it was me, and he pressed the buzzer to let me in. As I drove through, I noticed that the gate doors did not shut behind me. I thought that they were automatic, set to close soon after someone entered, but then, what did I really know about gates at a house like that?

I parked my car in the circular driveway, near the large portico. There were no other vehicles in sight. Nobody came out to greet me, so I got out of the car, walked up to the mammoth front door and rapped the shiny brass knocker a few times. It took longer than I expected for Archer to open it, considering that I had just spoken to him over the intercom less than a minute before. Unlike the previous night, he was dressed in a suit. An expensive one from the look of the fabric. He neither smiled nor offered me a hand, but instead just asked me to follow him. It reminded me of how the widow had greeted me the first time I came to her house. Despite the feeling that gave me, I did just that, and after a long walk through the house, I was brought to a study. Like the late doctor's, it wasn't a home office. It was a study, this one even more impressive, made to look like something out of an old English estate, even though it was clear from the construction material and details that the house was built sometime in the last ten years. In that way, it reminded me of all those new ballparks constructed to evoke the feeling of Fenway Park or Wrigley Field. The paneling on the wall resembled the bar of the country club, and the leather on the sofa was butter soft. I took a seat there without waiting to be asked. Archer remained standing.

"So which one did you remember?" I asked him.

"Wait right here a second," he said. "I've got something I want to show you first."

Before I could object, he was out the door, which he took the unusual step of closing behind him.

Ever since I was a child, I've had a fear of closed in spaces, particularly when I have no control over them. Although I had no specific reason to suspect that the door might be locked, I immediately got up and attempted to open it. It came free and, feeling relieved, I stepped out into the hallway. Wherever Archer went, he was no longer visible, although I could hear his footsteps somewhere not too far away. I returned to the room, leaving the door open when I did.

I was about to sit back down when I decided to go over to the window to take in the view. Looking back, it was apparent that Archer had little aptitude for undercover work or espionage. From my vantage point, I had a clear sightline to the gate I had just passed through, which allowed me to witness a nondescript black sedan driving through at a speed one wouldn't expect from a visitor to a house like the one I was currently standing in.

Archer soon appeared in my field of vision, running down the driveway waving his arms, signaling for the car to stop, which it did.

He skirted around the front to the driver's side window and waited while it powered down. When the driver stuck his head out to talk to Archer, I recognized him to be the older of the two men in suits I had encountered in the doctor's study just days before. A man I presumed to be the younger of the two was in the passenger seat next to him.

It was a brief conversation that included Archer throwing his hand in the direction of the house, and me, or so I presumed. He then backed up a step and pointed in the direction of what looked to be a service road that would take the car out of sight of the window from which I continued to stare.

I don't consider myself to be a man of action. I don't work out, and I have never been in a physical confrontation in my entire life. Not a single fistfight, even on the elementary school playground. It was just one of those things that I had managed to avoid over the course of my lifetime, leaving me to often wonder how I would respond if circumstances ever required me to use force to defend myself. Usually, I pictured me fleeing rather than fighting. However, that day I did a bit of both.

Given the direction in which Archer ordered the car to drive, I predicted that the two men would enter through some door in the back. That's why I made for the front. Not only did I know the way there, it was also closest to where my own car was parked. I thought that there was a possibility that I might encounter Archer if I did that, but I decided that running into him was preferable to the two men whose skills I had already witnessed.

However, Archer must have gone to the back to meet them, or maybe he simply went to some other part of the house, leaving them to deal with me alone. All I know is that I didn't see him again. Instead, I found a rather large man standing in the entranceway, blocking the front door. He was dark-skinned, but not African-American. More

Polynesian. Samoan perhaps, judging from his hair. He too was wearing a suit. A black one. Ill-fitting. And plain black shoes with thick rubber soles that reminded me of the military. To complete the picture, he had an earpiece in one ear and spoke into his wrist as soon as he saw me. I assumed that he was either a security guard in the employ of Archer or an associate of the two men in suits. Or both. At the time, it didn't matter much to me.

I stopped a few feet away to gauge what his intentions might be. That was settled rather quickly when he put up his left hand, the one without the microphone in the wrist, and told me I wasn't going anywhere.

I paused for a moment as if thinking of a response. Then I took a step toward him, which surprised and, judging by his smile, amused him. I think I might have mentioned that I was referred to in my family as "the smart one." That being the case, I didn't come to the house that morning without giving it some serious forethought and taking reasonable precautions. Thus, when the bodyguard advanced toward me, I slid an expandable baton from my jacket pocket and, with a flick of the wrist, opened it to its full sixteen-inch length and swung as hard as I could on that still-extended left arm. The sound of bone crunching under the solid steel almost made my stomach turn, although I have to admit that erasing the smile on his face did give me enormous pleasure.

He leaned over instinctively to grab his injured forearm, and when he did, I struck again on the outside of his left knee. He collapsed in a heap in the floor and I stepped behind him and out the door.

I confessed to never having had a physical confrontation, and on that subject I was not lying. However, as I've noted, a good part of my writing and study has involved risk assessment and contingency planning. In that regard, I was once brought in to teach a workshop to an upper echelon military group at the Pentagon, involving all four branches of the service. At the end of the session, a colonel in the Special Forces approached me and asked if I practiced what I preached. When I asked him what he meant by that, he wanted to know if I had ever studied the physical arts to augment the mental aspects of what I taught. I was forced to admit that I had not, and he generously offered to school me over a three day period at a facility somewhere out in rural Virginia. I never expected to have to use any of it in my line of work, but I craved the knowledge and accepted his offer. I came away from those sessions with three bits of advice which have stuck with me ever since: (1) when it comes to fighting for one's life, nothing is considered out-of-bounds; (2) surprise and brute force are the key to defeating an opponent; and (3) weapons trump all else. The baton was the colonel's gift to me at the end of our work together. It had remained on a shelf in my home office collecting dust until I left that previous morning for New Jersey.

Now you may wonder why I carried the weapon with me to this meeting and not also to the one the night before. I surely considered it then, but I also assumed that matters wouldn't get too far out of hand at an exclusive country club, not to mention that at that point Archer had given me no reason to suspect that he was anything but what I believed him to be: a businessman whose name was on the list and nothing more.

Not so that morning. After getting the phone call and being told to come to his house in some rural area, far from civilization, I suspected that he might be less than truthful about remembering one of the names. And if so, there was a chance that my two friends might show up, as turned out to be the case. So you might wonder, why did I even go? Well, for one, I could have been wrong, and Archer might indeed have had some helpful information to share with me. I didn't fully believe that to be the case, but I've also been wrong many times in my life. Besides, I had already made the journey to New Jersey to see him and wanted to take advantage of all the opportunities that meeting with him might provide. Of course, being who I am and thinking as I do, I also came prepared.

Once I was out the front door, I took a quick look around to see if the two men were nearby. If they were, I needed to be ready for them as well, although I had no specific plan in mind. However, it turned out that they must have still been in the house, so I jumped into my car and started it and stomped on the gas pedal, heading for the gate that, at that moment, was just beginning to close. Technically, there were two ten-foot-wide, eight-foot-high, wrought iron gates, with thick cables guiding them. And in a matter of seconds they would shut tight, leaving me to come up with an alternative means of escape, one that I hadn't yet contemplated. In the two seconds I had to decide, I was forced to weigh whether it was more advisable for me to head for the quickly closing gap between the gates or to aim for one or the other of them. Either way, I was determined to at least try to get through.

It always amazes me how quickly the brain can sort things out, especially in circumstances involving danger or death. Without really recalling having made the decision, I steered the car toward the gate on my right. Upon reflection, I must have concluded that the one on the left was the anchor, as indicated by the extra cable securing it. The one on the right would no doubt be just as solid once in place, but it had only one cable securing it to the pole to which it was hinged.

I made the correct choice. That gate came loose from both the cable and the pole and was sent flying to the side of the road leading to the house. Of course, my car sustained some damage to the front end in the process, but it was far less than I had feared. There was no steam coming from under the hood as I drove away, leaving me to conclude that the radiator was still functioning, at least for the time being. I didn't stop to check the wreckage until I was a good ten miles away, heading south, with no sign of anyone on my trail. When I did pull over, I found that I was right about the radiator, but saw that the entire headlight assembly on the passenger side was crumpled and destroyed, meaning that I would be susceptible to a stop by the police when driving at night, and I didn't want that. It was for that reason that I chose to drive directly to the Philadelphia airport only about an hour away.

Now I probably could have flown to whatever destination I wanted without the police in hot pursuit. For starters, if Archer had wanted to bring in the authorities, he could have simply called them before I got there and entertained me with some made up story about one of the names on the list until they arrived. And those men in suits could have easily brought them along with them. Instead, the behavior of all of them seemed to suggest that they were acting on their own.

It was safe to assume then that my most pressing concern was the threat posed by those men in suits. Who were they? Did they work alone or for someone else? Why was the list so important to them? And what were their capabilities when it came to finding me? Showing up at my office the day before was hardly an indication of them having any great resources at their disposal. Anyone with access to a computer could have found out where I lived and worked. Appearing at Archer's house was different. I had to believe it was Archer who called them, probably sometime after our meeting at the country club and they drove down from Connecticut or wherever they were to confront me at the house that morning. Nevertheless, I couldn't dismiss the possibility that they were working for or with someone who could provide them with the ability to track me via my phone or credit cards or both.

That's why I rented a car when I got to the airport and parked my own car in long-term parking. In an effort to further confuse them, I also purchased a one-way ticket to Los Angeles (home of another name on the list). Finally, before I left, I took out as much cash as allowed from a nearby ATM, the third time in three days that I had done so.

As I drove away from Philadelphia, I tried to determine the significance of Archer contacting the men in suits and them knowing who he was. They had to know he was on the list. That much was certain for the simple reason that I had told him so. But if they only found that out after my visit, how would he know to contact them in the first place and for what reason? On the other hand, if they knew Archer prior to the phone call, might that also mean that they knew the others on the list?

Based on everything that happened up to that point, I decided it was best to proceed as if they knew every name and, therefore, could show up at the location of any of them. Of course, they may have known Archer some other way, but not have known that his name was on the list until he told them. If that was the case, then the same might be said for the other eleven names. Still, I couldn't count on that. I had to assume that they knew those names as well as I did and could contact them - any of the other eight still living anyway - at any time.

It was also plausible for me to suppose that while Archer was clearly an ally of theirs, not all of the others might be. Again, I couldn't rely on that, but it was certainly possible. And if it were true, those men in suits probably wouldn't want to contact any who weren't confederates. That was enough for me to decide to take the risk of going to see at least one more of them before I changed my strategy. Considering what had happened at Archer's estate, though, I decided that I would have to be considerably more careful than I had been in choosing to go to see him.

The next closest living person on the list was in Virginia, not that far from where I was. Assuming once again that the men in suits knew the names as well as I did, it would be easy for them to predict that I might head for that location. After all, my going to New Jersey had indicated a choice based primarily upon proximity. Even if they assumed that I would wise up, there was no other obvious option. If I were them, that's where I would go. But I was planning to use a different criterion in deciding who to go see next.

The one name on the list that intrigued me the most was that of the man from Arkansas who appeared to have gone off the grid. Unlike Archer or the anti-trust lawyer, he was not presently employed, at least not in any role that would land him in the search results on Google, and the address that came up for him on the "people search" website was an old one from that suburb of Little Rock where he had attended high school. I couldn't even be sure that he was still in that state, let alone that town, but I felt that he was so different from the others that he was less likely to be an ally of those men in suits. I had nothing to base that upon other than his limited professional life and, I suppose, the felony drug conviction. Nevertheless, despite the challenge of actually finding him, I felt that it was the wise choice to go there.

Looking back, the fact that my brother happened to reside in the western part of that state may have influenced that decision as well.

CHAPTER 7

JUST IN CASE

IT'S MORE THAN a thousand miles and at least an eighteen-hour drive from the airport in Philadelphia to the Arkansas border, causing me to break up the trip into two legs. It probably would have been to my benefit to drive straight through before the men in suits could even get a sniff of where I might have gone, but as I've said, I'm not the world's greatest driver these days, and I find that I need at least eight hours of sleep a night to function. Besides, I wanted time to think about this next step so I stopped at a small roadside motel just across the Tennessee border, east of Knoxville. The clerk was kind enough to give me directions to one of the local eateries, and I managed to get them to serve me just before they closed for the night. After that, I went back to my room, double locked the door, and went to sleep. When I woke up two hours later to use the bathroom, I checked the parking lot for signs of the men in suits. It was purely reflex, reinforced by the events of the previous morning. I didn't see anything, but I put the desk chair up against the door with the handle nestled under the knob, just like you see in the movies.

I awoke the next morning somewhat refreshed and found a donut shop nearby where I purchased some coffee and cinnamon rolls, along with the local newspaper and the USA Today. There was nothing in the local paper about the events of the previous day, not that I would have expected there to be, but I could be certain of nothing at that point. I then scoured the national newspaper for anything that might relate to the doctor's widow, but came up empty there as well, to my great relief. When I got back to my room, I decided it was time to check in with Gloria back at my office, and so I waited until just after nine - her time - and called from my cell.

She answered on the third ring, as she almost always did, as per the instructions I gave her when I first opened the office. I told her then that I wanted us to appear to be busy, and that answering on the first ring smacked of desperation. If that gave her any idea about what I might be up to behind my closed door and why I might feel the need to pretend, she didn't say. It wasn't the signal I told her to use when I left that Monday should those men be in the office when I called. Instead, she just said "hello" although with a hint of question behind it.

"It's me," I said, only then realizing the reason for her hesitation.

"Oh," she said. "I didn't recognize the number."

"I got a new phone," I told her. "Different line."

"Oh, okay," she said. "Let me write it down."

"Don't," I told her, perhaps a bit more strongly than I should have.

She was silent, probably feeling a rebuke.

"Memorize it if you want," I said. "But don't give it out to anyone. Ever. In fact, if you need to reach me, just call the old one and leave a message. I'll get it."

She didn't ask me to explain nor did I volunteer to do so. She simply said okay once more. I could tell that she was confused and, if I was reading her correctly, concerned.

I asked her what was going on.

"The police were here yesterday," she said. "They were asking for you."

"Local?" I asked.

It took a moment for her to realize what I meant. "No," she said. "They were from New York. The state police. They were detectives."

This was precisely what I had expected to happen at some point, although it was still troubling to have it confirmed. "What did they want?" I asked.

"They said they needed to talk to you about something."

"They didn't tell you what?"

There was a brief pause that I couldn't quite characterize. "Not at first," she said.

"OK," I told her. "So what did they say?"

"At first they wanted to know where you were."

"And what did you say?"

"I told them you were away at a business meeting."

"Is that all?"

"No," she said. "They wanted to know where. So I told them exactly what you told me to say."

Which was that she didn't know exactly. That I often went places without telling her.

"Then they said that I must've had to make your travel arrangements," she said, sounding nervous.

"And?"

"I told them that you drove," she said. "Just like you told me to."

"I'll bet they weren't very happy."

"No," she said. "Anything but."

"And that's when they told you what it was all about," I said. A statement, not a question.

"They did."

"Tell me," I said.

"They said a woman died. The one who called. The doctor's wife. They said that a friend found her dead in her house two days after the funeral."

"Did they say what she died of?"

"They thought it was a heart attack," she said. "They were still checking."

I took that to be good news, at least in part. "So why did they want to talk to me?" I asked, emphasis on that last word.

"They said that according to their investigation, you were the last person seen with her."

I didn't respond to that. I didn't like their admission that they were investigating, let alone that I had been seen in her company.

"Is it true?" she asked me then.

I hadn't expected the question and didn't answer right away. "I wasn't the last, no," I said finally.

She didn't ask me what I meant by that. Instead, she wanted to know if I knew anything about it. It was clear to me that it was she who was asking that question, not them.

I didn't want to lie, but I also didn't want to elaborate. "She seemed fine the last time I talked to her," I told her. That much was true. I didn't say that she was fine the last time I *saw* her, which was most decidedly not true. If she detected any parsing on my part she didn't let on.

"OK," was all she said. I think she believed me, but I couldn't be sure.

"Anything else?" I asked.

"I told them you never said a word about the widow when you came back and that I was certain that you'd have reported it if you knew that something had happened to her."

I chose not to correct her. It was nice to hear that she had defended me like that. I hadn't asked her to. It must have been something she decided to do on her own, presumably based upon all our years together. Such was the nature of our relationship. Since my divorce, there was no one on the planet I was closer to than her. It had never been romantic nor would it ever be. It was more of a brother-sister relationship, with all the same dynamics, including a protective inclination on both our parts. I wanted to thank her anyway, but I chose not to. Instead, I simply asked her what they said to that.

"They said they still needed to talk to you. That her phone records showed that she called you after the funeral and that someone saw you leaving her house that afternoon."

Once again, I expected that they would find all that out, although I was surprised that they would share it with Gloria. I took it to mean that they were trying to plant some doubt with her about my veracity. I also thought that if that young boy on his bike hadn't seen me, they might not have had any reason to pull the woman's phone records and come to see me. The boy had to have said something to someone.

"How did you respond to that?" I asked, genuinely curious.

"I didn't," she said. "They could have been lying. In fact, I'm sure they were."

I didn't correct her on that score either. "What else did they tell you?"

"That was about it," she said. "One of them gave me their card and said the next time I talked to you I should tell you to call her."

"'Her'?"

"Yes, the one who asked all the questions was a woman."

"Right," I said.

"Do you want the number?" she asked.

I had no intention of calling her or any other member of the police. New York or otherwise. And that's what I told her.

"OK," she said. "Then I won't ask where you are or what you're doing."

"That's wise," I told her, and said that I would call again, but that I wasn't sure when.

She told me that was fine and said goodbye. I stopped her before she could hang up.

"Maybe you should give me that number," I said. "Just in case."

She didn't ask me in case of what. She simply gave me Detective Bridget O'Connell's name and phone number, which I promptly committed to memory. Then I told her she could take the rest of the day off.

She said thanks, and we hung up.

CHAPTER 8

ARKANSAS

Arkansas in late March is not exactly the Cote d'Azur. When I crossed the border that day, the trees had yet to show buds, the ground was still brown from the winter, and many of the leaves from the previous fall were clinging to the sod in spots. As I neared the greater Little Rock metropolitan area, the river was swollen and the sky was as gray as the widow's sweater. I should have taken all of that as a sign of things to come.

Like I said, I am cautious by nature and have studied and taught preparedness. In my own life that has meant doing things that I'd never have thought might come in handy, like taking that self-defense primer and using the baton. But such was the set of circumstances I seemed to have found myself in, almost as if I'd had some subconscious forewarning that this scenario might some day come to pass. I didn't dwell on that notion, at least not then. I merely implemented another of those contingencies.

I was once part of a panel featuring some of the best and brightest in the espionage and surveillance business, both government and private. While I offered my own expertise in the area of critical thinking and risk analysis, others contributed in other specialties, many of which I found fascinating, learner that I am. I had, of course, known about the practice of creating pseudonyms, but I had never bothered to research how they were put together and why. Most people think that only criminals create separate and false identities. And that's probably true for the most part. However, they are used by a wide variety of professionals for a wide assortment of reasons, some legal and some not. When I returned from the weekend conference, I decided that I would try to do what I had heard about. In my line of work, I never thought that having another name, social security number and credit card might come in handy. As far as I knew, I had no enemies nor did I anticipate ever having to go on the run. But I thought, like training with that Special Forces colonel, going through the process of acquiring a different identity would only add to my knowledge base and experience. Based on the research I did, I felt comfortable that it wasn't a crime to merely possess a false ID in most states. Indeed, the laws that prohibit such a practice are normally intended for underage kids looking to buy alcohol, not middle age adults trying to satisfy some professional curiosity. And possessing it was all I ever planned on.

Of course, that all goes out the window if you knowingly use the name and social security number of a living person. That's identity theft, even if you haven't yet stolen anything other than those two personal identifiers. In fact, the mere acquiring of such information can be a crime. However, as I learned at that workshop, all that can easily be avoided if you look up the name of someone who has died as an infant, before acquiring a social security number, and you obtain a copy of his or her birth certificate. After that, you can apply for the social security number and, from there, get a credit card, open a bank account and, if you know the right people, even obtain a driver's license. Pretty much anything you could get under your own name.

Since I was never actually planning to use that new identity, I limited myself to the social security number, license and credit card, and I never even considered taking them out of my safe at home until those men in suits showed up at my office. Along with the baton, they made the trip with me, reinforcing what I have taught for years about anticipating unexpected needs. And the need to shield my identity arose at around six thirty that night sometime after I crossed the border into Arkansas.

Now I can't say for certain that my use of the name and credit card wouldn't constitute a crime in that state, but it didn't matter since I felt it was imperative that I try to hide my location from those men in suits, once again assuming they had the wherewithal to track me under my given name. The clerk at the motel in Tennessee hadn't asked to see any ID and so I used the false name, but paid in cash. True, I could have used both the name and credit card in the rental car place at the Philadelphia airport, but if those men did indeed go there and were to inquire about me, I wanted them to think they were following someone who didn't take precautions and didn't think a step or two ahead. That's why I made it a point to ask the rental agent for a map that might show me a route to Michigan, thinking that creating a diversionary trip to the upper mid-west might provide me with enough time to find the mystery man from Arkansas. Of course, I declined the GPS option for the car as well.

Using my fake name and credit card, I checked into another Holiday Inn Express, this one in the town adjacent to the one that contained the last known address for the man whose name was Rafe Plum. Because of the hour, it wasn't possible for me to do much in the way of sleuthing, and so I did the only thing I could think of, if only to avoid feeling like I was doing nothing. I looked in the dog-eared phone book that came with the room. Apparently, they still provide them in that part of Arkansas, and I was hoping to see if my search might turn out to be an easy one.

There was no listing for a Rafe Plum or any other Plum, leaving me with nothing else to do but unpack and find something to eat. Paying with cash, I dined at an Applebee's near the hotel and then went back to the room and fell asleep after a half hour of watching ESPN to catch up on the latest news on the basketball tournament.

I didn't sleep particularly well, waking every hour or so after having the same dream play over and over. It was a near exact replay of the events that took place at Archer's house the day before, except that in the dream, the men in suits captured me before I could reach the car. Each time it ended when they threw me in the trunk of their vehicle - a closed in space - and shut the lid, causing me to wake with a start and short of breath. I only managed to get back asleep by downing three sleeping pills, two more than I normally use and, for that reason, I didn't wake up until just after ten the next morning.

When I did finally open my eyes, I felt both groggy and un-settled, so I went out for breakfast and downed three quick cups of coffee. After my head cleared, I formulated a plan to try and find Plum, or at least to take the first step in that direction. That turned out to be a trip to the town hall in the community where he was last known to reside. Upon locating the office of the clerk, I gave her my new name and pretended to be a long lost cousin looking for his "childhood companion" Rafe. I had no luck. And no further assistance either. Whether the clerk was generally tight-lipped and unaccommodating by nature or simply didn't buy my story, I don't know. She may have never heard of Mr. Plum or maybe she was just being protective. I couldn't tell. All I knew was that I wasn't going to get anywhere at the town hall. So then, as I was about to get back in my rental car, I got another idea, one that I should have thought of earlier and which seemed more likely to bear fruit. Asking directions from a parking meter attendant, I promptly drove over to the high school that Plum had graduated from, at least according to what my on-line search on Sunday had produced.

I had gotten the graduation and high school information from the dedicated website that listed those who had attended, as well as those who hadn't come to the twenty-year reunion for his class. Otherwise, I would have had no idea of where he went to high school or even how old he was. Apart from the "find-a-person" site information about the teller job from a decade earlier, and the even older drug conviction, there was nothing else on him. That's how small his on-line footprint was. The "comments" section of the reunion page revealed that no one had seen him "for years" and that his whereabouts were unknown. Apparently, they weren't aware of his criminal past, or if they were, they had spared him that embarrassment on the official reunion website.

Sitting across from the current principal, it didn't take much to determine that she hadn't been in that position at any time when Plum had gone to school there, since she appeared to be about the same age as he would be. I thought that might mean that my idea would bear no fruit after all, but I turned out to be wrong once more. She was far more eager to help than the town clerk, and she readily accepted my lost-cousin story. After thinking about it for a moment, she told me that she had an idea, and she made a phone call to the man who had served as principal just before her and who was now retired and still living in the town. Turns out he was there at the school with Rafe Plum, although as assistant principal at the time, and he remembered him quite well. Armed with carefully written directions, she sent me off to see him.

"He was a pretty quiet kid," the retired educator told me, as I was seated in the kitchen of his modest ranch home no more than three miles from the school. He then went on to inform me that Plum had come from a tough background, with a father who was "a petty thief and drifter" and a mother who was "never around."

"But I saw something in him," he told me.

I asked him what that was.

"I don't know," he said. "Potential, I guess. They all have it to some degree at that age. Maybe I was just looking for it in him because of his background."

"He won a scholarship, right?" I asked.

He nodded. "U of A," he said. "But he never finished. I always thought that if he applied himself a little more, who knows where he could have gone."

He seemed to have a soft spot for Plum, or at least for the student he was then. I asked him if he knew where he was and what he was doing now.

"I have no idea," he told me. "I haven't seen him since graduation." I was prepared for that answer, but not for the statement that he volunteered right after.

"But he does have a sister who lives here. She works over at the local hospital."

When he told me that, I found myself hoping that she was a doctor. I don't know why. Maybe because this whole affair started with a phone call concerning my former family physician. Or perhaps I thought that a doctor would be more likely to reveal things about her brother and help me find the reason why his name might appear on the same list as Archer and the others. Of course, I knew that a doctor would be forbidden to share private medical information. But I felt that she wouldn't be able to resist sharing non-medical knowledge about her own brother who might be involved in something mysterious and possibly dangerous.

As it turned out, she wasn't a doctor. Or even a nurse. She was a phlebotomist, one of those people who draw blood from patients, day after day, hour after hour, like some sort of mechanic or dairy farmer. Apparently, the local medical professionals order routine blood tests for all their patients, since I had to wait in the cafeteria for almost three hours until the blood draw clinic closed and I was able to see her. When I first arrived and asked the person at the check-in desk where I might find Amanda Banyon (nee Plum), she asked who I was and why I wanted to see her. I obviously couldn't use the same "long lost cousin" story, so I invented a new one: that I was a former college classmate of her brother's and was trying to locate him. Only half of it was true, of course. None of it was particularly convincing.

I suppose it was for that reason that Plum's sister was highly suspicious when she exited the clinic and found me waiting for her. I repeated the same story as she stood before me, and then I asked if she could help me find him. She looked me over, and then asked me what year we met, meaning her brother and me. I told her it was junior year and she nodded. Then she asked me what year that was. Having remembered the year of Rafe's high school graduation I simply added a couple of years to it, choosing October as the month, to both embellish and reinforce the lie. She stared at me and asked me if I was sure of that. I said yes, and gave her a reassuring smile. She then informed me that because of his two years of incarceration, his junior year was two years later.

I should have recalled the drug conviction and factored in the time gap, but I had forgotten about that and was disappointed in myself for having made such an obvious mistake. I tried to recover from the error and told her that it was my junior year and not his. She gave a little snort and then turned away without saying another word, hurrying down the long hallway toward the hospital exit.

I followed, trying not to look like I was stalking her, but several other hospital workers looked at me with obvious concern as I pursued her. When she got to the door, I blurted out that I was lying and that I had never met her brother at all. She turned to look at me briefly, then picked up the pace as she went out the door. Again, I followed and called out to her that I was not after anything from him and that she could trust that I would not be a threat to her or her brother in any way.

She didn't even break stride as she headed for the employees' parking lot. However, when she got there, she stopped to say something to the security guard who then looked up at me and nodded. I halted in my tracks and gave a feeble wave as if to indicate that I was giving up and had no intention of following her any more. He didn't seem to care and picked up the phone in his glassed-in booth and dialed someone. I took that as an indication that I should get the hell out of there, and when I turned to do so, I nearly ran over a woman who called my name behind me. My real name, not the one I had just used to try and talk to the phlebotomist.

"Someone said you're trying to find Amanda's brother," the woman said.

I thought about how open I should be with her, given that this woman knew my real identity and could cause some serious trouble if I said or did anything that could be perceived as even slightly unlawful. Despite all that, I took a chance and told her that I was.

"Why do you want to find him?" she asked.

"Look," I told her. "I made a mistake in coming here and I can assure you that I'm not a threat to anyone. I plan to drop the whole thing right here and now. No need to worry. I'll just be on my way."

I meant what I said and had turned to go when she told me that she might be able to help.

As per her suggestion that we talk somewhere else, I followed her to a Starbucks not far from the hospital, and we took a seat in the back, away from the line for all the lattes and macchiatos.

She told me her name was Amy Mendleson and that she was a doctor and had read "all" my books. She said she recognized me from the book jacket photo. I told her I was flattered, and I was, especially considering how old that photo was. She said that she knew Amanda only as a worker in the hospital and had learned of Amanda's brother through a combination of gossip and a few brief exchanges with Amanda herself on the topic. She said that those talks came after the one and only time she saw Rafe. That was at the hospital, where he had come to "rescue" Amanda from the "medical mafia." Naturally, Amanda resisted, resulting in a great deal of screaming and threatening on his part. Security was then called, a doctor from the psych ward appeared and tried negotiating, but in the end Plum had to be subdued by force and taken to another hospital for observation.

"Is he still there?" I asked.

"No," she told me. "He only stayed a night or two, as required by law, and then they let him go. This was about two years ago."

"Do you know where he is now?"

She shook her head.

"Then how might you be able to help?" I asked.

"I'll let you know after you tell me why you want to see him," she said.

There was something suspect about her manner and behavior. I said before that I had hoped that Plum's sister was a doctor and, because of that, might be inclined to help me. But that only applied to his sister, not to any doctor. I thought maybe I should turn the tables, and so I asked her what her specialty was at the hospital.

She replied that she was an internist. Basically, a GP. I asked her how long she had been there. She gave what appeared to be credible answers to that and my follow-up questions, but something about her continued to give me pause. She asked me once more why I wanted to see Rafe Plum.

Despite my concern, I decided to take a flyer and told her about the list, albeit in the most general terms. After telling her that I couldn't disclose who gave me the assignment, she asked about the others on the list. I told her that, like the identity of the person who gave me the list, I wasn't at liberty to tell her. She seemed to accept that.

"What do you think all those people have in common?" she asked.

I told her that I didn't have the foggiest notion and that was why I was there.

"Well," she said. "I might be able to help you then." She proceeded to tell me that she knew Plum's last known address and was "fairly confident" that he still lived there.

I asked how she could know such a thing, and she replied that the psychiatrist she mentioned earlier had told her.

"Why would he do that?" I asked. "Wouldn't that violate some sort of privacy law?"

"I'm sure it did," she told me. Then, she added with a smile that he was a friend, saying it in such a manner as to lead me to believe that theirs was more than a professional relationship. "He wouldn't expect me to ever pass it along," she added.

"Then why did you?" I asked, before I could think about whether I should.

"Because I like your books," she said. "And I trust that you have nothing sinister in mind."

"A few minutes ago you told me you didn't know where he was," I pointed out.

"I don't," she said. "Not exactly. All I have is his last known address."

I wasn't completely satisfied with all the parsing, but I was more interested in finding Plum than I was in proving that she might be lying. So I asked her to give me the address and, without hesitation, she wrote it down on a piece of paper and handed it to me. I noticed that it was not the last known address that I had, nor even the same suburb.

I got up then and thanked her for her assistance. She gave me another one of those smiles and told me it was her pleasure and wished me luck.

CHAPTER 9

PLUM

THE DRIVE TOOK no more than thirty minutes and brought me to a run-down ranch house with what looked like prairie grass growing in the front yard. The neighboring homes were all well kept, if modest, causing me to wonder just how unhappy those neighbors might be with the occupant of number 77. It was early evening by the time I arrived, with the sun beginning to set as I approached the front door. There were no lights on that I could see, and I wondered if maybe he wasn't home or possibly had even abandoned the place. That wasn't so difficult to conceive, judging by the condition of the exterior.

There was a doorbell, albeit with one of the anchoring screws missing, and so I pushed the button, but heard no sound. Thinking I might have missed it, or perhaps hadn't pushed hard enough, I tried again. Once more, it was silent, and I couldn't help but be reminded of my trip to Archer's house a few days before. As I mulled that, along with some other disturbing thoughts, the door swung open.

Standing before me was a man roughly the same age as me, at best a couple years younger. He was freshly shaved, his hair short and neatly combed, and he was attired in a suit, well tailored and stylish, along with a clean white shirt and a rep tie. I was certain that whoever it was, it couldn't be Plum.

My surprise must have shown when he welcomed me inside after I asked if Rafe Plum was available. The interior of the house was a sharp contrast with the outside - clean, uncluttered and well furnished. In fact, everything looked quite expensive, so much so that I wondered if the total value of the furnishings was greater than the home itself.

"Who shall I say is calling?" he asked, in an accent that I couldn't quite place. I found the question to be as odd as the man who was standing before me, the whole scene almost like something from an old movie.

I gave him my real name. If he recognized it, he didn't let it show. He also didn't ask me why I was there or what I wanted. He simply gestured toward a chair in the living room and disappeared into the back of the house.

In retrospect, the appearance of a man in a suit at the home of one of the names on the list should have caused me to fear that there might be a connection to those other men in suits. It was entirely plausible that he might be an associate of theirs and, therefore, a danger. However, I didn't think any such thing, although I guess it might be more accurate to say that it crossed my mind, but I dismissed it almost immediately. I'm not sure why, other than to say that I was completely convinced that the man who greeted me at the door was not one of them.

If I had needed any further convincing on that, it came when he returned to the room. Alone. With the suit jacket off and his tie loosened and the top button of his shirt undone. He went over to the sofa across from where I was seated and sat down. He seemed less friendly than he had just moments before. Not unfriendly, just less so. It was almost like his mood had changed in a matter of minutes.

"What can I do for you?" he asked.

I held up my hands as if to indicate that I had no answer for him.

"You must have come here for a reason," he said, never acknowledging the weirdness of disappearing and returning, with only a slight change in his appearance. And without Plum.

"I'm looking to speak with Rafe Plum," I told him. "If he's here."

"What if he's not?"

Considering all that had happened that day, I was hardly in the frame of mind for talking in riddles, but I also thought that I shouldn't bail out so soon on what might be my only chance to find Plum.

"If he's not here and you think you might see him again soon, then perhaps you can give him a message for me," I said.

"What's the message?" he asked.

As in my previous meetings with both Alden Archer and Plum's sister, I briefly considered how much or how little I should divulge. But then I recalled that telling the truth, or at least a small part of it, to Amy Mendleson had gotten me to where I was, so I told the man before me the same thing I told her.

He smiled. Why he found it amusing, I couldn't say.

"A list," he said. "My name is on a list?"

I hesitated for just a second before responding, not sure if I had heard him correctly. "You're Rafe Plum?"

"Live and in the flesh," he said. "But I want to know more about that list."

I didn't say anything at first. I had assumed that the man sitting before me was either a friend of Plum's or maybe even a conservator of some sort. If not, then maybe a bodyguard or attorney. I never for a moment thought that it was Plum himself. I guess it's always dangerous to assume anything, but his appearance was not what I expected. Not after the story Amy Mendleson had told me. The man before me was not a raving lunatic. He was not what I would call well adjusted, but he was also not deranged, at least not in the clinical sense.

"You're surprised," he said, as if reading my mind.

"A little," I told him.

"What do you know about me?" he asked. "Or I should say what did you know about me before you rang the bell?"

I told him about what I learned from an internet search, along with what his former assistant principal had said, and the doctor's story about the incident at the hospital that I had just heard minutes before.

He smiled. "Never happened."

"Which part?" I asked.

"All of it."

I was confused for just a moment. "All of it?"

"OK," he said. "The high school part is mostly true. And I didn't go to that reunion, so I suppose that's true, too."

"So the incident at the hospital--"

"Yeah, that happened too," he said.

I laughed. He laughed. Mine was a nervous one.

"Then again, maybe not," he said. "Now tell me more about the list."

It was clear to me by that point that I probably couldn't count on Plum to be completely candid with me, but then, his name did appear on the list and I couldn't see what harm it could do to tell him a little more about how I came to be there. So I did.

"Interesting," was all he said.

"Yes, very," I said.

"Am I the first one you found?"

I told him about the three who were dead. Then I told him about my visit with Archer. In complete detail.

"Wow," he said. "The same guys?"

"Yes," I said. "Have you ever had any visitors like them?"

"Not that I know of," he said. "And I like to think I'd know."

"Don't you want to know who the others are?"

"Not really," he said. "It doesn't sound very safe to know too much."

"But you might know something about them and why you're on that list with them."

That was when the doorbell rang, causing me to nearly jump out of my seat. Plum hardly reacted at all.

"The doorbell didn't make a sound when I pressed it," I told him.

"That's right," he said.

"Are you expecting someone?"

"It only rings when I want it to," he said, ignoring my question. Then he got up and went to the door. I got up myself, prepared to do whatever I needed to do, should the person or persons on the other side of that door turn out to be who I suspected they might be. By then, I wasn't sure of anything.

My apprehension turned quickly to confusion when he opened the door and greeted Amy Mendleson with a big smile.

As I've said, I like to plan ahead and prepare for just about any contingency. It's partly a result of my area of study and partly just my nature, but this whole experience was beyond anything I might have imagined when I got to Little Rock.

With her eyes on me the whole time, Amy Mendleson came over and sat on the couch. She was joined by Plum, who sat next to her in such a way as to confirm that their relationship was closer than doctor-patient. Maybe that was because he slid his hand suggestively between her panty-hosed thighs.

"You look surprised," she said.

"I am," I said. "Shocked in fact."

She smiled and Plum took her hand.

"You don't work at the hospital," I said, already knowing the answer.

She shook her head.

"You're not even a doctor, I'll bet."

"I have my masters," she said, with a smile. "Archeology. I really am Amy, though."

I looked at Plum who seemed to be enjoying the moment. "She's my girlfriend," he said. "Hot, no?"

I laughed. "And she looks out for you," I said. "Let me guess. Your sister called and you sent Amy to the hospital."

"You're pretty smart," he said.

"But what about your sister? Why would she refuse to talk to me?"

"Take a guess," he said.

"She's protecting you, too."

"We made up that hospital thing," Amy said. "Well, it happened, but it was a production. Staged, as it were."

"Provided a nice little back story," Plum said. "Crazy brother. Embarrasses sister at work. She won't have anything to do with him."

"So you really are concerned that people might be coming around?" I asked.

"Just being cautious," he said.

"Why?" I asked.

They turned and looked at one another, as if deciding how much to tell me. Finally, Amy shrugged and Plum nodded. "Do you like basketball?" he asked.

Thursday night is the beginning of the regional round of the NCAA men's basketball tournament when the sweet sixteen teams take the first step toward paring themselves down to the Final Four. The first game starts at seven o'clock eastern time, and it was just about that time when we went down to Plum's very cozy and well-appointed basement to watch the first of those games on a beautiful fifty inch LED flat screen TV. I don't know much about such things, but I guessed it to be the latest model, judging by the picture quality, especially compared to the one in my home that is about five years old. To add further to the contrast with the outside, the furniture down there was every bit as nice as that in Archer's country club, and the wood inlay walls were as richly textured and finished.

"Do you like Duke?" Plum asked me, after we sat down.

"To win the game?" I asked back.

He frowned. "I already know who's going to win. I mean as an institution of higher learning."

"They have a fine faculty," I said, confused. "They do some serious research there."

"I hate 'em," he said. "Something about the attitude they all share. From the students to the faculty to the damn landscapers probably."

"Did you say you knew who was going to win the game?"

"Yes," he said. "VCU. By three. Maybe four. First upset of three coming in this round."

"You think there will be three upsets in this round?"

"No," he said.

"But isn't that what you just said?"

"Correct," he said. "But I don't think that. I know it. Check back with me tomorrow night after the last west coast game. Another one of those upsets by the way."

I stared. Once again, he seemed less than stable, but not really crazy either.

"How do you think I make a living?" he asked, noting my confusion.

"I have no idea."

He smiled and looked around proudly.

"You're a professional gambler?"

Amy laughed. So did he. "No," he said. "I'm a predictor. And when it comes to certain sporting events, I'm right almost seventy-nine percent of the time. That makes it nearly a sure thing. And very lucrative."

"The only problem is finding a place to make the bet," Amy said. "You get a reputation."

I looked at the TV where VCU was currently on a run, up by twelve points in the early going. "And that's why you think people might be after you?" I asked.

"It tends to piss people off when they think they're being played," he said.

"Or fixing games," she added.

"They'll close the gap before halftime," he said, waving at the screen and meaning Duke, I presumed. "But VCU is a second half team. I could go into all the statistics, but I hate statistics. They just are. I don't need numbers to back up what I can see."

Without intending to, I accepted his invitation and stayed for all four games that night. Plum sent Amy out for Thai food - he said he didn't permit any kind of home delivery - and we had an assortment of drinks from his very well appointed bar. I managed to work in the names of the other people on the doctor's list, in between games and during the longer commercial breaks. True to what Plum had said earlier, he didn't recognize any of them, nor did he have any information about any, although he did ask a few questions about their background. I wasn't sure whether I should believe him, not after my experience with Archer, and particularly not after the way things transpired when I first encountered him. Nevertheless, the company was pleasant, the food was quite tasty and the games were all close and exciting. And Duke lost, just as he predicted.

He was also correct in picking the other three games. I know because I made sure to ask him before the tip-off of each, and he gave me the winners without hesitation. Clearly, he had studied the sport and used whatever mental process it was that allowed him to be so accurate in choosing the winning team. Don't get me wrong. It isn't a feat worthy of Nostradamus to select all four winners on the first night of the sweet sixteen round of the NCAA tournament. Thousands of fans probably do so every year, but to call them all within a five-point margin of the final score was rather impressive.

"If my usual percentage holds up, I'll probably lose one of the four games tomorrow," he said, when the final game ended. "Then again, I might not."

"How much do you have riding on the eventual winner?" I asked.

He smiled and stole a glance at his companion. "More than a Lexus, less than a Bentley."

I got up to leave then, seeing as it was nearing midnight. "Well," I said, "I'll have to call you tomorrow before the games start to see if you can match tonight."

"Nice try," he said.

I gave him a look indicating that I didn't quite understand.

"I don't have a phone," he said. "At least not one with a number I've ever shared."

"Not even with me," Amy said.

"You didn't object earlier when I guessed that your sister called you after I met with her," I pointed out.

"That's right," he said.

"He has a system," Amy said. "It's very sophisticated."

"And very effective," Plum added.

I shook my head. I had to admit that, despite his quirkiness and borderline crazy demeanor, I liked the guy. I thought he must have felt the same way about me because when he walked me to the door, he invited me to come back the next night to watch the other four sweet sixteen games to be played.

"Thanks," I said. Then I told him that I was leaving in the morning and uncertain if I would return. Which was essentially true.

With that, I left and made the thirty-minute drive back to my motel without careening off the road or getting stopped by the local police. Purely out of a recently acquired habit, I drove several times around the block before turning into the motel's parking lot, to see if there was any sign of my suited friends, but I detected nothing out of the ordinary.

After parking the rental car several doors down from my room, I made a cautious entrance, but found no sign of anyone having been in there, save for the maid. Still, I chained the door and used the chair as a secondary barrier and drifted off to sleep wondering how much money one could make if they had a seventy-nine percent success rate against the spread in predicting the outcome of sporting events.

I woke up fresh and without a hangover at around nine the next morning. I went to that same diner for breakfast and read each story on the games from the previous night, just to make sure the outcomes had really occurred as I remembered. They did, which only confirmed Plum's admission of how he made a living.

The diner was only half full when I finished my meal, and so I didn't earn any scowls from the waitress when I ordered yet another cup of coffee and put my newspaper aside and wrote down on a napkin the initials of the remaining seven on the list that I could potentially call upon. The nearest was an estimated three hundred and forty miles away.

I was at the point of wondering whether I was on a fool's errand, as Archer had suggested, and considered for the first time calling it quits. Once more, I weighed the consequences of handing it over to someone else, a lawyer perhaps. And with his or her help, I could then go to the authorities and give a statement, producing the list and the doctor's instructions to bolster my story. It was in my favor that I had no criminal record, not even a speeding ticket, and therefore had no reason for them to suspect me of any violence toward the widow. It might work, and I could be done with a task that I had neither asked for nor wanted. But then I was reminded once again of the doctor's warning in those same instructions and those two men coming to Archer's house in New Jersey. Even if I were to be absolved from blame for the widow's death, which was hardly a guarantee, those men weren't likely to let me go so easily. After all, they had to realize that I would still have those names, if only in my head, and that would seem to be reason enough for them to keep searching for me. And reason enough for me to try and stay one step ahead of them.

That being the case, I pushed away any thoughts of quitting and opted instead to pay a visit to my brother before deciding what to do next.

CHAPTER 10

SNATCH

MY BROTHER WAS born seven and a half months after my parents married. They told everyone he was a honeymoon baby and arrived early. I learned later from my paternal grandfather, drunk on peppermint schnapps one Christmas, that my brother came into the world right on time and was the driving force behind the nuptials. Maybe because his arrival was cloaked in a lie, one that was revealed to him when he was fourteen, the cards were stacked against him from the jump. That doesn't mean that he didn't enjoy any success or have any fun. For starters, he was a better athlete than I was, by far. While I was the last man on my high school basketball team (they didn't cut anyone at our small school), he set the scoring record in his four years on the varsity, a mark that stood for twenty more years after he graduated. Truth be told, he was the reason I grew to love the sport so much. I went to all his games and cheered loudly, more so probably because I had no aptitude for it myself. He also excelled at baseball and football, although he only played the latter for a year, wanting to avoid injury and risk missing any time at hoops, his favorite.

His athletic prowess made him popular in high school, with both the guys and girls. He had lots of friends and girlfriends throughout his entire time in school, but he struggled to graduate with his class, and it was rumored that he did so only because the basketball coach exerted considerable pressure on the principal, a scholarship to the local division one school hanging in the balance if he didn't matriculate. In the end, it didn't matter. It turned out that my brother couldn't handle the pressure of playing basketball and doing the work necessary at a college where academics actually mattered, and he dropped out after his freshman year. Don't misunderstand - my brother was not unintelligent. In fact, in many ways he had more sense than I did, and I believe that "sense" especially of the common variety, is an undervalued form of human intelligence. Perhaps the most valuable one of all.

Unfortunately, he didn't share that opinion, and resigned himself to a succession of jobs at places that didn't require a college education. He worked at various times as a logger, a car salesman, a grocery store manager and a limo driver. He married only once, like me. And again like me, he was divorced, although he left behind a daughter. Because of the somewhat unusual nature of our last name, he was often asked if he was any relation. He told the truth for the first few years after I became somewhat well known. After that, whenever someone inquired about the possible connection, he claimed to have never heard of me. I only know this because I kept in touch with his ex-wife who I liked a great deal and who often confided in me after their parting. I also liked my niece. Loved her, in fact. And when times were tough for them and my brother was unable to keep up the support payments, I helped out a bit financially. Rather than earning my brother's gratitude, it only bought me his scorn. That, and my keeping in touch with my former sister-in-law, something he viewed as betrayal, although I don't know exactly why.

I shouldn't have been surprised that he would react that way. There were signs even before he met and married his wife. While he was proud of me when I was young and sitting at the top of my class in high school, he started feeling resentment not long after he left college. He never told me so, but it wasn't that difficult to detect.

Upon reflection, I suppose it wasn't that hard to see why he might feel that we weren't dealt equal hands in life. His athletic prowess was a currency he was only able to enjoy for a limited time, whereas my intellect was a "gift" that had no apparent expiration date. With every book I wrote and every academic appointment and honor I received, he was reminded of that, I'm sure. The last time we spoke was after the last check I wrote to his ex-wife, one to help out with their daughter's tutoring, when he told me that he was sick of my "rubbing his nose in it." My niece has suffered from learning disabilities since grade school, something my former sister-in-law believes may have contributed to the breakup of the marriage, not because my brother was in any way frustrated or embarrassed by it, but because she thinks he might have suffered from the very same thing, albeit undiagnosed, and may have felt guilty for having "passed it on." It was a theory I couldn't easily dismiss.

He left his upstate New York home a few years after the divorce, around the same time that I was earning an endowed chair at my university. Because our parents were deceased by then, it was harder to keep up with him after he left. It was made harder still by his moving first to the Gulf Coast of Florida, then southern Alaska, northern California and east Texas, all before finally landing in Arkansas where, I was told by his ex-wife, he seemed to have settled into a position as a small engine repairman at a factory just outside of Fort Smith. She had provided me with his address long before the list had entered my life, and I hoped that he hadn't moved again in the year and a half since we last communicated.

It didn't take me long to find his house. It was a small, two-story cottage, nicely maintained, as one might expect from someone who fixes broken machinery for a living. Still, the brother I remembered was a bit of a slob, even after high school and college. I recall visiting him and his wife after they were first married, and their apartment was a wreck most of the time. I never made mention of it, but he volunteered that it was his wife's doing, and that he had given up trying to maintain any kind of order. I accepted that notion until they were divorced and I paid a visit to my former sister-in-law's home and found it to be well kept. By way of contrast, the few times I saw my brother after the divorce, the same disorder was evident, causing me to draw an additional insight into why their marriage might have fallen apart.

As I stood at the door awaiting the answer to my knock, I allowed myself to fantasize that my brother might have changed some since we last spent any time together. Turned out I was right, although not in the way I had hoped it might.

He opened the door and I almost didn't recognize him. He had a shaved head, buffed shiny, and his arms and chest were thick and muscular, to the point that he almost looked like a professional body builder. To further reinforce that impression, he had a tattoo on his right bicep, exposed by the sleeveless t-shirt he was wearing. Unlike most body art I've seen over the years, this one was not elaborate, but rather a simple depiction of a barbell, the bar bent by the weight of the bells on either end. No other image or embellishment. I couldn't ever recall seeing my brother with a tattoo, telling me it had to be of recent vintage. I tried to smile, despite the shock of seeing him looking like that. He didn't return the grin when he saw that it was me.

"What the hell are you doing here?" he asked.

I lied and told him I was in the area for business and thought I'd stop by to see him.

"Here?" he asked. "In Fort Smith?"

I told him my business was in Little Rock, which wasn't a big lie. Nevertheless, he looked at me like it was.

"I got a phone," he said, his voice even but unfriendly. "You could've called."

"I tried," I told him. "It went right to voicemail."

"When was that?"

"About a half an hour ago," I said. That was a lie. I hadn't called him. I hadn't wanted to warn him that I was coming and give him time to find a way not to see me.

He pulled a cell phone out of his pocket and looked at the screen. "I didn't get it," he said, making a face. "I get shitty reception here. You should've called earlier. When I was at work."

"Maybe you should get a land line," I said, more as a joke than a bit of advice.

He didn't take it that way. "We're not all rich like you," he said. "You probably got ten phones."

I chose to ignore the slam in the hopes of salvaging whatever chance there might be for us to have a civil visit. "Well, can I come in?" I asked. "I came all this way."

He didn't say anything. Instead, after a brief moment in which he sized me up once more, he backed away a step to allow me to enter, and then shut the door behind me a little harder than one might do after receiving a guest.

I didn't have to go exploring to find a place to sit. The entry was part of the living room, and the TV was on to some sports channel not associated with ESPN, which disappointed me, as I had hoped to catch some of the tournament games which were starting in an hour or so. I had planned the nearly four-hour trip according to the TV schedule. That and allowing him time to return home from work. I saw that there was some sort of rice dish on the coffee table, half-eaten, with a fork sticking out of it. Without waiting for him to offer, I went over to the only chair and sat down, leaving the sofa all to him.

"I was hoping maybe we could go out and get something to eat," I said, nodding toward the food on the table. "But if you've already made something, that's OK."

"You want to buy me dinner?" he asked.

"Only if you want to go," I said.

He answered by picking up the fork and going to work on the rice again.

"So what kind of business are you here for?" he asked. "Big talk at the university? You get another one of those awards?"

I debated telling another lie, but decided against it. I just told him it was private business. Consulting, I called it.

"What happened to teaching?" he asked.

"I don't teach anymore," I said.

His fork paused halfway to his mouth. "Why? You get fired or something?"

"I resigned," I told him. "I got tired of it. Decided to focus on my writing."

He grunted, and resumed eating. If he had more food made, he didn't offer me any, nor did he ask if I wanted something to drink.

"So what's this all about then?"

I assumed he was referring to my visit and not my decision to stop teaching. "Nothing," I told him. "You're my brother. I was close by. I just thought I'd come and say hi."

He looked at me like he didn't believe me. I had seen that look plenty of times over the years, not that I lied to him that often. It was more that he was always skeptical about anything I said, perhaps because he couldn't relate to me or maybe because he didn't want to.

"What're you writing?" he asked. It didn't sound like he was that curious, more like he just wanted to get the visit over with and that was something you might be expected to say in order to get the conversation moving in that direction.

"Nothing that you'd find very interesting," I said. Which was true. Technically. Since I was writing nothing.

"Right," he said. "I'd probably be too stupid to understand even if I was interested, isn't that what you meant?"

I didn't want to bother trying to correct him or make him feel better. That was our dance for so many years, and I wasn't keen on engaging in it again.

"I actually haven't written anything yet," I confessed. "People think I'm writing. My publisher certainly thinks so. But I haven't written a word. I don't even have a topic yet."

He put the fork down and stared at me. "You serious?"

I told him I was.

"You sick or something?"

"Not that I'm aware of."

He picked up the fork once more and resumed eating. "I guess you probably don't have to work if you don't want to," he said, between gulps. "Not like the rest of us."

"It's not that I don't want to exactly."

He gave me another one of those skeptical looks. "Writer's block?" he asked. "Isn't that what it's called?"

"I suppose," I said. "Although I don't think that applies in my case. I haven't even tried to write."

He finished his food and pushed his plate aside and hit the mute button on the TV. "You came all the way out here to tell me that?"

I shook my head. "I'm just making conversation. You asked me what I was doing. So I'm telling you."

He stared at me for a bit, probably trying to figure out what was different about me. "I fix motors," he said finally. "I never thought I'd be mechanically inclined, but turns out I am, and I like it. It gives me a feeling of accomplishment every time I get one running again. Happens at least once a day. No writer's block or repairman block or whatever-the-fuck block. My hands are always dirty. But I don't mind that either."

"Maybe I should try it," I said.

He shrugged. Flipped a few channels on the TV until he landed on the pre-game show. "You still follow basketball?" he asked.

"I do," I told him. "Some tournament this year, huh? Looks like anybody could win it."

He gave a dismissive gesture, almost exaggeratedly so. "I don't even know who's in it," he said. "I don't follow team sports anymore."

I found that to be odd, especially since he was such a team guy growing up, to the point of being named captain of the basketball team in both his junior and senior years.

"What do you follow?" I asked.

"Snatch," he said.

I must have raised an eyebrow because his expression showed his displeasure.

"Weight lifting," he said. "It's a specific form of weight lifting. And it's something people do. It may not have any brackets, but it's a real sport and people do it."

"It's also a slang term for a certain portion of the female anatomy," I noted.

"It's a strength sport," he said, ignoring me. "It's in the Olympics."

I looked him over once more. At least it explained his new look. "And do you do it, too? Apart from following it?"

"Yeah," he said defensively. "Not on an Olympic level. But I do it."

"What for?" I asked. It was probably the wrong question at the wrong time, us having only spent five minutes in each other's company for the first time in years, but I was curious.

"Why did you ever do anything?" he asked back.

"You got me there," I admitted. "I didn't mean to judge."

He was silent for what seemed like a minute. I wasn't sure if that meant he forgave me for the insult. I doubted it.

"Why don't you tell me why you're really here?" he said.

"I already did," I told him. "There's no hidden agenda." Which was true. I just came to see him. It had no connection to what happened with the doctor and his list. Of course, if I hadn't come to Arkansas to look up someone whose name appeared on it, I wouldn't have been sitting there in his tiny living room, but other than that they weren't connected.

He studied me for a brief time. Then he turned off the TV using the remote and stood up.

"Fuck it," he said. "Let's go out."

CHAPTER 11

I Know People Who Can Help

Mᵧ ʙʀᴏᴛʜᴇʀ ʙᴇɢᴀɴ drinking when he was a junior in high school. My parents weren't aware of the start date, but I sure was. We shared a small bedroom and I soon came to realize that the smell that accompanied him to bed on most Saturday nights was beer. Our parents went to sleep early and, at that time anyway, had developed a level of trust with regard to my brother. After all, he was both a star athlete and a popular student. They had no reason to suspect anything until they got a phone call one night during the winter of that same year when the police informed them that they had discovered my brother passed out in a snow bank several blocks from our home. He was suffering from frostbite and being treated at the local emergency room after having been brought there and revived.

As was the practice of most parents at the time, he was grounded for a couple of weeks, the leniency of the punishment reflecting the lie he had told that he'd succumbed to pressure from some friends (who he refused to name) and that it was the first time he had ever touched alcohol. I wasn't in the room when he said that. I found out later, from him, when he at first asked for my complicity and then, when I didn't answer fast enough, threatened to hurt me if I said anything to the contrary. I didn't. I wouldn't have anyway, even without the threat, but he must have worried that I might.

He got caught a half a dozen more times after that, with increasing levels of punishment that at first he endured, and then later ignored without consequence, until they finally gave up, thinking no doubt that he would soon be off to college and on his own, free to fuck up as much as he wanted. Because of the change in his appearance and his professed love for a form of physical exercise that would seem to require at least some level of discipline, I suppose I was hoping he had curtailed that particular bad habit. Turned out I was wrong, as was often the case with my brother.

He took me to a sports bar where he seemed to be one of the regulars. Before we even sat down, a waitress came by with a "seven and seven," hardly the drink of a man with the physical look of my brother. A little old school even. But he sure seemed to like them. While I nursed my Bushmills, he put back four of them in an hour. Other than waving and saying hello to several of those aforementioned regulars, he didn't engage in a lengthy conversation with anyone, nor did he introduce me to anybody. In between watching the game on one of the many big-screen TVs in the bar, I tried to get him to talk about his ex-wife and daughter, but he answered with few words and even less enthusiasm. When I moved the topic on to whether he might have a new woman in his life, he all but ignored me except for a quick shake of the head.

It went on like that throughout the first game, during which he had two more drinks. I noticed that while that game was on, he was paying particularly close attention to a man across the bar who looked like he might share some of the same training habits. The guy was watching him as well. Because of that, the thought crossed my mind that my brother might be gay and newly (or not) out of the closet. It wasn't so hard to picture, not because he ever did anything that caused me to suspect that he might be, but because he had always been so unpredictable and capable of surprising me, as reaffirmed by both his appearance and behavior that night.

Any further thoughts in that direction went out the window when he announced that we should get going and we walked - rather deliberately it seemed to me - in front of that guy on our way to the door. We weren't two feet past when the guy uttered an insult regarding my brother's manhood. While I had attended most of my brother's sporting events and even played some sports with him when we were younger, I couldn't ever recall seeing him move so fast. He had the guy by the throat before he could even react, and in a spilt second was bending him backward over the bar. But as I mentioned, the guy looked like he worked out as much as my brother, and he managed a move that I wasn't sure was possible when he swung his legs around my brother and used them as leverage to pull himself upright. At the same time, he delivered a couple of kidney punches, one on each side, causing my brother to let go of him and back off. By then, one of the bartenders and a bouncer I hadn't seen when we walked in came over and pushed them out the door, the bouncer exclaiming that they could "kill each other" if they wanted to, as long as they did so outside the bar.

I was right behind them, thinking that it was all over, when the bartender and bouncer let them loose and they started right up again. A crowd came pouring out of the bar to watch, and it was like something you might see on TV, with each man seeming to gain the upper hand before giving way to the other. Finally, a cop car showed up, sirens and lights going, and two members of the local force got out and put an end to it. Both men were handcuffed and my brother was thrown into the back of the cruiser while the other guy was forced to wait with one of the cops for a second squad car to arrive. I hopped in my car just as the one containing my brother turned around, and

I somehow managed to follow it a good two miles back to the station where I witnessed my brother being hauled in. Thankfully, he didn't resist or utter any objections, foul or otherwise.

After booking and assorted other police procedure, I was able to post bail and bring him back to the car. Observing the bruises on his face and seeing how gingerly he walked from the station, I asked if he wanted me to take him to the emergency room.

"I'm fine," he said, and closed the door firmly.

I started the car and pulled away in what I thought was the direction back to his house. "What was that all about?" I asked.

He opened the window, presumably to get some fresh air, and stuck his head out as we drove. I waited a little longer for him to answer, and as I started to repeat the question he cut me off.

"He works out at the same gym as me," he said, pulling his head back in the car. "He's always riding my ass about my weight."

"What for?" I asked. "You don't look heavy."

He frowned. "Not that weight," he said. "The weight I snatch. He says he was doing that when he was twelve. Which is pure bullshit."

I didn't know what to say to that so I drove on for a while before I realized that nothing looked vaguely familiar and I had no idea where I was going. He must have sensed what I was feeling because he told me to take a left at the next stop light. I did so, and from there he gave me directions back to his house in a voice about as animated as the one associated with your basic navigation system.

When I pulled into the driveway, he opened the door and stopped before getting out. "Thanks for posting bail," he said. "I'll pay you back. Every cent."

"Don't worry about it," I said. "They'll send me a check after you show up for the court date. I'm sure you won't be in any major trouble. At least that's what the desk sergeant said."

He nodded and looked down.

"You driving back to Little Rock now?" he asked, still not looking at me.

"I don't think so," I told him. "It's too far and I'm too tired."

There was an awkward moment when we both had to be thinking the same thing.

"I only got the one bedroom," he said, nodding back toward the house. "One bed."

"Sure," I said. "I understand."

He nodded again, and then gave me directions to a motel nearby. "It's pretty clean," he said. "And they got HBO."

I told him thanks and he got out. Then he leaned back in before walking away.

"Why are you here, really?" he asked.

"I already told you," I said.

He stared at me for a couple of seconds. Then he shook his head and closed the door, the window still open. "Have it your way," he said. "But if you're in some kind of trouble, you should tell me. I know people who can help."

He didn't wait for me to respond. Instead, he walked up to his front door, put his key in and unlocked it and entered, without ever turning back.

I waited there in the driveway until I saw the light go on in what I assumed to be his only bedroom.

Then I made my way to that motel he suggested.

CHAPTER 12

THE DEEP END

Now you may wonder why I never suspected that the men in suits would think to come looking for me in Arkansas. Well, in point of fact, I did. However, I relied on the proximity of the other names on the list to my first stop in New Jersey to point them in another direction. I also counted on the fact that if they were capable following me to my home in Connecticut, they were probably also capable of learning that my brother and I were hardly close and that I would have had little reason for going to see him. Of course, I recognized that I could be wrong and that they might in fact show up there, eventually. But there didn't seem to be a network of these guys, as proven by not sending someone else to Archer's house. They would have to decide which name to pursue first, and I simply reasoned that they would choose another city and another of those people on the list before choosing Arkansas. In the end, I was both right and wrong, which did little for my predicament. And when I woke up that morning in the motel outside of Fort Smith, I absolutely found myself in a predicament.

Someone was at my door, banging on it and calling my name. My real name, not the fake one I was registered under. I immediately thought the worst and dug the baton out of my duffel bag, put it behind my back, and peeked through the peephole in the door.

It would be an understatement to say that I was surprised to see the guy who my brother fought with at the bar standing there. I cracked open the door, keeping the chain on it.

"What do you want?" I asked him, through the crack.

"Your brother asked me to come by and get you. He wants to go to breakfast. He feels bad about last night."

"My brother?" I asked. "You talked to my brother? When?"

"About a half an hour ago."

"Bullshit."

He frowned. "I know it didn't look it, but we're actually friends."

"Right," I said. "And you're going out to breakfast with him?"

"Yeah," he said. "We go every Saturday."

"You've got to be kidding me," I said.

He must have realized that he was making little sense and that I might be in need of a bit more of an explanation. "Look, I don't expect you to understand," he said. "We get into a fight about once a month. Usually the cops don't get involved. But if they do, we just drop the charges against each other and forget about it."

"OK," was all I said.

"Good," he said. "Then let's get going. We gotta pick him up on the way."

He started to turn and walk away, as if I would be right behind him. I wasn't.

"This is crazy," I told him. "Why in hell would I agree to go anywhere with you after that story you just told?"

He stopped and turned. "I knew your name, didn't I? And I knew where you were staying. How would I do that if I didn't talk to your brother?"

I could think of a couple of reasons. But they didn't seem to jibe with someone who lived there in Fort Smith and whom my brother clearly knew. Still, my paranoia wouldn't permit me to move. He could see that and frowned once more.

"You're the smart one, right? The one who writes all those books and gives all those talks? Your brother told me all about you. Think about it for a second. Who would make up something like that?"

"My brother told you about me?" I asked, more surprised by that than anything he'd previously uttered.

"Yeah," he said. "A bunch of times."

"Alright," I said, hoping it was true, but still not thoroughly convinced. "Tell me something you couldn't know just by looking me up on the internet."

He seemed to think about that for a second. "You guys shared a room growing up. He used to come home drunk all the time in high school and you never ratted him out. He thought that was pretty cool."

With that, I undid the chain and opened the door.

"Let me throw some water on my face and grab my wallet," I told him.

About ten minutes later, we were on the way to my brother's house. He drove a huge pickup, a Dodge Ram, which seemed fitting for a guy like him.

"It's just something we do," he said, elaborating on the fight of the previous night. "To keep sharp. We act like we don't like each other and then one of us says something to the other. Then the other one comes back with something. Pretty soon we forget that we're just acting and start throwing lumber."

"You know that's nuts, right?" I asked.

He laughed as we turned the corner onto my brother's street. I was about to ask another question when he stomped on the brakes.

"What's wrong?" I asked.

"Look," he said, and pointed at my brother's house. There were two men standing in front of the door. Wearing suits. Black ones. Waiting.

"Shit," I said.

"You know them?"

"I think so," I said. At that moment, my brother's door opened, and the two men shoved their way in.

"What the fuck?" he said and turned to me.

"Does he have a back door?" I asked him.

Less than a minute later, we were parked around the corner and out of the car. He must have been familiar with my brother's house since he cut through a couple of yards and approached the adjacent garage about twenty feet from the porch and the back door. I followed and stopped behind him at the edge of the garage. From what I could see through the only window in the back, there was no movement inside.

"I know this is probably a stupid question, but can you handle yourself in a fight?" he asked, his eyes still on the porch.

"A fist fight?"

He turned to me and frowned. "Shit. Just try to keep one of them occupied and not get yourself killed. I can take 'em both if you can just buy me a minute or two."

I pulled out the baton then and flicked it open. "Is it alright if I use this?"

His frown gave way to a big smile. "You really are something. Just like he said."

"How do you want to do this?" I asked.

"I know where the back door key is," he said. Again, my look stopped him from continuing.

"You guys really are strange," I told him.

"Define strange," he said.

"Never mind," I told him. "You go in first. I'll count ten seconds and come in after you."

He looked at me for a bit, then shrugged. "Why not?" he said. Then he took off for the tiny back porch.

As he did, I couldn't help but think how bizarre this had all been, beginning with the phone message I'd received nine days before. Until that moment when I walked back into my office from lunch, I hadn't given much thought to my brother in months. I certainly didn't have any plans to visit Arkansas. Or New Jersey. Or anywhere else, for that matter. The only thing on my calendar was to watch the NCAA tournament, something I looked forward to for about three hundred and forty six days, from the end of the championship game the year before until the start of the new one the following March. And yet here I was, about to rush into the house belonging to my brother, where two men were probably looking for me for reasons I hadn't yet determined. And for the second time in three days, I found myself wondering if I was going to have to strike someone with intent to harm, something so out of character for me that I almost believed that it had to be a dream or some sort of prolonged hallucination. It was only the sound of shouting from inside the house that caused me to remember my end of the plan, and I ran into the house, considerably later than ten seconds after my brother's friend.

When I got in there, I saw my brother holding a man I had never seen before in some form of headlock, while simultaneously rifling through his pockets. The second man was unconscious on the floor, at the feet of my brother's friend, who was simply watching my brother conducting his search. There was something familiar about the man on the floor, although I didn't take the time then to try and figure out what it was. Whoever they were, they weren't the two I had encountered at the widow's house.

"What the hell is going on?" I asked.

My brother removed his empty hand from the man's pocket and threw him hard to the floor. He gave him a brief glance as if to determine how much fight he might have left in him, before he turned to look at me.

"You're late," said my brother's friend.

"Sorry," I said. "Looks like you didn't need me anyway."

My brother stared at me, and for the first time I noticed a bruise on his face that wasn't there the night before. It was new. As was the blood running down the side of his head.

"Now are you going to tell me what you're here for?" he asked.

I surveyed the scene for a second or two, and it was then that I realized where I had seen the unconscious man before. He was the guy who I had encountered in the entranceway of Alden Archer's house. The Samoan. The one I struck with the baton. His hair was short now, a buzz cut, and his arm was in a plaster cast. I turned back to my brother who was still waiting for my answer.

"I guess I owe you that much," I told him, and I meant it.

A short time later, the two men had their hands duct-taped in front of them and were seated together on the sofa, with kerchiefs tied around their mouths. Which was unnecessary, in my opinion, since they hadn't uttered a word before those gags were put on. I was in the kitchen, where I had just finished telling my brother and his friend the events of the past week, not leaving out a single detail.

"Fuck," my brother said.

"That's some weird shit," his friend chimed in.

"And you're sure that's the guy from New Jersey?" my brother asked, jerking his thumb in the direction of the man with the cast on his arm.

"Yeah," I said. "I did that to him." I picked up the baton again and showed it to him.

Both my brother and his friend looked at me with some new-found admiration. Or at least that's what I thought it was. It could have been something else. I didn't ask for a clarification. Instead, I walked back into the living room, followed by my brother and his friend. Then I went over to the Samoan and pulled off the kerchief to allow him to speak.

He looked at me without the slightest fear or concern.

"Who do you work for?" I asked.

He continued to stare and said nothing.

"What's so important about that list that you're chasing me all over the country?"

I waited a bit, hoping to get an answer, but his expression remained fixed. It seemed that he wasn't going to share any information with me, so I started to put the gag to him again, but he shook it away.

"You know how to swim?" he asked.

It was hardly the question I had expected, but I figured I ought to play along. So I told him I did.

"Good," he said. "Cause you're in way over your head."

My brother made a move for him, but I grabbed his arm to stop him. "Don't. Let him talk."

"I got nothing more to say," the man told me. "Except that you can't just walk away anymore. That ship has sailed."

My brother and his friend both turned to look at me. I shrugged. It sounded about right. I never really believed that I would have been able to hand over the list and simply walk away.

"Who are those guys who came to Archer's house?" I asked the Samoan.

"Wouldn't you like to know," he said.

"What are we, seven?" my brother said.

The man turned and smiled at him. Then he spit on his chest, the spume slowly running down his t-shirt. My brother looked down and watched it do so until it ran out of momentum and stopped just above his belt. He turned to look at me.

"Can I?" he asked.

I just shrugged. I figured I owed him that too. He nodded and turned back to the man and threw a vicious jab to his nose. I heard the crack, then watched as the blood began to flow down the front of the fat man's shirt. He didn't make a sound. If it hurt him, he wasn't about to let on.

I got his attention then by snapping my fingers. He looked toward me.

"What's this all about?" I asked him. "Maybe if you tell me, we can work it out."

He shook his head. "I already told you, it's too late. My orders were to find you and bring you back. Along with those papers. And not to say a word about any of it."

"You already violated that one," my brother told him.

The man shrugged. "Not gonna matter if you're gonna kill me."

"Who said anything about killing anybody?" I asked.

He looked a little surprised, though not necessarily relieved. "What are you gonna do with us then?"

It was a good question. The first thing we did was put the gag back on him. It took some effort, but my brother was more than happy to help hold him steady. The Samoan stared at him with more than a little hatred in his eyes as he did. When we were done, we left them in the living room and went out to the porch where they couldn't hear us talk.

"They were asking me where you were," my brother told me, touching the knot on his head.

"That's good," I said. "That means they didn't know. They probably didn't even know I was in the state."

"Or maybe they did, but just not where," he said.

"How would they know that?" I asked.

He shrugged. But he was right. Maybe they did and I was just hoping otherwise.

"What about the bail record from last night?" his friend asked. "That would have your name on it."

"Maybe," I said. "But they'd have to have a lot of juice to get that. Especially that fast."

"What about your rental car then?"

"Same thing," I said. "Plus they would've come straight to the motel instead of here."

We all chewed on that for a bit.

"How do you think they found me?" my brother asked.

"Wouldn't have been hard," I said. "A little digging around and they could find out I had a brother and where you live. I think that's why it's them and not the other two. They just took a shot."

"Well, they know you're here now," his friend pointed out. "What do you want to do?"

"You want to call the cops?" my brother asked.

I shook my head. For all the same reasons I didn't go to the police in New York, I didn't want to involve the cops in Arkansas and told those guys as much.

My brother looked at me and shrugged. "Can't just let 'em go."

He was right once more, and so we debated our options for a good half hour, drinking coffee and eating donuts back out on the porch. Just to make sure those guys hadn't figured out a way to free themselves, my brother's friend checked on them through the living room window every minute or so.

Ultimately, we decided upon a plan, one that I believed both suited my need to make a clean escape, while also not exposing us to a manslaughter charge. It was also more humane than some of the others we came up with, but that didn't really influence our decision.

CHAPTER 13

THEY'LL TAKE THEIR LUMPS

My brother's friend drove me back to the motel so that I could retrieve my car, while my brother remained behind at the house to watch the two men. When we returned, I pulled the car into the driveway and all the way around to the back stoop where my brother's friend and I had first entered the house just hours before. Out of the sight of any neighbors, we loaded the two men into the trunk and my brother got behind the wheel, while I rode in the passenger's seat. My brother's friend drove his truck and led us out of the neighborhood and, eventually, up into the hills outside the sleepy town.

I never bothered to ask my brother or his friend how they knew about the abandoned fishing camp. It didn't seem necessary. It was far outside of town and we didn't encounter a soul once we turned off the two lane state highway that took us to the one-room shack that was a good mile or so down a barely-passable road. Once we got there, we unloaded our captives and led them to the falling-down front porch. Then, with some physical persuasion, we got them to lie down on their stomachs and we duct-taped their feet together and then rolled them over on their backs once more. Once that was accomplished, my brother produced an old knife with just enough of a serrated edge to make it possible to cut through duct tape if one worked long and hard enough at it. He made sure to act that out for the benefit of the two now-miserable men on the porch. Then he tossed the knife into the woods some thirty feet away. As I'm sure he planned, their eyes followed the path it took into the trees. It would take some effort, but if they were willing to crawl on their bellies with nothing more than their elbows and knees to propel them, they might be able to find it. Hell, they might even break free from their taped ankles and hands just from the sheer effort of trying to get there. Either way, we were pretty certain that they weren't going to just lie there and wait for help that was never going to arrive. Indeed, based on the way the Samoan was staring at my brother, blood still dripping from his nose, it was obvious that he wanted to get his hands on him and would do whatever it might take in order to do so.

Finally, my brother's friend took two bottles of spring water from behind the seat of his truck and set them near the edge of the woods. When they were ultimately free of their bindings, they would have sufficient hydration to walk back to the highway and, eventually, civilization. And when they did finally get back to town and their own transportation, wherever they left it, we were likewise pretty certain that they weren't going to report what we had just done to them. Not unless they were prepared to tell the authorities why they happened to go to my brother's house in the first place that morning.

"They're professionals," my brother's friend said, in arguing the point. "They'll take their lumps and go back to get new orders."

We had a lively debate then about what those orders might entail. We didn't agree on anything except that their superiors, the other two men in suits, weren't simply going to leave me unmolested. Which is why, after we dropped off his friend, my brother offered to take a few days off of work and accompany me back to Little Rock and help me find out the meaning behind that list that I wished I'd never laid eyes on.

"Are we going to go see somebody else whose name is on it?" he asked, as I was throwing my belongings into my duffel bag back in my motel room in Fort Smith.

"Yes and no," I said.

"Explain," he said.

"I want to go back and talk to Plum first. Tell him what happened back at your house. I want to see how he reacts."

My brother stared at me and didn't say a word.

"You don't think that's a good idea?" I asked.

"I don't think you tell anybody anything they don't need to know," he said. "There's no point. If he could've helped you, he would have offered the other day."

He was probably right, but my gut was telling me to go there anyway. I acknowledged his concern, but told him I felt that in the course of talking to Plum, I might discover if he was in any way connected to those men in suits, seeing as their muscle had showed up less than forty eight hours after my visit. That was an angle we hadn't yet considered. Despite conceding the point, he remained steadfast in his opinion that I shouldn't go back there.

We arrived back in Little Rock and my motel room there later that night, and I could have gone straight over to Plum's once we did, but I was too tired from the day's activities and wanted to have my wits about me when I saw him. There were two beds in the room and my brother and I watched the last of the Saturday games of the east regional, each in our own bed, just like when we were kids sharing a room.

As we did, he surprised me when he said out of nowhere that his biggest regret was not trying harder when he was in college that year.

"I think I could have started as a freshman," he said. "Maybe even made all-conference."

"I always thought so," I told him. It was true. I always did. And I always wondered what might have happened if he had stuck it out.

He was quiet for a bit, maybe wondering the same thing, as the hoop action played out on the screen. "Ah, fuck it," he said, finally. "We are who we are."

I chose not to argue the point and we left it at that, eventually falling asleep with the game still on.

We didn't talk about it in the morning or even acknowledge it. Instead, we went and had breakfast at that same diner where I announced that I was going to go out to see Plum, and would be happy to go by myself. However, my brother capitulated without any prompting by me and said that I was probably right to do so, but that he ought be there with me.

When we got there, things looked largely the same as they did three days earlier. I watched as my brother took in the scene, and even though I had informed him of the condition of the exterior of the house, he still seemed surprised, probably because of the amount of money I told him that I estimated Plum was raking in from his gambling. I was looking forward to gauging my brother's reaction when we got inside, not having fully described the contrast between the interior and the outside, and so I stepped forward and rang the bell without pause. As before, it made no sound. My brother looked first at me and then at the bell as if he might be mistaken, and I remembered that I hadn't told him that part of the story either. I related it to him as we waited.

"What's the point of no sound?" he asked.

"He didn't tell me."

"Well, what do you think? You're the smart guy."

"I think it's a control thing," I said. "He probably has a light that goes off somewhere in the house to tell him that someone has rung it. He then decides whether to answer it, based on if he's expecting someone."

I then told him how it rang when Amy came to see him. "Telling me there's a switch that allows him to activate the sound when he wants," I added.

"Why would he do that?"

"Maybe the light is only in one room and he wants to be able to know someone is outside at the door," I said, with confidence.

"So like a normal person with a normal doorbell," my brother said.

I laughed. He was right. I had clearly over-thought it. He simply shook his head when no sound came after I pushed it once more.

As we waited, I looked up at the ceiling of the little roof that covered the front step and, for the first time, noticed a small hole revealing a tiny camera lens. You really had to look closely to find it. I hadn't seen it when I was there before, but it made sense that Plum would take such precautions. His strategy - if indeed it was a strategy - of keeping the outside of the house in terrible condition so as to cause visitors to make assumptions about both the house and its occupant had worked with me. I had no reason to look for a camera or any other form of security on my previous visit. It was also how he probably made a determination of whether he was going to answer the door. Again, there was logic to it, but I suddenly felt uncomfortable. I didn't like the feeling it gave me.

I elbowed my brother and pointed up at the camera, ignoring the likelihood that I was being observed doing so from inside. My brother didn't react. He just kept staring at it. I could tell he was going through the same mental calculations as I was about Plum's paranoia. With no other idea in mind, I gave a friendly wave at the camera to indicate that it was me and that he had nothing to be afraid of. My brother looked from the camera to me, and I pointed at him and mouthed the words "my brother." I hoped that doing so would cause Plum to open the door and let us in, regardless of whether he might be willing to offer any more information than he did two days before. At the very least, I thought he might be curious to meet my brother.

We waited on the porch for another minute or so, way past the time it would take Plum to come to the door and let us in, and certainly past the time it took him to do so the other day. I knocked on the door once more. Loudly. Loud enough that he couldn't miss it, even if he was in the basement watching the game and ignoring the monitor that must be somewhere inside. When that didn't bring a response, I tried the door and found it to be locked, which was hardly a surprise given Plum's abundant caution.

"Do you have a phone number?" my brother asked.

I told him that Plum wouldn't give it to me.

"If he's got that security camera and he's inside, he knows we're out here," my brother said. "And if he was friendly, he'd let us in. Something's not right."

I nodded. Then I turned to look around. There was a driveway leading to a garage in the rear of the house and, I guessed, a back door somewhere. I looked at my brother as if to ask what he thought about going around to the back. He shook his head.

"I'm out on bail, remember?" he said. "I'm not about to get caught trespassing."

"Alright then," I said. "Let's get out of here. I think we probably have our answer about him."

I stepped off the porch and was about halfway down the sidewalk leading to the street when a door opened on the house next door and a large man came out on the stoop. The guy was somewhere in age between forty and sixty, although it was impossible to tell because of the mop of graying hair and his bushy beard, not to mention his weight which had to be somewhere close to three hundred pounds.

"Are you looking for the fella who lives in there?" he asked.

"Yeah," my brother said, before I could. "You know if he's home?"

"You the po-po?" the neighbor asked.

I looked at my brother whose expression didn't change. He just kept staring at the guy with something less than approbation.

"No," I told the man. "We're friends of his. We're here to watch the basketball games with him."

"You like basketball?" the neighbor asked. It was a strange question, considering the circumstances.

"Yeah, that's why we watch it," my brother said, with that familiar edge to his voice.

The neighbor copped an attitude in response to that. "I was going to tell you the score, but now fuck it," he said. "And you probably should go find yourself a bar 'cause you ain't gonna be watching it in there anytime soon."

My brother and I exchanged a look. "Why is that?" I asked, turning back to the neighbor.

"Cause the moving truck left about half an hour ago," he said with a smug smile. "Emptied the whole place out. In record time. One of the moving guys told me they were getting a thousand dollar bonus to get it all done in three hours. Did it, too. With ten minutes to spare."

"He moved out?" I asked.

"Yeah," said the neighbor. "That's what I just said."

My brother looked at me. "Did he ever mention anything about moving?"

I shook my head. My brother made a face. I didn't know what it meant, but I had a good idea. I turned back to the neighbor.

"Did he say where he was going?"

"He don't talk to nobody around here," the guy said. "And nobody ever talks to him."

"Why did you think we were the police then?" my brother asked him.

The man made a face that seemed to indicate that we were a couple of complete fools to be asking such a thing.

"Fella lives here six months, I see trucks bringing all kinds of stuff that costs all kinds of coin. Only two ways for 'em to get it in there and I can see both. Hell, that TV had to cost a few grand all by itself."

"They've come down considerably in price these days," my brother told him. "Plus, you can pay on time. That doesn't make him a criminal."

The neighbor laughed, seeming to enjoy the back and forth. "Yeah, well, he never left the place that I could tell. Had all his food brought to him by that pretty bitch he hung around with. Only person I ever saw go in there. Until you come the other day."

He nodded his sizeable head toward me.

"He had to be up to something no good if he didn't have no job," he added.

"Maybe he worked from home," my brother said. "Lots of people do."

"Yeah, maybe," the man said. "Then again maybe he didn't. But then there was that gun."

Once more, my brother looked at me, as if I might know what he was talking about. And once again, I didn't.

"What gun was that?" I asked.

"The one he pointed at me just before he left," the man said.

The image of Rafe Plum holding a gun on his enormous neighbor would not register, even though I had only met him once and knew next to nothing about him. Nothing I could be sure of, anyway.

"He did that?" I asked.

The neighbor nodded. Smugly.

"In front of the movers?" my brother asked. It was a good question. It did seem implausible that Plum, or anyone else for that matter, would do such a thing and risk possible criminal exposure.

"The truck was halfway down the street," the neighbor said. "His girlfriend was in her car waiting for him. He told her to wait a minute, then walked over and pulled out the biggest fucking pistol I ever seen and stuck it in my chest. Told me if I said anything to anyone about what I saw he'd come back and kill me."

"And yet you just told us," my brother pointed out.

"I ain't afraid of that little prick," the neighbor told us. "He's running from something. And he sure as hell ain't coming back if he is."

"Why would he lock the door then?" my brother asked. "If he moved everything out, what's the point?"

The neighbor sneered. "What do I look like? The fucking answer man?"

With that, he turned and went back into his house and slammed the door, leaving my brother and me to stare at it for a few more seconds, as if waiting for some kind of encore.

When he didn't give us one, we went back to the car and drove back to my motel room to decide what to do next.

CHAPTER 14

You're Very Smart

M Y BROTHER STARED at the list I had retrieved from the rental car. While he did, I realized that the only two people other than me who had seen it were now dead. That's assuming the men in suits had never seen it before, which I was fairly certain was the case.

"I think we should go to Chicago," he said, suddenly looking up at me.

"Why Chicago?" I asked.

"It's the most interesting of the remaining names," he said. "Plus it's the closest."

I didn't necessarily agree with the first part, but couldn't debate the second.

"Are you sure you want to do this?" I asked.

"I took time off from work to help you and you want me to stop before we even get started?"

"I didn't say that," I said. "But if your friend and I didn't come along, you could have gotten hurt by those two guys back at your house. Or worse."

"That's touching," he said. "Really. Very touching. But that's exactly why I want to keep going. At least until we get a handle on things. Then maybe you can turn it all over to the cops or just forget the whole fucking thing and go live in Peru."

"I'm not turning it over to the cops," I said. "I already told you that."

"Well then, you better check on flights to Lima."

He was joking. Or at least I thought he was. He had something resembling a smile on his face. I took the list from him and looked at the name of the person living in Chicago, even though I knew it and needed no reminder. I guess I was stalling.

"What do you propose we do when we get there?" I asked.

"I've been thinking about that," he said.

"And?"

"I think you should let me talk to him," he said. "Alone."

I was surprised to hear him say that and told him so.

"Look," he said, "those guys are looking for you. Not me."

I guess he was figuring that our friends at the abandoned camp were back in civilization and in communication with their superiors.

"But they also know you're my brother and might know as much as me now about the whole situation."

He shrugged. "So what?" he said. "Doing something to me doesn't keep you from still checking out those names. That's assuming they even show up when I'm there."

"I don't think they're sticklers over who's the greatest threat to them," I said. "They killed the doctor's wife for less than you know now."

He didn't argue, and we sat in silence for a few more minutes.

"But it's not a bad idea," I said finally. "Assuming you're willing to take the risk. And there is a considerable risk."

He smiled wide. "Why the hell do you think I'm doing this in the first place? For you?"

Actually, I did and it must have registered on my face.

"Of course I'm doing it to help you," he said, backpedaling. "That goes without saying. But I had fun yesterday. More fun than I've had in years. My buddy and I pull that same fight routine to keep sharp and stay on our toes. But it gets boring. I know all his moves. He knows all of mine. This is the real thing. Combat. With live bullets."

"Very live," I told him.

"It's just an expression," he said.

"I wouldn't be so sure."

He smiled. I was making his day.

I looked at him and tried to figure out if he had shown any signs of this thrill seeking when he was younger. It then occurred to me that living life on the edge must have been what was at the heart of all that drinking. It wasn't because he liked the taste of it, although he probably did. And it wasn't just the feeling of getting a little buzzed. It was his way of testing the limits, whether it was with our parents or some guy in a bar fight, trying to see what he could get away with and how much punishment he could take. Not unlike playing sports. He wasn't an alcoholic. He was a thrill junkie. Hell, it must have been what led to the dissolution of his marriage. His ex-wife had told me stories of him not coming home on some nights. Of going away for weekends without telling her where he was going or where he'd been whenever he came back. I always assumed it was an affair or a series of them that explained the behavior. But from what I had experienced in the previous few days, it was clear to me that it was more complicated than that.

"So you're actually hoping those guys are going to be waiting for us when we get there?"

"I wouldn't say that," he said. "But if they are, I'll be ready for them."

"Alright then," I said. "Let's do it."

We had just gotten back into the car and as I reached to turn the key in the ignition, my phone began vibrating. I pulled my hand away from the key like it was on fire and looked at my brother. He shrugged, as if anticipating what I was about to ask him, which was whether I should answer it.

"It's probably my secretary," I told him, although I left out the part where I had instructed her to only call me under certain circumstances, none of which were of the positive variety.

I pulled out the phone and looked at the number on the screen. It wasn't her, but I recognized the area code. In truth, I should have been expecting it.

I answered without giving my name.

The female voice on the other end of the line said it for me - in the form of a question.

"Yes," was all I said.

There was a pause, as if I had surprised her by actually picking up.

"This is Detective O'Connell from the New York State Police," she said. "How are you doing?"

She sounded young. Certainly younger than me. Probably less than forty. "Are you really that interested in how I'm doing?" I asked.

"Actually, I am," she said. "I heard about last night."

That, of course, was the reason for me expecting the call. When I bailed out my brother, I used my real name on the form, as my brother's friend had noted. I made a calculated decision not to give my alias. I hadn't told my brother about that and feared that he might use my real name in front of the police. Plus, they had seen my car and I didn't know if they might run a quick check on it, not really knowing the whole story of my brother and his friend at that point. I knew the risk of using my real name and assumed it, thinking that getting caught with a fake name and credentials might be an even bigger risk. Nevertheless, it was still somewhat disconcerting to be talking to the very people who could put me away for a long time.

"I wasn't involved in the scuffle," I told the detective. "I'm perfectly fine."

"Good," she said. "That's good."

There was another silence that stretched on for longer than was comfortable for me.

"So I was wondering if you might be headed back this way anytime soon," she said. "We have some questions for you in connection with the death of Mrs. Condon."

I thought of acting surprised at her reference to the widow's death, pretending that it was news to me, but I knew that after having already talked with Gloria she would probably assume that I knew about her demise. Instead, I asked her what kind of questions.

"Just the usual," she said.

"Why don't we do it now then?" I asked. "On the phone."

"I'd feel much better about a face-to-face meeting," she said.

My brother sat watching this with a look of concern. I had told him about the detective and he must have gathered that she was the person on the other end of the line.

"When I last talked to the widow she was fine," I told the detective.

"That may be," she said. "But I suspect you know quite a bit more about her death than we do at the moment."

"Do you think I killed her?" I asked.

"Did you?"

"Of course not," I said.

"Then you don't have anything to worry about," she said.

I laughed. So did she. We both knew how silly that statement was.

"Anyone is capable of killing," she said. "Depending on the circumstances."

"Ah," I said. "A psychology lesson."

She laughed again. "I've looked you up," she said. "You're very smart."

"That's debatable. I'm talking to you, aren't I?

"Certainly smart enough to kill someone and make it look like a heart attack," she said, ignoring my question.

So they had done an autopsy and found what I suspected. That was enough for me to think that I had no reason to keep talking, and I was just about to hang up when I heard her say, "But I don't think you did that."

"Is that right?"

"Yes," she said. "But I still believe you know more than you're letting on."

"And why do you believe that?"

"What are you doing in Arkansas?" she asked, again ignoring my question.

"Visiting my brother," I told her.

Again, she laughed. "I'm really enjoying this," she said. "But I'd enjoy it a whole lot more if you were here in my office telling me everything you know."

"I told you I don't know anything."

"You didn't actually say that," she pointed out. Of course, she was right.

"Look, I think you might be in the middle of something that could spin out of control," she said. "There's something going on here. I don't know what it is just yet, but I know it's something. And you could be the next one who has a heart attack."

"So you're looking to protect me, is that it?"

"We will. Absolutely. If you come back and tell us everything you know. I'm afraid we can't do much for you if you elect to stay out there."

"If I come back you're going to arrest me," I said.

"Is that what you think?" she asked.

"Yeah," I said. "I come back and talk and you twist my words and suddenly you have probable cause."

"I told you. I don't think you did it. But if we were to arrest you, we could keep you in custody. And therefore safe."

"You don't have the evidence to do that, though, do you? Otherwise I'd be sitting in an Arkansas jail cell right now."

There was a brief pause. "Like I said, you're very smart."

"Well, that being the case, I think I'm going to continue my visit with my brother."

"Your choice," she said, sounding disappointed. "I sure hope this isn't the last time we talk. If you disappear, I fear that we'll never really know what happened to Mrs. Condon and that would make me very sad."

"Sorry to disappoint you," I said.

I didn't give her a chance to respond and hung up.

I waited a bit before I started the car to see if she would call back. My brother waited wordlessly as well, both of us staring at the phone. When it was finally clear that our conversation was over, at least for time being, my brother told me that I should let him drive since he knew the fastest way to Chicago.

CHAPTER 16

IT LASTS FOREVER

W E WERE ON the interstate when my brother handed me his phone and asked me to plug the Chicago address into the GPS on it.

I took it, and instead of doing as he asked, I removed the back and took out the battery and the SIM card. I threw all of it out the window onto the highway where everything bounced and disappeared under the cars behind us. He watched in the rearview mirror and then looked over at me.

"What the hell did you do that for?"

"They know about you now," I told him. "And you've probably got your location services turned on. If they're as wired as I think they might be, they can track it. They can do it even without the GPS. Although that's much harder. But that doesn't mean they won't try."

"That's my only phone," he said.

"I know. Sorry."

He turned back to the road. "What about yours?" he asked.

"What about it?"

"You just used it a few minutes ago," he said.

"That wasn't my phone."

He looked over at me again. "Whose is it?"

I explained my second identity and my reasons for having it. "I bought the phone in the second name back in the Philadelphia airport," I said. "I'm having all my calls forwarded to it."

"They can't track that?"

"Not unless they know the new name or number."

"Well, can't they find out your calls are being forwarded?"

"I suppose. With some effort. But they'd have to think of it first."

"What if they have already?"

"Like I said, they would have showed up back at the motel."

He seemed to ponder that a bit. "You thought of all that? Back in Philadelphia?"

"Yeah. I tried to anyway."

He nodded. "Smart," was all he said. I couldn't tell whether he really meant it, although it sounded different than when he usually uttered that word in my presence.

We were headed toward Missouri and interstate 44, a route that would take us up to St. Louis and more than halfway to Chicago.

"Did you ever wonder why you were so smart and I was so dumb?" he asked.

"You're not dumb," I said. "I never thought of you as dumb."

He kept his eyes on the road. "Don't patronize me. I don't mean overall. I meant in school."

I gave it some thought. In truth, I had often wondered why I won the genetic lottery and he didn't, especially being the first-born.

"I just think the right sperm met the right egg at the right time," I told him.

"Right," he said. I didn't laugh at his attempt at a joke.

"Did you ever wonder why you were such a natural athlete and I couldn't hit a baseball or sink a foul shot to save my life?" I asked.

"Actually, I never did."

"Same thing," I told him. "With every sexual encounter between mom and dad the possibilities were endless."

"That's a picture I didn't need."

"I might have been a top-notch billiard player," I said, ignoring the comment. "Or fly fisherman. Whatever. Everybody is born with some sort of natural talent or inclination. It's how it's worked ever since the beginning of mankind."

We drove on in silence for the next minute or so.

"I was always jealous of you," he said finally.

I looked over at him to see if he was serious. "Really?" I asked.

"You're telling me it never occurred to you?"

"No," I said. And it was true. I never did think of him as jealous, at least not when we were kids. Wronged perhaps. But not jealous really. After all, he was the star athlete.

"Maybe when I was teaching and making all that money," I told him. "Never before that."

"It was just the opposite," he said. "I never cared about the money. And I never would've wanted to be a college professor or consultant or whatever the fuck you were."

"So why as a kid?" I asked. "You were the prom king. I never even got to go."

He shrugged. "I don't care what any jock ever says. They all wish they were the smart kid. At least in the classroom. And at home. Don't get me wrong. Sports are fun. You get the girls, but it's not the same. There's something about being called smart. Or in my case, never being called that. It lasts forever."

I'm terrible at emotional issues. I operate on a surface level in that regard, preferring logic to feelings. Just ask my ex-wife. It was the basis for most of our arguments. So I wasn't particularly comfortable with my brother's confession, and I had no idea what to do with it.

"Don't be so sure," I said finally. "Just like you might lose your jump shot or run a little slower now, the smart stuff fades too. The brain ages just like the rest of the body."

"What's that supposed to mean?"

I told him again about the trouble I was having with the book.

"That doesn't sound so bad," he said. "I'd still trade with you."

"And I might just take you up on it," I said.

He smirked and held up his callused and stained hands. "That'd be a pretty shitty deal. Maybe you have lost a step."

It was a joke, I'm sure, and we both laughed. I thought he might want to continue the conversation, but whatever it was that he was seeking, he seemed to have found.

About an hour or so later, I told him to pull off the interstate and, when he did, I directed him to pull into a strip mall. We were somewhere north of Springfield, Missouri, just before sundown.

At my urging, he parked at the far end of the lot and turned the car off. "What are we doing here?" he asked.

I gestured at the rental car outlet at the opposite end of shopping area.

He turned back to look at me. "We already have a car," he pointed out.

"We have to assume those two goons have the plate now," I said. "They'll tell those other guys who might be able trace it. I haven't seen any indication that they have, but that doesn't mean we should take the chance."

"Back at my house you weren't so worried."

"I never said I wasn't worried," I said. "I'm just being safe."

He didn't argue any further. Instead, he followed me into the rental place and listened while I inquired about a mid-sized American sedan. The more ordinary, the better.

After filling out the paper work and handing over a credit card, the rental agent processed the transaction. He never asked how we got there. He only asked if we planned to go out of state, to which I said yes. I pre-paid for two weeks rental and declined the GPS option for obvious reasons. When we came in, he was listening to music on his phone and the ear buds were still hanging over his shoulder. He was no more than twenty-five, with that earnest attitude that one often associates with people from the mid-west.

"Thanks Mr. Pinckney," he said, handing me back the card and a receipt. "If you'll follow me outside, I'll show you to your car."

My brother turned to look at me when he heard the name. His expression was part surprise, part amusement, if I read it correctly. He didn't say anything.

I nodded for him to follow as the agent and I exited the tiny storefront. We then walked around to the back of the strip mall where there was a smaller lot containing six cars, each of which had the unmistakable look of a rental. The agent pushed a button on the key fob, and the lights flashed on a metallic blue Chevrolet. After walking us around to inspect the car for dents, he opened the driver's side door and waited for me to get in.

When I did, he thanked me and shut the door. Then he stared at my brother waiting for him to move from where he stood near the back, almost frozen in place. As if getting the cue, my brother walked around to the passenger side and got in, and I started the car and pretended to adjust the seat belt. The agent waved to us and walked around the corner of the building to the front of the tiny strip mall. As he did so, he was already putting his ear buds back in and looked to be picking out a song on his phone.

I waited a sufficient amount of time to give the young rental agent the opportunity to get back inside the store. Then I put the car in gear and drove around the building to the front parking lot.

"Mr. Pinckney?" my brother asked.

I then explained to him how I created the new identity with the birth certificate of a dead child. "I got lucky," I added. "Found one with a last name that was easy to remember."

He smiled. "Villanova-Georgetown nineteen eighty-five."

"Biggest upset in NCAA tournament history," I said. "Ed Pinckney scored sixteen points. Grabbed six rebounds."

"Tourney MVP," he said.

"We watched it together, remember?"

"Yeah," he said. "I do."

"It was the last time we did that."

His smile faded a bit. "Really?"

I nodded. "Well, except for the other night."

He stared, as if hoping it wasn't so. "Well, let's try not go another thirty years," he said finally.

I told him sure. Then I pulled into the spot next to my original rental, watching to make sure the agent wasn't eyeing us from the store. Then I handed my brother the keys to that car and told him to get in it and follow me.

"What for?" he said.

"Like I said, they might be able to track that one. If we leave it here, the first thing they're going to do is go into that rental place and ask about their latest renters."

I saw it dawn on him. "And learn about Mr. Pinckney."

I nodded.

"I should've thought of that," he said.

"That's OK. I wouldn't know one end of a small engine from the other."

"They don't have ends," he said, with a smirk.

I laughed as he exited and got in the first rental. Then we both drove out of the lot and got back on the interstate and headed south, back the way we came. When we hit the third exit, I pulled off the highway and into another strip mall. My brother pulled in seconds later.

I gestured for him to get in the new rental and he did.

"Actually, some do have ends," he said.

I looked at him, confused.

"Engines," he said.

"Like I said, I wouldn't know," I said with a laugh. Then I put the car back in gear, and we headed back onto the interstate, north-bound again, with Chicago still many hours away.

We stopped for the night just past St. Louis at a rest stop that had a small motel next to the twenty-pump gas station and all-American looking restaurant. It seemed to me like it might be a good place to spend the night, given all the tractor-trailers parked in the lot. It also had a large general store that sold everything from pork rinds to portable heaters. I veered from the path to the motel toward the store entrance and parked in front of it. When my brother asked what we were doing, I told him that I had to pick up something.

He didn't protest and followed me inside, where I went up to the cash register and asked if they had any pre-paid cell phones. The sixty-something year old woman didn't even respond. Instead, she swiveled around on her stool and grabbed a couple of plastic pack-ages from somewhere behind her and spun back around and laid them on the counter. Each contained a rather outdated looking cell phone. She pointed at the one I picked up.

"That one has twice the minutes for just a few dollars more," she said.

I thanked her and told her I'd take it. I paid with cash and walked out, all while my brother watched without uttering a word. Until we got outside.

"A burner?" he said.

"A what?"

"Burner," he said, once more. "That's what they call them. They're non-traceable. Didn't you ever watch The Wire?"

"What's that?"

He frowned. "A TV show? On HBO?"

I told him I didn't watch a lot of TV, except for sports.

He nodded, like he wasn't surprised. "So you're going to get rid of your phone after all?"

"It's for you," I said, and handed it to him. "You don't have one, remember?"

He frowned, but took it. Then we got back in the car and drove across the lot to the motel where we checked in and went right to the room.

We were both up by six the next morning and, after a quick shower, were eating at the surprisingly large and crowded restaurant attached to the motel and part of the whole rest stop complex. My brother was using my phone to check the route to Oak Park, just southwest of Chicago. That was the home of the retired violinist who we targeted to go see next.

"It says a little more than four hours," he said. "Depending on traffic."

"Sounds good," I told him. He handed me back my phone.

"Why didn't you get a burner?" he asked. "Back in Philly? Why risk using the name?"

"I didn't want to run out of minutes and have to keep changing. Besides, I like the features on this." I held my smartphone.

"GPS," he said.

"For starters."

He nodded. Then asked me what my plan was.

"I think we ought to scout the house first. Then find a place for me to wait. You can take the car. If he's being watched and someone runs the plate, there won't be any connection to me."

"Other than me," he said.

"They'd have to get awful close to find out who you are," I said.

He grabbed the burner and stood. "That'll never happen," he said. "If they even show up."

I liked his confidence. I liked also that I was no longer alone on this quest. I didn't realize how good it would feel for me to have someone along to talk things over with. Especially my brother. I thought those days were well behind us and was happy to be wrong about that.

As my brother had predicted, the drive to the western suburbs of Chicago took us less than five hours, with a stop for a bathroom break that I elongated to watch for anyone who might be following us. I didn't see any signs of it, so we drove from there straight to Oak Park.

After arriving and parking half a block from the house, my brother asked where I wanted to wait while he went to see the violinist. We argued the merits of a few different spots before agreeing on a Panera store in a busy mall about three miles down the road. It was pretty well occupied and I could blend in for as long as I needed to. I bought a cup of coffee and a sandwich while my brother used the rest room. Then he handed me a napkin on which he had written down the number of the disposable phone.

"Do you know what you're going to say?" I asked him. "We should have rehearsed this."

I said this even though I had done a rather poor job preparing for the two meetings I'd already had with Archer and Plum.

"Not to worry," he said. "I got it covered."

"How's that?"

He took a seat and looked around even though no one there could have any idea of what we were talking about or what he was about to do.

"I'm going to pretend to be one of the names on the list," he said. "I'll tell him that someone mailed it to me anonymously. Crazy note attached. Told me to find out what it was all about."

"You think he'll believe that you came all the way out here just to check out some names on a list that you got out of nowhere?"

"He will when I tell him that three people on it are already dead and that another one just disappeared."

I considered this for a moment. Like all good lies, there was just enough truth in there to make it believable, but it seemed to me that it still had some flaws.

"Why go see him though?" I asked. "Why not someone else?"

"I'm going to tell him his name is first on the list. That ought to get his attention."

Again, I could think of a lot of things wrong with that scenario, but I decided that it didn't matter. He was right. Somebody receiving that kind of information from a total stranger who shows up unexpectedly at his door is unlikely to dismiss it out of hand.

"He's going to ask why you haven't gone to the police. He might even call the cops himself."

"Not when I tell him that calling the cops is exactly what Plum did right before he disappeared."

It sounded even crazier then. And maybe just bold enough to work. After all, the truth was even crazier. "I guess it's as good a plan as any," I said.

"Brilliant is how I see it," he said with a smile.

"Well, you can always fall back on the truth if anything goes wrong or he calls the cops while you're sipping his coffee."

"Won't happen," he said.

Once again, I admired his confidence. Then I held up the phone. "If you need some help, I'm just a phone call away."

He nodded. And with that, he was out the door.

CHAPTER 16

TOYLAND

THE SUN WASN'T anywhere near setting when my brother hurried into the Panera and over to the table where I was still sitting. I could see that he was stirred up and so could several other patrons of the restaurant.

"C'mon," he said. "You gotta see this guy."

I remained seated and looked for signs that something might be different about him, that he might be under some kind of duress. Forced in some manner to bring me with him. It wasn't what I expected.

"Why?" I asked. "What happened?"

"You need to see for yourself," he said.

Rather than create an even bigger scene than the one he just had, I pushed from the table and headed for the door, trailing my brother who was moving like the place was on fire.

We didn't speak for the five minutes it took to get back to the house belonging to Michael Toyland, the retired violinist. His was a stately brick colonial, well kept and expensive, as apparent from the neighborhood and my limited knowledge of Chicago real estate. My brother parked in the driveway, as if he had already been given permission to do so.

Before we even got to the door, it opened and a woman who appeared to be in her late sixties greeted us. She was well dressed and adorned. She called my brother by name and he introduced me. Her last name was different than Toyland's, but my brother told me that she was Toyland's cousin. She nodded in agreement and escorted us inside.

Unlike Rafe Plum's residence, the inside matched the exterior. Toyland had obviously earned enough from playing the violin to both live in that house and furnish it accordingly. Cousin Betsy, as my brother referred to her, walked us through the center hallway, past a living room with a blazing fire and back into a room that had been converted into a combination bedroom and sick room. It was difficult to tell what its use had been prior to that. I'd hate to think it was yet another study.

A man whom I assumed was Toyland was in a hospital bed that was set up in the center of the room, surrounded by medical equipment. He had IV tubes in his arm, wires for what could only be heart monitors running under the covers and his gown, and an oxygen mask over his mouth connected to a tank with a computerized monitor that emitted whooshing sounds with each breath. His eyes were closed and I didn't think he was asleep, nor did I think he was just resting. The place smelled like it was awash in hand sanitizer.

Betsy stepped aside to allow my brother and me to enter. My brother took a spot on the side of the bed near the oxygen tank. I stopped at the foot of the bed and looked first at Betsy, then my brother.

"I take it he hasn't been able to communicate in that condition."

"No," he said, "but Betsy here has been a big help."

I didn't turn to look at her but kept my gaze on my brother. He got my drift.

"Don't worry. She knows the whole story."

I turned to her then and she smiled. "It's quite a tale. I hope you get some answers soon. I know Michael would have liked to have known what's going on."

"What's wrong with him?" I asked.

"What isn't?" she replied.

"What do you mean?"

She looked at the man in the bed before turning back to me. "He's had several forms of cancer, both a minor heart attack and a major stroke, not to mention adult-onset diabetes."

"Jesus," was all I could think of to say.

"Yes," she said. "And it would probably take some kind of miracle by him to do anything for Michael at this point."

"Look at him," my brother said to me, referring to Toyland. "He's only a year younger than I am."

I did as my brother said, and doing the math, compared Toyland's age to that of the others on the list who had died. Four dead out of twelve would most definitely make it a statistical anomaly. And Michael Toyland looked like his journey's end was right around the corner. It might not happen while we were standing there, but it wouldn't come as a surprise if he passed on before the week was out.

"When did all this start?" I asked Betsy.

"About two years ago," she said.

"One thing after another?"

"A couple were contemporaneous," she said. "Otherwise, yes."

"What do the doctors say?"

"They've asked permission to keep his body when he passes," she said, ruefully. "For research. They're rather dumbfounded."

"How long have you been taking care of him?"

"Since his wife left," she said. "That was this past Christmas."

I turned to my brother who raised his eyebrows. As he had implied, it was a hell of a story. I turned back to her.

"Had he ever mentioned anything to you about a list?"

She laughed. "No. The first I heard of any list was just a couple of hours ago when your brother told me about it."

"Does he ever wake up?" I asked.

"He'll open his eyes on occasion," she said. "It's hard to tell if he has any awareness. He hasn't spoken a word in weeks now."

I feared that might be the case. So instead of counting on Toyland, I went through some of the names on the list with her, in case any of them could be a friend or relative. She listened attentively, and then told me she had no idea who any of them were.

"Has he had any other visitors recently?" I asked.

She shook her head. "Except for his doctors and nurses, no one but me has stepped foot in here."

I looked at my brother. "Why did you bring me here to see him if he can't talk?"

He looked surprised. "Look at him," he said. "There's something going on here."

He was probably right, but I was at a loss to figure out what it might be. I turned back to Betsy.

"Had anything unusual happened to him just before he got sick?"

"Well, I wasn't here then," she said. "But there's nothing in his medical records that I'm aware of."

"No distant travel? No contact with items from exotic places?"

She shook her head once more. "I'm sure he would have mentioned that to the doctors."

I looked back at the bed and the almost lifeless figure in it. Then I turned to Betsy again. "I'm sorry if we wasted your time."

"You didn't," she said. She sounded like she meant it. "I'd be happy to let you look through his things before you go. Who knows? You might find something I might have missed."

I told her that that was generous of her and sounded like a good idea. Privately, I felt it would most likely be a waste of our time, but the one thing we had going, it seemed, was time.

She then led us upstairs into what must have been his bedroom before he got so sick. It still showed the influence of a woman, between the furnishings and the wallpaper that featured a gaudy floral design. It was also tidy and clean, save for some boxes of files on the floor near his dresser. She gestured at them.

"You're free to see if there's anything in there. Other than the medical records, it's mostly credit card accounts and old bills. I'm afraid his wife took everything else."

"Money as well?" I asked.

If she was offended by the question, she didn't show it. "A big chunk of it," she said. "But we ought to be able to keep a roof over our heads for the foreseeable future. Or at least until..."

She let that idea trail off, and I simply nodded. She told us to meet her back downstairs when we were done and then she left.

It took about an hour or so for my brother and me to go through all the files and confirm what Betsy had told us, at least from a medical standpoint.

I did manage to find some papers relating to his time as violinist with the symphony. In working his way up from smaller orchestras, he had made quite a name for himself and received numerous awards. He had also been in demand as a recording artist over the years, getting regular work not only there in Chicago, but in New York and Los Angeles as well, some of the latter related to the movie business. It appeared that, together with some timely investments, he made himself quite wealthy, and it looked like he worked right up until his health began to deteriorate.

When we were finished, my brother and I rejoined Betsy in the kitchen. Obligingly, we sat down for some tea and pastries, none of which I ate, but which were a hit with my brother. We were engaged in some banal small talk about the weather when a buzzer went off on a small monitor sitting on the counter. Betsy spun her head in that direction and froze.

"What is it?" my brother asked.

She continued to stare until the buzzing stopped.

"It's the call button," she said, standing up quickly. "From his bedside."

She rushed out, and I followed her down the hall, with my brother close behind.

When we entered the room, we found Toyland in the same position as we left him, although something seemed different. His eyes were still closed, but his arms were slightly askew. Before I could ask Betsy whether he had any motor control left, his eyes sprang open.

"Michael?" she asked.

He blinked a few times, and then examined each of our faces, before returning to Betsy's. It appeared as though he wanted to say something, and she quickly removed the oxygen mask along with the tube that was in his mouth to prevent him from choking on his own saliva.

He put his lips together and then ran his tongue over them, as if feeling them for the first time. Then he mumbled something I couldn't hear.

She moved to the bedside chair where she took his hand in hers.

"Can you speak?" she asked him.

"I thought I just did," he said. His voice was weak and somewhat strained, but those words were clear enough for us all to hear.

"How do you feel?" she asked.

"Like shit," he said.

My brother laughed, and Toyland's eyes went to him. He looked at me then, before looking back at Betsy.

"More doctors?" he asked.

She shook her head. "They're visitors."

He narrowed his eyes. He obviously didn't recognize us and seemed suspicious.

"Can I speak with him?" I asked Betsy.

"I'm not sure that's such a good idea," she said. Neither of us tried to hide what we were saying, and Toyland looked back and forth between us. Before I could respond, he said I could "sure as hell" talk to him.

Betsy looked torn, but finally nodded. "I'll stop it if I think he's getting too upset," she warned me.

I told her that was fair enough and then grabbed a chair and pulled it up to the bedside opposite of where she was.

"This doesn't look good," Toyland said. His voice sounded a bit weaker then, and I was worried that his lucidity might not last much longer, so I got right to the point and explained the whole of my experience over the past week, leaving nothing out.

He listened, sometimes with his eyes open, and other times with them closed. Each time he shut them, I feared that we might lose any chance to learn what he might have to share. But each time I thought that, he opened them again and they finally remained open until I finished.

He didn't say anything for what seemed like an eternity but was probably only a minute or so.

"I spent the last five years thinking I was going to die," he said. "Even before all this happened."

I didn't know what to say to that.

"Maybe I brought it on myself," he said. "They say that's possible."

"That's nonsense," Betsy said.

He turned to her, but didn't say anything.

Then he turned back to me. "I wasn't like that before. Then all of a sudden, I began feeling like I was going to die. I went to see a bunch of doctors who found nothing. Well, at least until all of this. I even saw a psychiatrist."

Again, I didn't know what to say, so I remained silent, hoping he would go on.

"If I die, then that makes a third of those people on your list," he said to me.

I told him that was correct.

"What if they're going to kill us all?" he asked. "What if that's why we're on that list?"

"I don't think that's it," I said.

"What if you're wrong?"

I hadn't thought of that. But when I did it made no sense. "Two of them had cancer," I said, referring to the others who had died. "They could make a death look like a heart attack maybe. But not cancer. Besides, Archer is on the list and he's fine. So is Plum."

He tried to say something but no words came out. Then he started coughing badly. Betsy stood up then and put a hand out.

"I think that's enough for now," she said.

"I think your cousin is probably right," I told him.

When the coughing finally subsided, he shook his head in frustration. Then he gestured to me with the hand that didn't contain an IV, indicating that he wanted me to come closer. So I did.

He grabbed me with the same hand and pulled me to him, or tried to anyway. I got what he was asking and leaned in. Somehow he managed to turn his head so that he could speak into my ear. I could feel his hot breath that smelled like a sour combination of sulfur and ash.

"She's not my cousin," he said, in a voice that was barely loud enough for me to hear.

He made another sound, like he was about to say something else, but then let his head fall back on the pillow and let out a deep groan.

I feared that his heart might have given out right there, but the monitor showed that it was still beating, albeit at a faster rate than when we first came in. It soon settled down to that earlier rhythm and his eyes remained closed. We all watched him for a time to see if he might come around again. He didn't.

"What did he say?" my brother asked.

I looked at him but didn't answer. Instead, I turned to Betsy. If that was even her name.

"Who are you?" I asked.

She looked genuinely confused, meaning that she was either for real or one hell of an actor. I don't believe she had heard what Toyland told me.

"What do you mean?" she asked.

I told her what Toyland had just said. Her expression changed from curiosity to umbrage.

"He gets confused," she said. "I can assure you that he's my cousin."

"On what side?"

"My mother's," she said, almost immediately.

My brother looked back and forth between the two of us.

"You don't believe me?" she asked, angrily.

I didn't have an answer right away. I wasn't sure.

"Look at him," she said. "He just spoke for the first time in two weeks. He's lucky he even knows who he is."

My brother started to say something, but I put up my hand. I wanted him to remain quiet and see if Betsy might say something to give me some idea of whether she was telling the truth. She wasn't willing to go along.

"I let you in here to see him. I let you go through his things. And now you accuse me of what? Being some sort of thief? A gold digger? I think you should leave before I call the police."

As much as I wanted to question her more, I also didn't want to involve the police, and so we did as she asked, without another word spoken by any of us.

My brother drove and within fifteen minutes, we found a bar that was both comfortable and empty enough to offer a modicum of privacy.

"What do you think?" he asked, after our drinks arrived.

I told him I didn't know. That maybe she was right. Maybe he was just confused.

He shook his head. "I think she's lying."

"Why would she do that?"

"I don't know," he said. "But I don't like it."

Clearly, Toyland's words to me had changed his opinion of Betsy, and so I asked him if he thought she might be working for them. I didn't specify who I was talking about. It was clear enough.

"What else could it be?" he asked.

"I don't see it," I said. "She's got to be in her late sixties. What would she be doing for them? Besides, it looks like she's taking pretty good care of him. And he didn't appear to be afraid of her."

He agreed as to the last of those observations, but didn't seem any more convinced that she was who she said she was.

"How did she act when you first told her about the list?" I asked.

"The same as you saw when you were there," he said. "Maybe a little surprised."

"Did that seem weird to you?"

He appeared to think on that for a few seconds. "It does now," he said.

"Did you tell her the truth right from the start or change your story after you saw him?"

"I changed it," he said. "Sort of."

"So you went with the idea you told me?"

He shook his head. "When she asked who I was and why I wanted to see him, I just told her that I had an important message for him. I had no idea he was in that condition when I walked in."

"And she took you right in to see him?"

"Not right then," he said. "She told me I should tell her whatever message I had and that she'd pass it along. I said it was private and Toyland had to hear it directly from me."

"What did she say to that?" I asked.

"She told me to follow her and she took me to the room where you saw him."

"So then you told her about the list," I said.

He nodded. "After she explained what was wrong with him and how long he's been sick."

"I feel like we're missing something," I said.

"What about the hypochondria?" my brother asked. "Why would he tell us that?"

"Damn good question. I've been thinking about that too."

"You think that was a lie?"

"No," I told him. "That came from him. And it's embarrassing for someone to admit something like that. There had to be a reason."

"Well, I hope to hell you think of it because I'd sure as hell like to know what's going on." He gestured for the bartender to bring us another round, even though he hadn't finished his.

"So what do we do next?" I asked.

He shook his head. "I don't know," he said.

"The next closest name is in Boulder," I told him. "We should probably try there."

"I don't think that's a good idea," he said.

I hadn't expected that and asked him why not.

"Think about it. If we go see somebody else on that list it'll probably just be more of the same. Either they won't know shit or they won't tell us shit. Or there'll be another Cousin Betsy."

"We don't know that she's not who she said she was," I said. "We may be over-reacting."

"Maybe," he said. "But I can't go any way. That's too much time off of work."

He was right. It would be a long trip there and back. And probably just as futile as it was with Toyland. If so, that would be two or three days wasted.

"So what do you think I should do then?" I asked.

He shrugged. "Maybe try something different."

"Like what?" I asked.

"I don't know," he said. "Maybe go to the cops."

I reminded him that the doctor had warned me not to do that.

"He also told you not to tell anyone. And you told me. And that guy back there in the bed. Not to mention Betsy. The cat's already out of the bag."

I gave him a look.

He shrugged. "I don't like what I saw back there. This is pretty fucked up."

"I thought that's why you were doing this."

"It was," he said. "But it's more fucked up than I thought. I don't know if I want to go any further."

"Well, that's fine," I told him. "But I can't just quit. The doctor asked me to do this. He did that for a reason. He could've gone to the police any time he wanted. Or had some detective do it. But he didn't. He chose me instead."

He stared at me for a couple of seconds. Then he nodded.

"So that brings us back to the original question," I said. "What do you think I should do?"

"Tell you what," he said. "Why don't you come back to the house with me. Stay for a couple of days. We'll figure out what you should do next."

"I thought you only had the one bedroom," I said, before I could stop myself.

My brother had never been one to show much brotherly affection. Concern perhaps. Although that was only when I was younger. Affection, not so much. And the rare times when he did, he almost always pulled back, almost out of reflex. I had just called him out on his earlier excuse and expected the same reaction. Perhaps something even harsher. So I was surprised by what came out next.

"You can have mine," he said, ignoring the elephant in the room. "I fall asleep on the couch most nights anyway."

"OK," I said. "Thanks."

And that was the end of it. We had a plan of sorts.

The bartender came over then to bring us the new round. When he set the drinks down, I asked him if he could put ESPN on the TV so I could hear what happened with the games the day before. I had never thought about watching them or even checking the highlights. I realized then that I hadn't missed a round to determine the Final Four since I was about eleven years old. Nearly a lifetime ago.

Along with everything else that happened in the previous four days, it was something I would have never imagined.

CHAPTER 17

Sorry About Your Brother

I was laying out the cash for the bar tab when my phone began vibrating in my pocket. It took me a second or two to find it, and then pull it out. By then, the vibrating noise had alerted my brother who turned from the TV to see what I was doing.

I set the phone on the bar, almost as if it were radioactive, fully expecting the call to be from the detective from the New York State Police, if for no other reason than we were talking about the police just moments before. Instead, the screen displayed a number I didn't recognize, from an area code that was equally unfamiliar.

"Should I answer it?" I asked.

He looked at me without expression. "At this point? Why not?"

So I picked it up and did so.

"He's dead," said the female voice. "I hope you're happy." She didn't bother to identify herself, as if she expected that I would know who it was just from her speaking. Or the message. I didn't.

The voice did sound familiar, but it wasn't Cousin Betsy or whoever she was. Of that much I was certain. Meaning that the 'he' she referred to wasn't Toyland, who was the first person that came to mind when I heard those words, especially considering the condition in which we'd just left him.

"Who is this?" I asked, finally. "And who's 'he'?"

"It's Amanda Banyon," she said. "Or have you forgotten me already."

In all that had happened, it seemed that I had.

"Rafe Plum's sister," she added, when I didn't respond. "You followed me out of the hospital where I work. Just a few days ago. You don't remember that?"

Of course I did. Once she said it. "Yes, right," I said. "Wait. Are you telling me that your brother is dead?"

She told me that was exactly what she was saying.

I asked her what happened and when.

She told me a fire swept through his room in a roadside motel. In New Mexico. The night before.

"Are you sure?" I asked.

"The police came to my door to tell me," she said, again not hiding her disdain. "I don't think they do that if they're just guessing."

I realized the stupidity of my remark but, in my own defense, I was once again being upended by news that was beyond any reasonable expectation.

"What about Amy?" I asked. "Was she there with him?"

"They said there was another person in the room. The body hasn't been identified yet. "

"But they confirmed the other one was your brother? They're sure?"

"They found his ID. And the room was registered to him. I think it's pretty safe to say it was him."

A thought then came to me in a rush. A disturbing one,

"How did you get this number?" I asked her.

"Those two men gave it to me," she said. "The ones who came after the police."

"Which two men?" I asked, already knowing the answer.

"His friends," she said. "They were looking for him."

"Suits," I said. A statement. Not a question.

"Yes," she said, sounding confused. "They were wearing suits. Is that what you're asking?"

I ignored her question. Instead, I asked her why they came to see her.

She paused for a second, as if she hadn't thought of that. "I just told you. They were looking for him. I guess they thought he might be with me. I had to tell them about the fire. Can you imagine how horrible that was? To have them ask me about him not thirty minutes after the police came to tell me he was dead?"

"Why did they give you my number?"

Again, she paused before answering. "They asked me if anything unusual happened in the last few days. Why he might have left town. I told them about you and your visit the other day. They said I should call you and tell you what happened."

"Why?"

"They said you weren't his friend. Which I already knew. They said it would keep you from coming back. And I hope it does."

Their logic didn't seem particularly convincing to me, but she didn't appear to have a problem with it, as evidenced by the fact that she had just called. "Did they say who they were and why they wanted to see your brother?"

"They told me they were from the government. That he was working with them and that they had a meeting scheduled and he didn't show."

Again, that was something I hadn't expected. At the same time, the notion that those two men might be working for the government, if true, added a new bit of concern to the already worrisome nature of the whole affair. But I doubted that Plum was working with them or that they'd had any kind of meeting scheduled. It made no sense. What made more sense was that they killed him or had him killed.

"Did you ask to see any ID?"

She didn't answer me. I took that to mean that she didn't or they didn't show any. Most often, when someone tells regular folks that they're in the presence of a cop or a government agent of some kind, they don't ask to see a badge or photo ID. The more convincing the person, the less likely they get asked.

"Right," I said. "And did they tell you where they were going when they left?"

"No," she said, defensively. "I didn't ask. Why would I?"

I could think of about a hundred reasons, but I didn't answer. Instead, another thought came to me.

"What's the area code?" I asked her.

"What are you talking about?" she said.

"The number you just called. Mine. What's the area code?"

There was a pause, probably because she was looking at the number that she must have written down somewhere. As with the ID, if you ask a regular person a question with enough authority behind it, they're likely to answer you.

She recited the area code for my cell phone. The one registered in my name. Not the new one I was currently holding in my hand. Meaning that the call had been forwarded and that those men did not know of the new phone.

"I call to tell you my brother's dead and you ask me about your phone number?" she asked.

"I'm sorry about your brother," I told her, ignoring her question.

She told me to go fuck myself and hung up.

I looked at my phone again before setting it down. Then I filled in my brother on what I learned. He had probably pieced together most of it based on hearing only my side of the conversation. Still, he listened intently until I got to the part where she hung up, and then we both sat staring at the TV.

"At least they don't know about the phone," he said.

"Not yet anyway."

We sat there silent for another minute or so.

"Toyland might be right," he said. "Maybe they're killing all of them."

"I don't think so," I said. "Archer's still alive."

"How do you know that?" he asked.

I paused before answering. He was right. How did I know? I grabbed my phone again and logged onto the internet and ran a search under Archer's name. My brother watched as I did. When the results came up, I looked at him and shook my head.

"Nothing," I said. "If he was dead, he's important enough that it would be reported."

"It doesn't matter," he said. "That's four dead now. Five if you count Toyland. Which I do. That's way too many for me. It should be for you, too. I think you need to drop this. Go into hiding or something."

I wanted to tell him again that I couldn't. That I had started something that I had to finish. Whether I wanted to admit it or not, I took it on the minute I saw the doctor's widow on the floor and those two men standing over her. I couldn't quit even if I wanted to.

But I didn't say anything. Instead, we paid the tab, got back in the car and started the drive back to Arkansas.

CHAPTER 18

IT'S COMPLICATED

I T WAS NIGHTTIME when we pulled into another of those highway rest stops, this one a little smaller than the one we stopped at on the northbound side of the interstate, but it was just as busy. There was also a motor court there, and we debated whether we should stay the night and get going early in the morning or just grab something to eat and gas up and power through until we got to his house. Looking back, I wonder how much of a difference it might have made in both of our lives had we chosen not to stay.

After a quick dinner, we checked into a room using my alternate identity, and we turned out the lights just before ten o'clock. As we did on the way to Chicago, we chose not to keep watch, figuring the name on the motel register and the credit card we used to pay for it would prevent them from finding us. After all, they hadn't come to either of my rooms in Little Rock or Fort Smith, which told me that they weren't yet aware of that identity. Buoyed by that confidence, we both drifted off to sleep right away.

My brother woke up first. He claimed later that he heard the pick go into the lock on the door. This particular motor court had actual room keys, not the kind you see in nicer hotels, those plastic cards that slide into a slot to unlock the door. I've wondered if he would have heard that noise had that been the nature of this motel's security. In any event, he was up and out of the bed and at the door just as it opened to the length of the chain that he had wisely secured prior to getting in bed. Before he could even make an attempt at shoving the door closed, a very thick and ominous looking wire cutter emerged from outside, the jaws positioned on either side of the now-vulnerable looking metal links.

He swiftly shoved the cutter away and back out the door before it could do its job, and then body-slammed the door shut.

By that time, I was sitting up in my bed, trying to figure out what was going on. I managed to get that question out just as my brother lodged a chair under the doorknob.

"It's them," he said, without turning. "Call 911." He put his shoulder to the door to keep it shut.

"What do I tell them?" I asked.

"Who cares," he said. "We don't have time to fuck around here."

I rummaged around on the nightstand until I found my phone. Then turned it on and pressed "9" followed by "1" and was poised over that same number again when I realized that bringing in the cops would reveal my false identity and, depending on who those men were on the other side of the door, possibly the list and everything else. There was no way to avoid at least one of those things coming to light, and matters could quickly start to unravel from there. I told my brother what I was thinking.

"Well then help me with this door," he said.

And so I did, as best I could. They somehow had the door unlocked and were pushing hard from the other side. The noise seemed loud enough from where we were inside of the room, but I wasn't sure how it might sound to those in the ones on either side of us or beyond. I tried to remember if I saw any lights in the rooms near us, but couldn't recall.

Then the shoving from the other side stopped almost as quickly as it started. My brother and I both sensed it at the same time and shared a look. As if anticipating my question, he shook his head, which I took to mean that they had not gone away. Indeed, I heard no footsteps. His assessment was confirmed a few seconds later.

"You can't hide anymore," a voice said from the other side. It was more than a whisper, but less than a normal speaking tone. From that, I got the feeling that they weren't interested in calling attention to themselves.

My brother didn't look at me. He didn't need to. I wasn't about to answer.

"We need that list," the same voice said. "And all of those papers." I wasn't positive, but I thought it belonged to the older of the two men in suits who I had encountered at the widow's house.

"Your fat friend told us it was too late for that," my brother said, without waiting for me to answer. His voice was strong and showed no sign of fear. I was glad for that.

"He's rather exuberant," the voice said. "And he doesn't call the shots. It's never too late."

"If you don't go away I'm going to call the police," I said, deciding to test my theory about them wishing to remain undetected.

"Go right ahead," the voice replied. "Be my guest." Neither they nor we were expending much energy in pushing or holding the door at that point.

I hesitated, unsure about what was going on. My brother nodded at the phone still in my hand, clearly in favor of taking that route.

I deliberated for a few seconds trying to determine the least harmful action I could take. Then I turned on the screen. I decided that my calling 911 would likely cause them to leave, making my true identity the only thing I had to somehow keep from the police. Believing that it was our best option, I dialed the three numbers, unsure of what I was going to tell the emergency operator when they answered. I was still trying to think of what to say when I noticed that the call wasn't going through.

"Having trouble?" asked the voice from the other side of the door.

"Fuck," I said.

"What?" my brother asked.

"They're blocking the signal," I told him. "I can't call out."

"There's a way to do that?" he asked.

"There is," I said. "Unfortunately."

"He's right," said the voice from outside. "You can't call anyone. Sorry. We insist."

I immediately turned to the nightstand and the motel phone sitting there. I grabbed the receiver and punched zero on the dial pad.

Nothing. The line was dead.

"Yeah," said the voice. "That won't work either. We're not stupid."

That much was certainly true. They were nothing if not proficient. By now, my brother had let go of the door, although he did secure the bolt. Regardless, they were making no attempt to open it.

"What do you say you let us in so we can have a talk," the voice said. "That's it. Just a talk."

My brother looked at me and shook his head.

"If we let you in here you could probably kill us both without making a whole lot of noise," my brother told him. "Forget it."

"There aren't that many other places to talk around here," the voice said, after a moment in which he must have taken a look around.

"Tough shit," said my brother. "We're not stupid either."

I stared at the door, just as my brother did, waiting to see how he would respond to that. The silence went on longer than I expected. So much so that I thought for a moment that they might have left.

"I just sent my associate over to the restaurant to secure a table in the back," the voice said finally. "It's a public place. You'll be safe in there. And we ought to be able to grab a little privacy as well."

"How's that going to work?" my brother asked. "I'm not going to just open the door and walk out there."

There was a short pause before the man spoke again. "OK then, I'm going to back away from the door now. But you'll still be able to see me through the peephole. After I do, one of you can come out and go meet my associate in the restaurant. When that one's safely inside, the other one can come out and we'll both go to the restaurant together."

My brother and I looked at one another. I shrugged. He turned back to the door.

"Why should we trust you?" my brother asked. "You could do anything to us out there."

"There are a lot of people coming and going out here," the man said. "And there's a camera right outside the restaurant. I doubt we'd get away with very much."

We looked at each other again. I asked my brother in a whisper if he had any better ideas.

"We could wait until it gets light," he whispered back. "They'd look awful suspicious just waiting outside the door."

"I suppose," I said. "But they could also just wait in their car and then follow us wherever we go. Someplace where no one's around."

He frowned, and then nodded. Unless we could somehow call the police, we were trapped in the room. So I went over and rummaged through my duffel bag and pulled out my baton. Then I put on my jeans and a sweatshirt and stuffed it - unopened - in the waistband.

"We're waiting," the voice called from outside.

We both looked at the door, then I turned to my brother.

"You go first. But if they're both out there, let me know and I'll be right out. Otherwise, I'll do what he said and meet you in the restaurant. Then we'll hear what they have to say."

My brother thought about it for a bit, and then he nodded and turned to the door.

"Back off," he said. "I'm coming out."

He looked through the peephole for a few seconds, and then turned to me.

"Somebody in a suit is standing outside the restaurant," he said. "Somebody else is in the parking lot."

He looked back through the peephole and told me that the first person had just re-entered the restaurant. Then he slowly opened the door wide enough to allow both of us to see. There was no one immediately on the other side, but someone was indeed standing in the lot about twenty feet away. It was dark where he was, but I could tell that he was wearing a suit, although I couldn't make out his face. From what I could recall, his overall height and weight seemed to match that of the older of the two men.

My brother studied him for a few seconds, then stuck his head out and checked either side of the door. Apparently satisfied, he walked out and left the door open so I could see.

I watched as my brother looked first at the man standing in the parking lot, then toward the restaurant where he and I had eaten right after we pulled in that night. Keeping his eye on the man in the lot, he walked toward the restaurant. When he got to the door, he turned around and looked back at me. Then he held up a finger as if to tell me to hold on and entered the restaurant.

While I waited to see what he was going to do, I kept my eye on the man in the suit. He did the same with me. A few seconds later, the restaurant door opened and we both turned at the same time. My brother stepped out. Alone. He nodded at me, then turned and went back inside.

Taking my cue, I walked out and shut the door firmly behind me, making sure it locked. I suppose that was for the benefit of the man waiting in the parking lot who watched as I circled away from him and in the general direction of the restaurant. After I took a few more steps in that direction, I noticed that he hadn't moved. So I stopped.

"You first," I said.

A truck pulled away from the gas pumps just then and its lights swept across the man, illuminating him as if in a spotlight. I didn't like his expression any more than I did back at the widow's house. And it was him. The older of the two. There was no doubt.

He glanced over at the truck, now coasting in the general direction of the motor court, and he nodded at me and started walking toward the restaurant. I followed behind and to one side of him, keeping a safe distance, although I was certainly well within sight of whoever was behind the wheel of that truck. A part of me worried that the driver might be working with those men and that he might suddenly accelerate and turn in my direction. I stopped and waited to see what he would do, ready to run if need be.

To my great relief, the truck lumbered past our room and toward the part of the lot where some other rigs were parked, their drivers presumably asleep either in their trucks or in one of the rooms.

When the man in the suit got to the door, he opened it and turned in my direction. I waved with the back of my hand indicating that should go inside first. He frowned, but did as I suggested.

I got to the door a few seconds later and looked through the glass before entering the restaurant. He was not in front of me, and so I looked around until I saw my brother sitting alone on one side of a table in the back, across from the two men in suits.

I took a deep breath and walked slowly to the table, where a waitress appeared with a coffee pot in hand. She asked if I wanted a cup as I approached. I shook my head and told her we would wave to her when we were ready to order, something I had no intention of doing.

The younger of the two men smiled at me as I took a seat next to my brother. I ignored him and turned to the older of the two men, assuming he was the one in charge. His right hand was resting on the table, and in it he held a lighter. It was one of those old school metal ones with a cap that you had to flip open in order to light it. He did just that as my brother and I watched. Given what we had been told had happened to Plum, it seemed a rather obvious and clumsy attempt to send some sort of message.

"Betsy?" I asked, looking up from the flame to his face.

He didn't seem to understand what I was asking at first, but then it dawned on him. He nodded and closed the lighter.

"She works for you?" I asked.

"She's on the payroll, yes," he said, opening the lighter again. This time he snapped it closed without lighting it.

"And she gave you our license plate," I said, trying to ignore the distraction.

"Better than that," said the young one.

His partner winced slightly, and put his hand on his arm and shook his head. Then he turned to look directly at me, opening the lighter and sparking it once more.

"Forget how we managed to find you. This whole affair can end as quick as a cat if you'll just give us that list and those other papers the woman gave you."

"You still want it?" I asked. "The actual list?"

He looked confused for a moment.

"It isn't hard to memorize twelve names," I told him. "A child could do it."

He smiled and closed the lighter. "Then you shouldn't have any problem giving it to us."

I shrugged. "I've got a few questions first," I said.

The younger one leaned forward with a finger pointed at me.

"Fuck your questions--"

My brother's hand shot out and grabbed the finger. At the same time, he grabbed the back of the guy's wrist with his other hand, no doubt ready to snap the digit. The younger man began to rise from his seat, but my brother bent the finger further back, causing him to grimace and freeze.

The older of the two men held up his hands in a sort of surrender.

"There's no need for any of that," he said, in a calm and low tone. Then he turned to me. "Please forgive my young friend here. He doesn't realize that not every dispute calls for a physical response."

"Tell that to the doctor's wife," I said.

"We did. And we're here to give you the same chance we gave her."

He turned to his younger partner and shook his head once more, the expression on his face indicating that he had probably had to reprimand him more than once for his behavior.

The young one sat back down and my brother let go when he did. Everyone took a deep breath and reset for a moment. I took a second to look around to see if anyone else in the place had noticed. It appeared not.

I turned back just as the older man uncapped the lighter again. As soon as he did, the waitress appeared at the table, seemingly out of nowhere.

"There's no smoking in here," she told him.

He looked up at her with a smile. "I don't smoke," he said. "I don't even have a cigarette on me."

She stared. "Well, I'd appreciate it if you'd put that away then. We don't want to give the other diners any ideas."

He pursed his lips, and then shrugged. "Sure," he said. " Happy to oblige." Then he made a bit of a show pocketing the lighter.

She nodded and walked away. I waited until she was gone before I turned to him again.

"You don't care that I could hand over those papers and still have the names in my head?"

"Why? What're you going to do with them?" he asked. His tone was almost mocking.

"The same thing I'm doing now," I said.

"And do you think anyone will believe your story without the list?"

"Why not? I can be pretty convincing."

He looked amused by that. "And have you been? Convincing, I mean?"

I paused to consider that. I suppose that I had. Alden Archer surely seemed convinced, but then he was obviously in league with those two men and needed no convincing. As for Rafe Plum, I must have convinced him of something or he wouldn't have left in such a rush.

"Yeah," I said, as confidently as I could. "I think I have been."

"Are you talking about our friend the gambler?"

It was as if he had read my mind. I tried not to react. I may have failed.

"Rafe Plum," said the younger of the two. "You remember him, right?"

"He left two days after we were there," my brother said, staring the young man in the eye. "He must have been persuaded of something."

"And where did that get him?" the younger one asked.

"Dead apparently," my brother said.

The older one held out both hands as if the point was made. "Enough," he said.

"So what's your offer?" I asked, ignoring the indifferent manner in which he seemed to acknowledge Plum's demise.

The man laughed. "No offer, other than you giving us those papers and us leaving."

My brother turned to look at me. I continued to stare at the older man, trying to size him up.

"Tell you what," I said. "You tell me why this is so important that you'd be willing to kill for it and, if you're convincing enough, you can have them."

He frowned. "I'm afraid if we did that, we wouldn't be able to let you go. I admit it's a bit of a conundrum."

He was right. His lack of concern that I could turn over those papers and still know those names made no sense to me. Unless he was bluffing, I was missing something.

"Are you really with the government?" my brother asked then, interrupting my thoughts.

The older one turned to him. "Who told you that?"

"His sister," my brother said, referring to Amanda Banyon.

"You told her to call us, remember?" I added.

"I did indeed," he said.

"Why?" I asked. "Why have her tell us about her brother? It makes no sense."

"Perhaps I wanted to get your attention," he said.

He paused for a moment, and then he picked up the menu and opened it. "Is anyone hungry?"

The waitress must have taken that as a cue and appeared once again. I shook my head and she frowned and walked away. Then I reached over and pulled the menu down so that I could see the man's face.

"You didn't answer the question," I said. "Are you with the government?"

"It's complicated," he said.

"No it's not," my brother said. "Either you are or you're not."

The older man shrugged. "It's not technically an employer-employee relationship."

"Somebody signs your paychecks," my brother said.

The younger man smiled. "It's all direct deposit these days. Nobody signs anything."

"You must have IDs," my brother said, ignoring the comment.

The older one frowned. "This isn't the movies. We're not the FBI."

"They're not from the government," my brother said, turning to me. "It's all bullshit."

The older man shrugged once more. I wasn't sure what that was supposed to mean.

"Let's suppose you were to agree to wait here while I went back and got the list and brought it to you," I said. "What would happen after that? You'd just sit here and drink your coffee and let us drive off?"

My brother made a face indicating he was not in favor of that. Neither was I, but I had a reason for asking.

"Would you believe me if I said yes?" the older man asked.

I shook my head.

He set the menu down. "Then I guess we'll have to think of something else," he said.

"I have to go to the bathroom," my brother said then, and he stood abruptly and left the table before anyone could say or do anything to stop him. We all watched as he walked to the opposite corner of the restaurant, away from the entrance, and into the men's room.

"Should I go after him?" the younger man asked his partner.

"Nah," he said. "Let him piss in private. What's he going to do in there?"

He looked in the direction of the bathroom for a few more seconds before turning back to me.

"It's actually good that he left. I do have an offer for you. But I wanted to present it in private." He stole another look at the bathroom door. "I know you two aren't close."

I told him to go fuck himself.

"I understand your anger," he said. "But I think you'll want to hear me out."

"I don't care about your offer," I told him. "What I want is for you to tell me what that list is all about."

He looked like he was about to say something when the bathroom door opened and my brother walked out, accompanied by a man even bigger than him and wearing a leather vest and trucker hat. Or at least that's what I later learned it was called. They spoke to one another outside the door for a few more seconds as all three of us watched. Then the man in the hat looked over at us briefly and nodded. After that, they walked up to the table together.

When they got there, they stopped, with the stranger standing next to the table on the side where the two men in suits were seated.

"Are these them?" the man asked my brother, gesturing at the two across from me.

"Yeah," my brother said.

"What the fuck do you want?" the younger of the two suits asked the trucker.

"I want you to shut the fuck up," he said.

The younger one raised his eyebrows in response. Then he turned to the older one as if to ask what he should do. Once more, the older one chose discretion and shook his head. The younger one looked disappointed.

"We're having a private discussion here," the older one said to the trucker. His tone was polite and conciliatory. "I'd appreciate it a great deal if you'd let us continue."

The trucker stared at him for a beat, then turned to my brother. "How long did you say?"

"An hour," my brother said. "Two if you can swing it."

"Alright then," the stranger said. "We got a deal."

My brother handed him something that I couldn't see, then turned back to me. "C'mon, let's get going."

I paused to see what our suited friends might do in reaction to my brother's announcement, but they just continued to stare at him. So I stood up.

"Wait a minute," the younger of the two men said, and he started to rise.

My brother's new friend reached out and shoved him back into his seat. He reacted quickly and started to get up once more and the trucker thrust his hand out again to stop him. The older man pulled his partner back into the chair, but didn't say a word.

As he did, my brother started tugging me toward the door. I turned then and noticed that four more men looking a lot like my brother's newfound friend had entered the restaurant and were headed toward our table.

We passed them as they did, and by the time we got to the door, they were surrounding the table, blocking our pursuers from getting out. It was clear that if the men in suits wanted to come after us, they were going to have to go through five rather large men in order to do so. And that would cause a commotion that they seemed to be hoping to avoid.

When we got outside, my brother began running toward our room. I followed closely behind.

Once we got inside, I asked him what the hell he'd just done.

"I paid for security for you," he said. "Like the rock star you are."

I told him I didn't get it.

"I saw that trucker go in the bathroom and followed him in," he told me as he stuffed his belongings into his bag. "I told him that those guys were giving us shit and that we'd pay handsomely if he could get some of his friends to come by and keep them in the restaurant until we could make our way out of here."

"How much did you offer him?" I asked.

He zipped his bag closed and threw mine at me. "All I had. Two hundred bucks."

"He agreed for that little?"

"Not until I told them that our friends were with the highway transportation department. Undercover. Checking on hours-of-service. Truck narcs."

I laughed at the sheer lunacy of that.

"I think they would have done it for free at that point," he added.

"How the hell did you think of that?" I asked.

"I saw a notice on the wall when we checked in," he said. "Something about some new regulations cutting down on the number of hours these guys can drive. I guess it really eats into their potential earnings. Somebody wrote 'fuck you Nazis' on it. I figured anybody having anything to do with it wouldn't be too popular around here."

I laughed again and began stuffing my bag. "Pretty smart," I told him. "I wish I thought of it."

I expected him to make some sort of wisecrack, but he just smiled and shoved me toward the door.

When we got out to the car, I told him to wait a second and walked around the back. While he watched, I bent down under the trunk and looked until I found what I thought might be there, based upon the younger man's slip back at the restaurant. I pulled it loose with some effort and stood to show my brother the square metal object with a red light blinking.

"What is it?" he asked.

"Tracking device," I told him. "Cops use them to follow people."

"Shit," he said. "Maybe they really are with the government."

"Not necessarily," I said. "You can find one on-line, if you know where to look."

"We've only had the car for a day," he said. "When did they do that?"

I was about to respond when I saw the answer come to him.

"Fucking Betsy," he said.

I nodded. Then I told him to get in and start the car.

As he did, I ran over to the truck I had seen coming toward me as I was approaching the restaurant earlier. It was parked now, with the engine off, outside one of the rooms at the end of the motor court. I ducked below the rear bumper and attached the device to the metal frame there. The magnet on the back held it firmly in place. Then I ran to back to the car where my brother was waiting.

Before I got in, I looked back at the restaurant, but there was no sign of the two men. Satisfied, I got in and we pulled out and onto the interstate without another look back.

CHAPTER 19

I'll Treasure It Always

My brother was right. It was decidedly more dangerous now. The ability of our suited friends to track us down was even greater than I had thought. And he was right also that I wasn't equipped to solve this puzzle by merely looking up the people on the list. I had to come up with something else. And I needed to think about what that something else might be before I did anything.

So we agreed to keep heading south and eventually to the airport in St. Louis where I was going to buy a ticket back to New York and my brother was going to rent a car to get him back to Fort Smith. The idea of me going back and staying with him for a few days was off the table. Both of us thought that it was a bad idea in light of what had just happened at the rest stop. We did argue over whether it was wise for him to go back to where they obviously knew he lived. As an alternative, I tried to convince him to take some more time off from work and come back east with me, but he couldn't be persuaded.

"I'm not the one they're worried about," he said. "I don't have the list."

"You could know the names, same as me," I pointed out. "In fact, I'm sure they already believe that."

"They don't care if I know the names," he said. "It's figuring out what they actually mean and why he gave them to you. I can't do that. They know that."

He was partially right. It wasn't the names alone, although they had to be important. It had to be something more. What the older one said back at the rest stop seemed to indicate that. I told him what I was thinking.

"You mean like there's a message in what he wrote on the papers?" he asked. "Some kind of code?"

I shook my head. "I don't think so. The doctor was no cryptologist. Neither am I."

"Fingerprints then?" he asked. "Can they get fingerprints off paper?"

"They can," I said. "It's difficult. But they can do it. But I don't think that's it."

"What then?" he asked.

I shrugged. "I don't know," I said.

We were silent for a minute or so, both staring at the road.

"You know what?" he said, turning to me.

"What?" I asked.

"This is pretty fucked up."

I laughed. "Yeah, you said that already."

He laughed as well, and looked back at the road.

We arrived in St. Louis about three hours after leaving the rest stop. If those truckers were true to their word, the men in suits had to be at least an hour behind us, and that was assuming they were heading where we were and not following that tractor trailer with the tracking device on it wherever it was going. We both agreed that Betsy must have put it on our car while we were upstairs looking through Toyland's files, a ploy she probably came up with to allow her to do so, only further confirming that she was in their employ. She had to have been hired to keep an eye on Toyland for some reason. At the same time, it seemed to me that they didn't have any motive to kill him since he was going to be dead on his own soon enough. Yet they were still watching him anyway. I had no idea why. Unless it was to look out for us.

It was somewhat reassuring that they hadn't tracked us by the license place since that would have given them the name I was now using to rent the car. From that, they might have gotten curious and checked for a phone in that same name. I couldn't be certain that they didn't have the capability to track the plate, but the device I found told me that they probably hadn't done so, at least not at that point.

When we got to the airport, we pulled into long term parking and left the car on the highest floor, as far away from the elevators as we could, just to make it harder should they come looking for it. Then we retrieved our stuff and made our way into the main terminal. My brother had decided that it was more important for me to get a ticket on the soonest possible flight out and be on my way rather than for him to get a rental car, since the latter was likely to be easier to obtain than a last minute ticket to New York.

And that turned out to be the case. As we soon learned, unless I was willing to wait an additional eight hours for a direct flight, I was going to have to be flexible about my destination. So after visits to several carriers, I opted for a flight to Boston leaving in two and a half hours, the soonest departure we could find that would get me close to New York and home.

Before purchasing the ticket, my brother asked me if I was going to use my own ID or that of Mr. Pinckney.

"I can't take the chance of trying to fly under that name." I said. "I don't know for sure, but I suspect the TSA has internal checks for things like that. It's a name that's never been flown under."

"Well then," he said. "If you use your real name and those guys are really with the government, they can find out where you're going."

"Maybe," I said. "But at least I'll have a head start. "

He didn't like it, but he didn't argue. However, he did object when I insisted on paying him back the money he gave those truckers back at the rest stop.

"I don't need it," he said, pushing it away.

We both knew that not to be true, but I didn't say so. My having more money than him had always been a thing between us. Not on my end, but certainly on his, and that was probably behind his refusing it. At least in part. So I reminded him that he was going to need to eventually replace his old phone and could use it to buy a new one.

He snatched the bills from me and smirked. "I didn't think of that," he said. "I'll send you a bill for the rest."

I told him to go fuck himself and that he could buy me breakfast now.

After getting my ticket, we ended up in one of those airport chain restaurants to wait out the time until my departure. My brother was plowing through a cheese omelet that looked like it could close a major artery when I asked him how often he went to see Doctor Condon when we were kids.

"Not as much as you," he said.

"What's that supposed to mean?" I asked.

"We had a different doctor when I was young," he said.

"Who was that?"

"Doc Harding," he said. "Nice guy. Pretty wife. She was his nurse. I loved dropping my drawers when she came with him to do our team physicals."

I ignored his attempt at boyish humor. "What happened to him?"

"Nothing that I know of," he said. "When you got sick that time, Mom switched doctors. Condon treated you at the hospital. I guess she liked him better."

He was referring to the respiratory infection I had contracted just before the start of fourth grade. They were never able to determine how I got it, although there was some talk that I might have picked it up swimming in a pond on the farm of a friend, something my parents warned against, but which as a nine year old boy, I ignored. Whatever the cause, it kept me from starting school that year and since nothing seemed to help me get better, they finally admitted me to the local hospital. I don't remember much about being in there, except for being scared at night, since I was isolated from the other patients in what was only a slightly less frightening version of the legendary "iron lung," this one a zipped-in enclosure made of heavy plastic. As I look back on it, I think my confinement there was probably what began my fear of closed in spaces. Luckily, I was only in it for a few days before being allowed to go home, where I was laid up for another week or two, although I can't remember exactly how long.

Doctor Condon was the only doctor I could ever remember going to, although when my brother mentioned Harding, I did have a fleeting glimpse of going to see him, probably for a check-up or two. I couldn't recall his pretty wife at all.

"Do you remember anything about Condon that would make you think he could be tied up in something like this?" I asked.

He shook his head. "I only saw him a few times, but he seemed like a regular guy as far as I could tell. What about you?"

"I've been thinking about it. A lot. I can't recall ever hearing anyone say a single thing that would make me think he was anything but a small town doctor with a regular life. Unless there's something in his background that he managed to keep a secret from everyone."

"Maybe he worked somewhere else before he came to our town," he said. "That could explain how he might have met those people on the list."

I shook my head. "Those people are from all over the country. He would have had to work in twelve different places. There's no indication that they were ever all in the same place at the same time."

He pushed his plate away, finished with the meal. "Well, I give up. When you find out what's going on, you let me know."

"I will," I said. "Find out, I mean."

He stared at me for a couple of seconds before he spoke again.

"Let me ask you something," he said, his expression turning serious.

"What?" I asked.

"Why are you so intent on doing this?"

"I already told you," I said. "The doctor picked me to do it. And after what happened to his wife, I'm not going to stop till I do."

"You think maybe there might be another reason?" he asked.

"Like what?" I asked back.

"Like maybe you're trying to prove something. To yourself. To me. Hell, maybe to the whole world."

"Why would I be doing that?" I asked.

He stared. "Maybe you think that if you can solve this, then you can write that book. No more writer's block. Or whatever it is that's holding you back."

For once, I didn't have a ready answer. I wanted to tell him that he didn't know what he was talking about. That he was way off base. But I couldn't. Because it had the ring of truth to it. Prior to him saying that, it may have only been buried somewhere down in my subconscious. But once he said it, once it was out in the open, it made sense. More than I cared to admit.

"So what if you're right? What difference does it make? I still need to do it."

"Look what happened to Plum," he said. "And what might have happened back at the rest stop. You can't do this by yourself. It's too dangerous."

"What are you suggesting?"

"I think you have to go to the cops now. Maybe that one who called you. The woman."

I shook my head. "The doctor said to avoid the police. You said yourself that those guys might be part of the government. Which includes the police."

"They didn't seem to want them to show up back at that rest stop," he said.

He was right. I had thought the same thing. Despite telling me to call 911, which I was unable to do thanks to them, they seemed to want to avoid acting in any way that would alert the authorities.

"I've been thinking about it," he said. " Maybe it's not the police themselves. Maybe it's just that they can find out what they know. Like with the bail thing back in Fort Smith."

"Maybe," I said. "But even if you're right. I don't think I can take that chance."

He nodded finally. "Well, at least tell me that you'll think about it. I don't want to hear that something happened to my little brother and I wasn't there to help him."

For the second time in twenty-four hours, he was showing me some sentiment, and I marveled at the thought. I half-expected him to change the subject or make a joke, as he might have in the past, but he just kept staring. Waiting for my answer. "Alright," I told him. "I'll think about it."

After he paid the check, I told him to wait a second before getting up to go. I reached into my duffel and took out the baton. I looked around to make sure no one was watching before I handed it to him.

"What do you want me to do with that?" he asked.

"It's illegal to carry in about twenty states. I'm pretty sure I can't take it through security."

"Well, I don't want it," he said, trying to hand it back. "Just toss it in the trash or something."

I pushed it back to him. "You don't have to go through any kind of security to rent a car. And you might want to have it if those guys ever show up at your house again."

He frowned as if I had insulted him and his ability to defend himself.

"Consider it a gift then," I said. "A memento of our trip. From your little brother."

He smirked at that, but it did the trick. He stuffed it in his bag.

"I'll treasure it always," he said.

Again, I told him to go fuck himself, and we got up so I could get to my gate.

He walked with me to the security line, and as he did, I told him that just to be on the safe side, he shouldn't get a new phone until we figured out what was going on and to only use the burner till then. He looked like he wanted to argue, but nodded.

Then we said a quick and awkward goodbye, more like the old days, and he went off on his own to go find a car to rent. I watched as he walked down the terminal and couldn't help but think that I was going to miss having him with me. Despite the danger, I had enjoyed the time together and was struck by how differently things had turned out from when I first knocked on his door just five days before. I continued to watch until he disappeared into the crowd.

Then I ducked out of the line to do one last thing before I boarded the plane. Something that I knew had to be done after our sit-down with those two men back at the rest stop.

CHAPTER 20

A CLOSED IN SPACE

O NCE I WAS safely on board and the plane took off, I drifted into a dreamless sleep and woke up only when I heard the announcement that we were about to land at Logan airport.

It was a rainy spring night in eastern Massachusetts, and the harbor was as black as the sky as we descended to the tarmac. Snow stuck stubbornly to a few parts of the city, but the lights from the waterfront to the Common and Back Bay were a reassuring sight to see. Over the previous two decades or so, I'd spent a lot of time in Boston, giving talks and attending conferences at the various institutions of higher learning that the region is famous for. But I had no plans to stay there that night. My goal was to go straight from the airport to South Station where I would grab the late train back to Connecticut. It was risky to be sure. If those men in suits had access to flight rosters from the airlines, they could easily presume that I might do such a thing and show up at any point along my proposed journey.

I'm not a big fan of public transportation. I never have been. Whenever I've spent time in New York City, which has become increasingly rare in recent years, I've made it a rule to travel above ground, meaning that I take a taxi wherever I need to go. It's not a matter of elitism. It's just that I don't like being below ground in a metal tube full of people. Not an unreasonable choice, I think, given my fear of being trapped in small spaces. However, that option was limited that night when I exited the terminal and found a long line waiting for just a few taxis, most likely due to the rain which had picked up significantly then. I was resigned to simply endure getting soaked until someone at the back of the line suggested taking the bus that runs to and from the train station. That seemed like a reasonable alternative, so I followed a number of others to the bus stop only to discover an employee of the transit service standing there informing everyone that they were down two buses and that service would be slowed considerably. He then directed everyone to the airport's sub-way stop, telling us that even though we'd have to change trains twice to reach South Station, we'd still get there sooner than the bus. Given my aforementioned rule, I considered going back to the taxi line, but then chose to keep following the others, not wanting to risk missing that train and having to wait until morning to get home.

I took it as a positive sign that I was able to catch the blue line car only seconds before it left the station, and I breathed a sigh of relief as I got on and found a seat. As the train pulled away from the loading platform, I began to do the breathing exercises and mental imaging I often employ when I find myself in a situation that I fear might cause me to become phobic. I have become pretty skilled at it, and it usually does the trick, especially when I can convince myself that the situation will improve rather quickly, as I expected to be the case on such a short ride.

I had just closed my eyes and began to picture the comfort and quiet of the Acela, Amtrak's super fast train, racing above ground past the many towns along the coast in Massachusetts, Rhode Island and Connecticut, when the subway car made a loud, screeching noise and shuddered to a stop. The lights remained on for only a few precious seconds before they went out, leaving just a bare bulb outside in the tunnel to provide any kind of illumination.

As the train emitted some sort of compressed air, sounding vaguely like a dying animal, a few of my fellow passengers began to grumble and swear at the inconvenience. I tried to remain calm, but found it to be a difficult task. As I said, in recent years, I've been able to manage my phobia through a combination of behavioral techniques, together with avoiding situations where I am most likely to have trouble. Unfortunately for me, a subway train broken down in a dark tunnel under the Boston harbor is one of those situations. Not quite up to the level of my nightmare of being trapped in a submarine, but close. Even before I could tell myself that a breakdown was a fairly common occurrence and something that was likely to resolve itself in minutes rather than hours, my breathing rate skyrocketed and I could feel my heart pounding in my ears. I've found in the past that if I don't tame those reactions within the first couple of minutes, things can quickly spiral out of control. And that is exactly what happened.

The car was crowded with people and their belongings, which only added to the feeling of confinement. Looking around, I could see no clear exit out of the car, but I was hardly thinking straight at that point. After trying and failing to contain my growing panic, I leapt from my seat and pushed my way to the far end of the car, jostling several passengers in the process. When I got there, I stopped short only to find that there was no door leading out to the tunnel, unlike on an Amtrak train. To escape, I would have to use the door in the center of the car that everyone uses to board and de-board. Of course, that remained closed. So I elbowed my way back to the middle of the car in hopes of trying to pry my way out.

By then, I had caused quite a stir and people were shouting at me to calm down while others simply moved away, as often happens when folks find themselves in the presence of someone they perceive to be unbalanced. In my agitated state, I ignored not only their objections, but also anything else happening around me. It was for that reason that I didn't see the person who approached me from behind and grabbed my shoulder.

Without taking the time to determine who that hand might belong to, I flung an elbow back and felt it connect. If the police officer had been a few inches taller, I probably would have struck him in the chest and perhaps he would have been a bit more forgiving. Of course, that was assuming it was a "he" which it most definitely was not. Instead, I turned around to face a policewoman several inches shorter than me, holding her hand over a nose that was now dripping blood.

She obviously had much better training in the physical arts than I did, and she quickly had me face down on the grimy and wet floor, with a forearm pressed firmly against the back of my neck. A circle quickly formed around us as she did, and everyone in the car watched as I was handcuffed and then jerked back to my feet. To add to my growing humiliation, that action was accompanied by cheering from the other riders that was abruptly cut off when the lights came back on and the train started to move once more. I would estimate that the entire episode lasted less than ten minutes, my being that close to a clean escape back to Connecticut and home.

From there it was all a bit of a blur. The train pulled into the next stop. The officer and I exited, once again to applause, and were promptly greeted by four more burly (and male) Boston police officers that she had radioed ahead to meet us. That led to a quick trip up the escalator, and then out of the station and onto the surprisingly busy street where I was shoved into the back of a waiting cruiser. Within an even shorter period of time, we pulled up to the nearest police station and I was escorted out of the squad car and inside to the booking area. There I was quickly fingerprinted and stripped of my possessions, including shoelaces.

During the booking process, I tried to explain my claustrophobia, but no one seemed to care. I was informed that I was being charged with misdemeanor assault on a police officer and told that I would have to wait in a holding cell until I could appear before a judge the next morning to determine bail. When a second officer came to the desk to escort me down there, I begged him to let me make a phone call before he did so.

It's not exactly like you see in the movies. They don't inform you of that right, if indeed one actually has a constitutional right to "one phone call." Lucky for me, the veteran desk sergeant was sympathetic to my plight and agreed to let me use my cell phone before he stowed it away with my other possessions. He told me that he recognized my name and that his son had read my books when he was a graduate student living at home, where the sergeant often saw them laying around the house.

I thanked him and promptly called my attorney back in Connecticut who, as a contract specialist, was unaccustomed to being awakened in the middle of the night for any sort of legal matter. After a brief and well-edited recitation of where I was and why, I asked if he could find a Boston criminal attorney to represent me at the arraignment the next day. He told me that he would make an inquiry and that I should expect to hear from someone first thing in the morning. After thanking him and telling him that I would be sure to come see him when I was back in Connecticut, he asked if there was anything else I wanted to tell him.

"No," I said. "Why?"

Even I wasn't convinced by my feigned ignorance. He didn't answer right away, so I filled the void.

"It's just what I told you. The train. My claustrophobia. You know about all that."

"I do," he said. "That's not what I'm talking about."

I immediately tensed, assuming that something must have gotten out regarding the widow and the funeral or, worse, everything that happened after that.

"What are you talking about then?" I asked, still trying to sound innocent.

He cleared his throat. "I stopped by the office the other day to say hello. You weren't there obviously. When I asked Gloria how you were doing and how the writing was going, well, let's just say she wasn't a very good liar."

"Why? What did she tell you?"

"That she's worried about you. She said you'd left town to go off somewhere without telling her where you were going or when you were coming back."

"I do that sometimes," I said defensively. "It's not all that unusual. Is that it?"

"No," he said. "When I reminded her that you were already past the due date for the book, she told me that she doesn't think you've written a word yet."

I didn't respond to that. After all, there wasn't much for me to say. It was obvious from his statement that I hadn't hidden my lack of production from Gloria as well I had hoped. Regardless, I tried to convince him that I had been working on an extensive outline at home and could get it all done in a month or so.

"Sure," he said. "And now you're in jail in Boston for assaulting a police officer. On the subway. In the middle of the night. After coming back from God knows where. I know something is going on and if you don't want to tell me, that's fine. But you'd be wise to tell that criminal lawyer tomorrow morning. That's my best advice."

I thanked him once more and assured him that everything was fine and he needn't worry. He said goodbye without offering any further counsel and hung up.

The officer who was to escort me down to the holding cell had drifted away by then and was in the middle of a conversation across the room, so I decided to push my luck and asked the desk sergeant if I could make another quick call. He looked at me with what appeared to be suspicion, and I wondered if he might have been able to piece together anything from just my side of the exchange with my attorney. I played it over quickly in my head and thought it unlikely. That seemed to be confirmed a few seconds later when he told me I could make "just one more" but to be quick about it.

I thanked him and punched in the number for Detective O'Connell, the woman with the New York state police, who my brother had urged me to call. Unfortunately, she didn't answer, and I soon discovered that the number that she had called me from (and that Gloria had given me) was for the detective's unit, and neither a direct line nor her cell phone. The person who answered listened for about ten seconds before he cut me off to tell me that he'd give her the message that I called. Before he could hang up, I shouted that this had to do with the death of Mrs. Condon and that Detective O'Connell wanted to speak with me about it. He came back on the line and had me repeat my name. Then I told him where I was and why and that I couldn't be reached on my cell phone. He said that someone would get back to me. Then he hung up.

The desk sergeant looked at me a little differently when I handed him the phone back.

"Was that a homicide you were talking about?" he asked.

I told him that I was informed that it was. He had heard me shout the widow's name. With a bit of investigation, he'd probably be able to find that out on his own. Better not to lie, I thought.

"Are you a suspect?" he asked.

That was a good question. As far as I knew, I was only being asked to come in and answer questions, or so the detective had told me. I wasn't sure if that qualified as a "suspect" in the eyes of the law.

"Of course not," I said. "I'm a friend of the family. I've been away. They've been calling me to see if I can help figure out what might have happened."

To say that those words were greeted with skepticism would be an understatement, but he didn't press me any further, and I wondered if maybe he saw me as crazy or intoxicated. I decided that either of those would be preferable to a possible murderer.

When my possessions were finally bagged and sealed, the other officer returned to the desk and brought me down two floors and put me in the holding area. As he closed the door, I asked how long I would be in there. He informed me that arraignments started at ten in the morning and that I should get comfortable, meaning that I would be spending the night.

To my great relief, the holding cell was one large room rather than one of those tiny ones they have in prisons, and this one wasn't full of rapists and murderers. There was but one skinny twenty-something who looked to be a college kid coming off a bender of some kind, and an elderly man in tattered clothes who was no doubt homeless or at least trying his best to appear to be. He didn't speak. I have no idea what put him in there.

After sizing things up, I quickly retreated to a neutral corner to wile away the hours and use some of those same behavioral techniques that had failed me so badly in the subway car just an hour or so before.

CHAPTER 21

NOT YET

M Y REPRIEVE CAME sometime the next morning, when a different cop called my name and woke me up from a not-so-gentle slumber. Without a watch or phone to tell me, I didn't know the time. The homeless gent had already been taken out some time in the night and the younger cellmate was still asleep, having crawled into a different corner than the one he was in when I arrived. I immediately stood up and followed the officer out of the cell, up in the elevator, and to a room somewhere on the main floor.

I had assumed that I would soon be going to court and that I was being brought into some sort of waiting area. When the officer opened the door, I found a well-dressed man, mid-forties and balding, standing by a table, talking quietly on his cell phone. When he saw me in the doorway, he said something into the phone and hung up. He then he introduced himself as my attorney, the one referred by my lawyer friend in Connecticut.

"Why don't you have a seat," he said, as the officer left and the door was closed and we were alone.

"What time is the arraignment?" I asked him.

"I don't know," he said.

"But it's today, right?"

He looked at me for a moment before answering. "Probably not."

My heart sank. "Why not?" I asked, my mind racing through all the reasons why it might be delayed. I didn't like any of them.

He paused for a second before he took out his phone again and hit a couple of buttons.

"They looked through all your possessions after the arrest," he said. "An inventory search, they call it. But really they're just looking for things that they might be able to use against you."

He finally found what he was looking for on the phone and turned the screen toward me.

"They found these," he said.

It was a photo someone had taken of the driver's license and credit card bearing the name of James Pinckney. My alternate ID. I had intended to dispose of them before going through security back at the St. Louis airport, but in my haste to run that other errand and get to the plane on time I had forgotten. Since they were in my bag and not liquids, or anything that resembled a bomb, they passed through the airport scanner undetected. However, they were pretty easy to find by a Boston police officer conducting a search of my things, as the attorney had just informed me.

I looked up at him. He raised his eyebrows in a questioning manner.

"Not good, right?" I asked.

He shook his head.

"A crime?"

He nodded. "Carrying a false ID," he said.

"Felony?"

"Misdemeanor by itself," he said. "Felony if it's used for fraudulent purposes. They're checking on that to see whose identity it is and if it's been reported stolen. That's the mother lode for them. That's why the arraignment's been delayed."

I explained to him how I had obtained the identity and that there was no such living person. He nodded again, although he hardly seemed sympathetic.

"I understand how you did it," he said. "Now do you want to tell me why you have it and what you used it for?"

"Not really," I said. I briefly considered telling him the whole story, from beginning to end, or at least to the point of us being in that room together. After all, he was an attorney bound by lawyer-client privilege, but my gut was telling me that I shouldn't. It seemed to me that over-sharing hadn't done much for me so far.

He stared at me for a good ten seconds. "I might have been able to work with the claustrophobia thing," he said. "But this is going to make it harder. It's also likely to make the newspapers."

I felt my stomach sink as those words settled in. I'm not exactly what you might call People Magazine famous, but I do have my own Wikipedia page and I'm well known enough to probably be of some interest to the media, particularly in a set of circumstances like the one I was embroiled in. In addition to the obvious desire to avoid the bad light I might be put in, I didn't want to make it so easy for those men in suits to find me, a fear I kept to myself of course. So I asked him if there was any way he could keep my arrest out of the press.

"I'll talk to someone I know out there," he said, meaning the police station. "But I can't make any promises."

After that, we went back and forth for a while with him trying his best to find out what I had been doing out in St. Louis before coming to Boston. I just told him that I went to visit my brother in Arkansas and that we drove to Chicago to see a friend and that on the way back, I decided it was time to fly home.

"Why wouldn't you fly to New York?" he asked.

I told him that the next available flight was much later and that I was happy to get to Boston and take a train.

He looked at me skeptically. "Which would take just about as long to get you to Connecticut as if you'd taken that later flight."

I simply shrugged. Again, I wasn't about to tell him why I didn't want to wait around the St. Louis airport.

He nodded. Then he opened his briefcase and took out a business card. "Well, let's see what they come up with. If it's anything more than you're telling me now, you're either going to have to tell me what you're hiding or get yourself someone else to represent you."

He didn't wait for me to respond and simply walked out of the room, leaving his card on the table.

A few seconds later, the same officer came back in and escorted me back to the same holding cell where I found a new set of bunkmates, although they appeared to be just as harmless as the ones from the previous night. I wondered how long my luck was going to hold out in that regard.

I spent the rest of that day and most of the following one wondering what the Commonwealth was going to do to me. I wasn't that concerned about a fraud charge. The motels where I had registered as Mr. Pinckney wouldn't be out any money. Other than the one at the second rest stop - the one we were forced to race away from - I paid cash at checkout. As for that one where the charge must have gone on the card bearing his name, as long as the credit card company paid the motel, the latter wouldn't be out anything. And since I had pre-paid a thousand dollars on Mr. Pinckney's credit card before I left Connecticut, the credit card company wouldn't be either. Same for the rental car under that name.

The lawyer had informed me that possessing the false ID was in itself a crime, but I hadn't used it to avoid law enforcement or to unfairly gain any kind of advantage with anyone. It was simply a way to pay for things without using my real identity. In fact, I had decided that when I saw him next that would be my defense - I was obsessed with privacy and wanted to keep my identity a secret when traveling.

Even if the prosecutor didn't buy that, the lack of any evidence of fraud would mean that an additional misdemeanor charge was all that they were likely to add to the assault. Which left me to wonder what was taking so long for the arraignment.

Of course I was worried that those men in suits would find out where I was before I was released. If they really were connected with the government and in possession of all of its resources, I suppose they could find out about my arrest without a newspaper story. And if they did, I wondered if they would possess the necessary credentials and paperwork to convince the Boston police to turn me over to them? Did they have that kind of sway? And, if so, would I be able to convince Boston law enforcement not to do so, that I would be in harm's way if they were to release me to them?

All those thoughts kept me occupied well past the time when the court would still be in session, leaving me to believe that I would be spending another night in the holding area. Just as I surrendered myself to that eventuality, a sergeant appeared outside the bars and informed me that I was being let go.

He opened the doors and instructed me to follow him upstairs where I could get my things. Of course, my worst fear came to mind. Nevertheless, I tried not to show it and asked him who had posted bail.

He pushed the button for the elevator and told me that no one had, that the arresting officer had been convinced to dismiss the complaint and drop the charges.

"All of them?" I asked.

"Whatever ones there were," he said. "Otherwise you'd still be our guest."

"Who would be able to do all that?" I asked, as we stepped into the elevator. I was hoping at least to learn what governmental body those men were masquerading under.

"Someone with a lot of juice apparently," he said.

When the elevator reached the main floor, we walked to the booking area where I expected to find my two friends waiting for me. Instead, the only person not wearing a Boston P.D. uniform was a woman dressed in tight jeans, an expensive looking t-shirt and a black leather jacket. As I approached the sergeant's desk, she turned around and extended her hand.

"Bridget O'Connell," she said. "New York State Police."

I'm sure my relief was visible and she smiled a little when she saw my reaction.

After collecting my personal items, I followed her out of the building to an unmarked car bearing New York State plates parked brazenly in front of the station.

She opened the front passenger side door and closed it behind me after I got in. Then she walked around to the driver's side and got in, almost as if we were a couple performing a daily ritual. She started the car and pulled away without saying a word.

"Where are we going?" I asked, when we were a short distance from the police station.

"Your choice," she said. "Albany or Connecticut."

"Really?"

"No," she said. "But I wanted to hear which one you'd choose."

"I don't care," I told her. "Either one is fine with me. As long as I'm out of there."

"We'll see how it goes then," she said.

"Am I under arrest?"

"Do you think you'd be riding up front with me if that was the case?" she asked.

The question didn't seem to require an answer, so I remained quiet as we drove through the streets of the Back Bay, the sun just beginning to set, sending its last rays of the day through the windshield. She seemed to have a pretty good handle on the city, causing me to wonder about her background.

"I understand how you might have talked that cop out of pursuing the assault charge, but how'd you get them to drop the ID thing?" I asked.

"Wasn't that hard," she said, her eyes still on the road. "It seems you didn't use the credit card or ID anywhere in Massachusetts. And you don't live here. They agreed with me that it would be a monumental waste of the Commonwealth's time and money to go the distance on a misdemeanor charge of possession. Of course, they had to confiscate them."

Reflexively, I pulled my new phone out of my pocket. The fact that it was returned to me had to mean that the police were unaware of the name it was under or they probably would have taken that as well. The detective looked over as I turned it back on, but said nothing, indicating to me that perhaps she didn't know either. We didn't say another word until we crossed over the bridge into Cambridge.

"Where are we going?" I asked.

"Somewhere nice," she said.

I assumed she was being facetious, but her statement turned out to be true, much to my surprise. In short time, we pulled into a pleasant little neighborhood with a tiny park at the center. Based on my limited knowledge of the area, I guessed that we were somewhere beyond Kendall Square and not quite near Harvard. She took the first available parking spot and got out of the car and walked toward a nearby bench without waiting for me. It was a cool spring night, and between the old fashioned streetlights and the glow from inside the houses, the place had a distinctively small town feel to it.

I hesitated about twenty seconds or so, and then I got out and followed her to the bench, which is what I had assumed she had wanted me to do from the start.

"Why are we here?" I asked, as I took a seat next to her.

She didn't turn to look at me and took her time before answering.

"I went to school near here," she said.

"High school?" I asked.

She smiled slightly. "College."

I quickly ran down the list of institutions of higher learning based in Cambridge, of which I knew there were close to a dozen. I worried that guessing the wrong one might reveal what I thought of her and decided that it might put me on her bad side, so I remained mum.

"MIT," she said, as if sensing my reluctance.

Had I taken a stab at it, I would have missed the mark by a wide margin. MIT was probably the closest to where we were geographically, but farthest from what I would have chosen off the list of possibilities I'd been considering. I tried to think of all the reasons why an MIT grad might want to become a New York state police detective. Once again, I decided not to guess and, instead, simply asked her.

She turned to look at me then. "Because it's what I wanted to do." She didn't sound insulted. It was merely an answer to my question.

"Sorry," I said, even though I didn't think I needed to apologize.

"I've read your books," she said, ignoring my apology.

"All of them?"

"The first two," she said.

"When you were in school?"

She shook her head. "After the widow's body was discovered and your name came up."

"You didn't want to read the third?" I asked.

She smiled. "I haven't been able to find it in any of the bookstores I go to."

I nodded. "I'm afraid it doesn't sell as well as the others," I told her.

She didn't answer.

"So what did you think?" I asked.

Regardless of what most people might imagine, all writers are insecure and constantly on the lookout for positive reinforcement, regardless of their level of success. She seemed to give the question some serious thought.

"I like the first one best," she said.

"Me too," I said, truthfully. Then I wondered what she thought of the other.

"They both have their merits though," she said, once again reading my mind.

"I suppose," I said, feeling somewhat unnerved by her intuition, if that's what it was.

We were quiet for a while after that. Then she asked me to tell her what happened, beginning with when I first heard about the doctor's death.

I briefly considered soft-selling much of the story and leaving out most of the juicier details, but I decided that my brother was right and that it might be time to get everything off my chest. After all, it was her, and not those two men who had come to my rescue. So I did just that.

I related every aspect that I could recall of the previous fourteen days, while she sat silently staring at the ground in front of her. She never once interrupted me to ask a question or have me repeat something. She simply listened.

"That's some story," she said, when I was finally finished.

I agreed with her. It was difficult not to.

"Men in suits?" she asked.

I nodded. "The same ones, too, I think. The suits, I mean. The men were definitely the same. They must get them cleaned every couple of days or maybe they own several."

I said that last thing in the way of a joke, and she smiled, almost the way one might after hearing a child tell of some incident that happened on the playground. I decided then that I liked her. She was about the age that I had guessed her to be from talking to her on the phone, maybe a little younger, but she looked nothing like I had envisioned. Her voice had a husky tone with an accent that definitely originated in one of Massachusetts' tougher towns, so I had assumed she might have some heft to her. Instead, she was willowy, with a runner's body and short blonde hair that framed her face perfectly. I found her to be quite attractive.

She took out a small notebook and wrote some notes for a time, apparently chronicling everything I had just told her, asking the occasional clarifying question. When she was done, I told her whom she could call for an alibi for Plum, giving her the name of my brother and his friend.

"Do you have one for Mrs. Condon?" she asked me then.

"One what?"

"Alibi."

I shook my head. "But I can promise you I never laid a hand on her and had nothing to do with her death."

"Do you know how she died?"

"No," I said. "Do you?"

"We found a substance in her blood," she said. "And what looks like a mark indicating an injection at the base of her neck."

"Causing her heart to stop," I said, repeating what she had insinuated before.

She nodded. Then tapped the notebook. "Naturally, I'll be checking all of this."

"You don't believe me?"

"Not yet," she said.

I nodded, disappointed though not surprised. "So what now?"

"I'll need you to give me that list along with the other papers you were given."

"I don't have them," I told her.

For the first time, she looked at me skeptically. "Why? Where are they?"

"I'm afraid I can't tell you that."

"Because you don't know or because you don't want to."

"The latter," I said. "Sorry."

"You don't trust me?"

"Not yet," I said.

She smiled. If she was angry, she didn't let on.

"You think if those men are in some way associated with the government, that I might be in cahoots with them?" she asked.

"Cahoots is not the word I would have used," I said. "But, yes, I'm worried that you might be taking orders from someone at a higher pay grade."

"I am," she said. "But not from anyone outside of my department. And I have no idea who those men are and I'm not working on their behalf in any manner whatsoever. Nor is my captain. And I'd like to think I'd know if he was."

I just shrugged. Then she asked if she could have the names that appeared on the list at least. I told her that I didn't see why not, and then recited them from memory. She asked for the spelling on each and I obliged, watching as she wrote them all down.

"So what do you think all this means?" she asked, again tapping the notepad when she was done. "The list? These names?"

"I don't know," I confessed. "I'm still trying to figure it out."

She nodded. I couldn't read her expression or tell what she might be thinking.

"Do you feel safe going back to your place in Connecticut?"

"I'm not sure," I told her. "Maybe if there were a police car outside around the clock. Is there any way you can arrange that?"

She stood up then and pocketed her notebook. "I'll see what I can do, but I can't promise anything."

After getting back in the car, we drove back over the bridge to Boston and South Station, where she double-parked out front and came inside with me and watched as I bought the ticket for home. Before I boarded, she gave me her card with her cell phone number written on it and told me to call if those men turned up or if anything suspicious happened before she could get back to me. I thanked her and we shook hands rather formally. Then she walked back through the station toward the entrance where she had parked and I got on the train.

Despite having little reason to do so, I believed her when she said she had nothing to do with those men. Of course, if they truly were connected with the government, I wondered if having her alone on my side would be enough to keep me alive.

CHAPTER 22

WHO IS THIS?

THE TRAIN ARRIVED at my local station on time, and I was able to hail a taxi and get to my building and inside the lobby without incident. It was just past eleven p.m. when I did, and if there was a police car anywhere in the vicinity, it must have been unmarked. Since that wouldn't provide much of a deterrent, I had to assume that there wasn't one and that Detective O'Connell had either had her request denied or failed to make one. I wondered which would be worse.

I went straight up to my unit, which I found to be in the same condition as when I left it. The cup that I had used for my coffee that morning I left for New Jersey was still in the sink, rinsed but not washed. I then checked all the drawers and closets, looking in particular for signs that they'd been opened. I had employed some of the methods one can use when seeking to detect such a thing. Everything I checked appeared to be undisturbed. I looked everywhere, even under the bed, to see if anything seemed to be amiss. As far as I could tell, no one had been inside, or if they had, they'd done a professional job of leaving no trace of it. However, I didn't believe they would have been so careful had they been there looking for that list.

As I told Detective O'Connell, I was no longer in possession of it. After the incident with those men at the rest stop, I had decided that it would be best if all of those papers were somewhere far away from me, in a safe place. It was the conversation with the Samoan back in

Fort Smith that first got me thinking that there might be something about all of them, not just the list, that was of concern to them. It wasn't anything specific he said. Just an inking really. But then the statements of the older man back at the rest area seemed to confirm that. And so, for that reason, before I boarded the plane back in St. Louis, I found a Fed Ex store and sent them to someone to hold for a while. Someone I could trust. Someone I was pretty certain that those men would have no reason to suspect might have them.

After checking the house, I turned on the TV to catch some news about the Final Four that was to begin in two days. Having missed the quarterfinal games the previous weekend, I was thinking that it might be nice to catch up on all the highlights and hear some of the interviews of the coaches and players. However, after about a half hour of watching, I found my thoughts drifting back to the events of the previous two weeks, so much so that I couldn't have told you which teams were favored in the semis or even which game was the first to be played on the weekend. Rather than try to pay closer attention, I turned off the set and went to bed, taking only one sleeping pill, and I drifted quickly off to sleep.

The ringing of my cell phone woke me at exactly 3:47 a.m. according to the bedside clock. I struggled to find the phone on my nightstand, and when I finally did, I opened it to reveal a number I didn't recognize from another unfamiliar area code. After briefly considering whether I should simply send it straight to voicemail, I hit "answer" but didn't say a word. Whoever was on the other side didn't either. I waited and watched as the call timer counted the seconds. When it neared ten, I finally asked who was on the other end of the line.

Again, there was no answer. I thought for a moment it might be those men in suits, but I couldn't fathom why they would be silent for so long. It simply wasn't in their nature. Then it occurred to me that the number might be from the burner phone that I had given my brother. I hadn't entered it into my contacts list and couldn't recall the number off the top of my head. Remembering that he had written it down on a napkin that I had put in my jacket pocket, I sprang out of bed and grabbed the coat from my closet and rifled through the pockets until I found it.

The numbers matched.

I spoke his name in the hope that it would be him on the other end of the line, but there was no response. Not right away anyway. All I could hear were what I believed to be night sounds, like the person holding the phone was outside somewhere.

Then I heard the faint sound of a siren.

I prayed that it would wane without getting any closer, but that was not the case. I then listened helplessly, as it grew louder and louder and finally stopped, only to be replaced by the sound of car doors opening and closing and footsteps beating the pavement.

I began shouting my brother's name as the sounds of movement and rustling took over, along with lots of clipped medical phrases and orders. I continued to scream his name until someone must have finally heard me and picked up the phone.

"Who is this?" a male voice asked. It was urgent and sounded annoyed. It was not my brother.

I told the person my name and asked him to tell me what was going on. Whoever was on the other end paused, and then asked who I was calling.

I told them that the person with the phone had called me and that it was last in the possession of my brother. I told him his name.

He asked me to describe him. I did as he asked.

I then heard him say the name, not to me, but presumably to the person they were attending to. He repeated it several times, all while the others around him were talking over one another and making noises I couldn't readily identify.

He came back on the line and asked if my brother had a tattoo on his right bicep. My reply was not a word, more of a guttural sound, but I had no doubt that he understood what it meant. He then said someone would call me back as soon as they could and hung up.

I found out later that morning that my brother died at the scene, which was on a quiet side street in his neighborhood, not too far from his home. The medical people were stumped when it came to the cause of death. There were no obvious signs of any illness, violence or accident. After a quick examination at the hospital, that included a full toxicology report and routine blood work, they were also able to rule out any kind of drug overdose. That left them to conclude that it must be something natural, like a heart attack or stroke. They said that the enzyme markers did seem to point to a cardiac event, but they were somewhat troubled that it didn't present itself in the customary manner. This was all explained to me by the doctor who had performed the examination.

"What do you mean?" I asked him.

"Most people who have a heart attack don't get up and walk out of their house in the middle of the night," he said. "Not three blocks anyway. At least that's what the police said he did. Personally I don't know how. Your brother must have had one strong heart."

I told him he did, nearly choking on the words.

Then I asked if they found any signs of struggle in the house.

If that seemed like an odd question coming from me when everything seemed to be pointing toward a possible heart attack, he didn't let on.

"No," he said. "But it's funny you should ask. The police told me they found some kind of billy club on the kitchen table."

My heart sank. "A baton" I said, correcting him.

"Excuse me?" he said.

"It's a baton," I said once more. "Not a billy club. I gave it to him. It's different. You open it up to use it."

"Oh," he said. "Well, that explains it. They told me it wasn't extended. I didn't know what they meant. Anyway, they said it was just sitting there, almost like it was on display."

I knew the reason for that, of course. The message they were sending. But I didn't bother to explain.

"Is that all?" I asked.

He paused for a few seconds, probably trying to figure out what I wasn't telling him. "They said they found the front door wide open but no one inside. His bed looked like it had been slept in. They don't know if he was asleep and woke up or why he left the house or why he walked so far."

"I do," I said softly.

He was quiet again, waiting for me to go on, I suppose. But I didn't see the point in telling him that my brother got shitty cell phone reception in his house and didn't have a land line and that he was obviously trying to acquire a signal so that he could call his younger brother to warn him that he might be the next one in line to have a heart attack. It didn't matter. Some emergency room doctor out in Arkansas didn't need to know all of that. However, I did suggest that he might want to search my brother's body for signs of an injection in a location where it was unlikely that he could have done such a thing to himself.

When he asked what would cause me to make such a request, I told him that I watched a lot of television and hung up.

In the meantime, I was forced to confront the notion that I had killed my only brother, not in any direct fashion, of course, but by needlessly involving him in the matter of the list. Of that there could be no doubt. Nor could there be any question as to who was behind his death, not after the message that was left with the baton. Of course, when the police in Arkansas eventually got around to calling to ask what I knew, I decided I would not to go through the same recitation of facts that I had with Detective O'Connell back in Boston. Telling them that I suspected it to be the work of "two men in suits" whose identities I didn't know and who might or might not be associated with the government in some murky fashion was more likely to move them further away from finding the truth, not closer.

When I called the detective later that morning to inform her of what had happened, she seemed to think otherwise. She was confident that if those men could be found, then evidence could be gathered to arrest them and charge them with my brother's murder.

"I don't want them arrested," I told her.

"What do you mean?" she asked.

"I want whatever happened to my brother to happen to them," I said, struggling to control my emotion.

She didn't answer right away. "Don't make me think that I'm making a mistake by trying to help you."

"Are you?"

"Am I what?" she asked.

"Trying to help."

"I will," she said. "But you're going to have to trust me."

I suppose that was true. I was going to have to trust her. But I was still undecided on that.

She must have taken my silence as agreement and asked me what I was going to do next. I told her that the only thing I had in mind was to go see my brother's daughter and his former wife to try and be of some comfort to them.

"Do you think that's a good idea?" she asked.

"What do you mean?" I asked back.

"In light of what just happened," she said. "You could be putting them in danger, too."

I thought about that before answering. I suppose she was right. I didn't care so much about myself, but I certainly didn't want to put them in harm's way. Then again, there were other considerations.

"I'll take every precaution," I told her. "And I'll only stay one night. Those men don't know where I am or it would be me laying on a slab in a morgue somewhere."

She was quiet for a couple of seconds. Then she told me to be careful and to stay in touch and that she would call me if she came into any new information.

My sister-in-law lives in Vermont, about a four-hour drive from my home in Connecticut. There was no way to fly there, not directly anyway, nor was there any train route that would take me anywhere nearby. And my severely damaged car was still sitting in the long term parking garage in the Philadelphia airport. I didn't want to use any of those methods of transportation anyway. They were all too traceable.

Instead, a series of bus rides would get me close enough that she could come pick me up, and she agreed to do just that after I called to tell her the grim news about her former husband. Her reaction was about what I expected. She was stunned at first, then saddened, and maybe a little resigned, as if him dying so young wasn't such a surprise. More than anything, she was concerned about her daughter, my niece. I didn't tell her about my being in Arkansas with my brother or our traveling together just days before his death. In fact, I told her nothing of what had been happening with me over the past two weeks, and I answered her question honestly when I said that I didn't know what caused his death.

When I asked if I could come to see them, she not only agreed, but insisted. She also told me that she'd inform their daughter about her father's death right away, and long before I got there. She graciously offered to have me stay with them and only asked that I help provide support for her daughter. While I would have opted for a hotel and the solitude that I normally crave, I immediately agreed to both the invitation and her request.

I left early the next morning. As I boarded the bus and found a seat, I took out my phone to turn off the ringer. When I did, I saw that Gloria had called an hour or so before, probably when I was in the shower. I considered waiting until I got to Vermont before I returned it, but then decided it would be better to get it over with. The Greyhound was only half full and I had whatever privacy comes from having a few empty seats next to me.

Gloria answered on the first ring, unlike the silly routine at the office, and she greeted me with both surprise and what sounded like relief.

"Are you alright?" she asked. "I heard about your brother."

I assured her that I was. Then I asked how she found out.

She told me that the medical examiner out in Arkansas had called the office and wanted to talk to me before the autopsy. "I didn't know what to tell him," she said.

I told her that was fine. Then I asked for the number and said I would call him when I had the chance. And I was going to. Though not right away. I didn't tell her that.

There was a moment of silence. Then she told me how sorry she was. "And you haven't seen him in so long," she added.

I told her that that wasn't actually the case. I then proceeded to fill her in on my visit with him and our reconciliation, leaving out most of the details. I didn't mention the list or the reason why I was in Arkansas in the first place. I also didn't offer any speculation about what might have killed him. Instead, I told her that it looked like a heart attack and that the autopsy would tell us for sure. Once again, we didn't speak for a couple of seconds.

"I feel like this is my fault somehow," I said then.

"Because you were just with him?" she asked.

"Yes," I said honestly.

"That's crazy."

"I suppose," I said.

"There's more to this than you're telling me, isn't there?" she asked.

I told her that there was and that I thought it was best to keep it that way. The implication was clear, and she must have made the association with the doctor's widow and those two men who had visited the office two weeks before because she asked me then if I had ever talked to that detective in New York.

I told her that I did and that we were going to meet up sometime soon, which I hoped to be the case.

Without waiting for her to respond, I asked if anything noteworthy had taken place at the office in my absence.

Once again, she hesitated before answering. "You got a certified letter from your publisher. They said they want the manuscript by the end of the month."

I wasn't surprised. As my attorney had noted, the book was already two months past due. A fair number of authors miss their due date, most without any consequences, but I suspected that the publisher was beginning to catch on to my inactivity and maybe even the reason for it.

"I hope you don't mind," she said, "I went on your computer to see if there was something I could send them, but I couldn't find anything that looked like a book on there." She paused a second before going on. "They're threatening to sue you for the advance if it's not in by then."

I told her not to worry about it. That I'd take care of everything when I got back. Then I told her about going to see my niece and former sister-in-law, which she thought was a good idea.

"I'm glad you called me back," she said then. "There's something else I want to talk to you about."

"Sure," I said, somewhat wary. "What is it?"

She went on to tell me that she had been offered a job back at the university. In our old department. I didn't ask nor did she tell me whether she had sought it out or if they came to her.

"Is it something you want to do?" I asked instead.

"I think so," she said.

I couldn't tell if she was fishing for me to ask her to stay or merely underselling a decision she had already made. I went in a different direction.

"Is it something I've done?" I asked.

"Heavens no," she said. "It's just that I feel like I'm not really doing that much for you here and that it's unfair for you to pay me so much for so little work."

I knew that there had to be more to it than that. That she was probably trying to soften the blow and, understandably, tired of the charade we were both playing a part in for the past three years or so.

"If it's a good opportunity, I think you should take it," I told her. "I'll be sorry to see you go, but you're right. There hasn't been a whole lot going on lately. Frankly, I'm not sure there will be in the future either." I meant that last bit to cover any number of possibilities, most of which I was trying not to think about.

She thanked me then and said that she was relieved I felt that way. She promised not to begin the new position until after I returned and had a chance to find a suitable replacement. I told her that there was no need to wait until then. That I didn't know how long I might be away and that she should just make arrangements for an answering service to take calls for the time being. I ended the conversation by telling her how happy I was for her and that I would be just fine.

If she were pressed, I'm sure she would have admitted that she thought the latter to be more of a lie than the former.

CHAPTER 23

THIS ISN'T NEW YORK CITY

THE BUS RIDE to Vermont was unremarkable, save for the beauty of the local landscape, even in the early spring. As she had assured me she would, my former sister-in-law was waiting in her car when the bus pulled up to the stop on the picturesque main street of her town. She came out and greeted me with a warm hug as soon as I got off. I've never been much of a hugger, but in that moment I began to understand the appeal of it to most people. When we finally disengaged, I looked around and asked her where my niece was. She told me that she was home waiting for us.

"By herself?" I asked, trying my best not to sound alarmed.

"She's almost seventeen," she said, looking at me oddly.

"I just meant shouldn't she have some company. You know. With all that's happened."

"We'll be there soon enough," she assured me.

In retrospect, as the detective had suggested I should, I had more than a few concerns about their safety, with visions of those men in suits showing up at their house at some point. I had even considered changing my mind just prior to boarding the bus, in order to avoid that very possibility. But in the end, I felt that I couldn't very well call to inform them of my brother's death and then give excuses as to why I couldn't make the trip up to see them. No matter what reason I might give, it simply wouldn't suffice. I didn't know what would be worse: to expose them to some possible danger or prove to be some-one without an ounce of decency.

It helped my decision that nothing had taken place since my return to Connecticut to indicate that those men could track my phone or my method for getting there, given that the bus didn't even require me to provide any form of identification.

I then asked how my niece was doing with the news.

"About as well as you might expect," she told me. "But she's a strong kid. She's mostly just trying to understand why."

The bus driver had finished unloading the luggage at that point, and I spotted my duffel bag and went over to retrieve it, saving me from having to come up with something to say to that. A minute later, we were in her car and on the way to her house.

My sister-in-law has worked steadily as a school nurse since split-ting up with my brother, and told me she's picked up additional money by doing private duty nursing for some elderly neighbors. Together with the settlement from the divorce, she was able to pur-chase a nice little three-bedroom home in one of the more quaint towns in that scenic state. I experienced a pang of envy as we pulled up to the very well maintained exterior. In fact, her house looked so well taken care of that I wondered if there might be a new man in her life, not that keeping a nice home requires a steady supply of testosterone.

After parking in the driveway and retrieving my bag, we entered the back door into the kitchen where my niece was waiting at the table with a cup of tea in front of her. She leapt to her feet at the sound of the door opening and immediately ran into my arms. I could feel her sobbing and trembling as soon as she did. We hadn't even spoken a word.

It turns out that I'm no better at comforting folks than I am at hugging them, but I did my best to do both under the circumstances. I looked at my sister-in-law over the girl's shoulder and saw a look of sadness that I hadn't detected prior to that moment. It was only then that I realized why. There were tears running down my cheeks as well. For some reason, I hadn't felt them, maybe because crying was something that happened so rarely for me. The last time I could recall doing so was when I had to put down the dog I had gotten custody of after my divorce. I had grown quite close to it, living alone as I did, and the loss was profound, much more than I had expected. Of course, I knew that that was going to be nothing compared to the loss of my brother.

I managed to utter several words of consolation to my niece as we continued to hold one another. They sounded phony to me as I said them, even though I meant them as sincerely as anything I have ever said. Eventually, just before it got to the point of awkward, she let go of my embrace and backed away, wiping her eyes. I took the opportunity to do the same. Then she asked if I found out yet how her father had died.

I repeated the same story I told her mother about how it looked like a heart attack but that they were going to have to perform an autopsy to be sure.

"What else could it be?" she asked.

I had thought long and hard about how I would answer any questions regarding the cause of death, and I decided that I would be honest, at least up to the point where the two men in suits might enter the equation.

"I don't know," I said. "It's probably just that, a heart attack, but I thought it was important to make sure. That's the reason for the autopsy."

She continued to examine my face as if to see whether I might have anything more to say.

"I'm sure your uncle is right," my sister-in-law said, rescuing me. "It's the most likely explanation."

My niece looked at her mother before turning back to me. "Do you think it could have had something to do with all that weight-lifting he's been doing?"

"I don't know," I said. "Maybe. But I'm certainly no doctor."

"Mom thinks it could be," she said.

"Well, I certainly wouldn't argue with your mother. She knew him better than I did."

"I'm not so sure about that," my sister-in-law said.

I shrugged to both concede the point and to avoid having to discuss who was further in the dark on the subject.

While my sister-in-law went about preparing dinner, I sat down at the table with my niece to look at photographs of her father, almost all of them from before the divorce. I'd forgotten how handsome he was and how different his body looked - slimmer and more sinewy than what I saw the week before. I wondered if he might have been using steroids or growth hormone in recent years. It sure looked it to me.

"I think I look more like him than Mom," my niece said to me at one point.

"You do," I said. "And even more like your grandmother. That's a good thing. She was quite a beauty."

It was true. I hadn't seen my niece in over two years and she had grown into a lovely young woman, with more than a little resemblance to my mother.

"I've only seen pictures," she said. She was right. My mother died when she was still a toddler. She couldn't have had any memories of her own.

When we finished with the photos, she asked what we were going to do about her father's burial.

"I'm not sure yet," I said. "What do you think?"

"I think we should bring him back here," she said.

Her mother turned from the sink to look at us then. From her reaction, I gathered that they hadn't discussed it.

"We'll have to see what his will says about that," I said. "It would be his choice."

"He doesn't have one," my sister-in-law said. She then dried her hands and came over to the table.

"A choice?" I asked.

"No, a will," she said.

I was relieved. For a moment, I was worried that she was trying to usurp my brother's wishes, something I would have thought to be out of character for her.

"Do you know that for sure?" I asked.

"That's what he told me anyway."

"When was that?"

"Not too long ago," she said. "In the fall sometime. He said he didn't need one. That he didn't have much besides the house and he wanted it all to go to his daughter. Which was fine with me."

I nodded. It sounded like something my brother would say.

"We were talking about college," she said, nodding toward my niece. "It's coming up next year and I wanted to make sure that we knew what we had available before we made any decisions about where she's going."

She sat down then and we all stared at the tabletop for a while.

"What's it like to be so smart?" my niece asked me, finally breaking the silence.

I looked up, surprised by the question.

"I don't know," I said. "I think it's all relative. I don't feel all that smart sometimes."

"But you are," she said. I could feel her mother eyeing me, anxious I suppose to hear my response.

"I guess some people think I am," I said. "But it's not really that important. If I am, it doesn't make me better than anyone else."

"Yes it does," my sister-in-law said, causing me to turn to her.

"No," I said. "It might make it easier to make a living, but that's about it. Even then, there are people out there with genius IQs driving cabs and waiting on tables."

"Well, I wouldn't," my niece said.

I turned to her. "Why? What would you do?"

"I'd be a doctor," she said. "Maybe find a cure for some really bad disease. One that kids get."

I nodded, wondering at the same time if that was an unintended indictment of me and my choice of profession, it being one that regular people had trouble finding much value in.

"That would be great," I told her.

"I tell her she can still do that," her mother said. "She's plenty smart. She just doesn't believe me."

I asked my niece if she did OK in school. She just shrugged.

"She gets Bs mostly, which is better than I did," her mother said.

"That's with tutors and special help," my niece said. "It's all I'll ever do. And I know it."

"You're wrong," I told her. "There've been a lot of people who've had learning issues but went on to do some pretty amazing things. Groundbreaking things even. Albert Einstein. Thomas Edison. Walt Disney. Just to name a few."

"Really?" she asked, her face lighting up.

"Absolutely," I said. "Happens all the time."

Her mother smiled at her and then me. I suppose I had probably reinforced a belief that she'd been trying to instill in her daughter over the years.

"See?" she said. "You should listen to your uncle."

After dinner, my niece borrowed the car to go over to a friend's house to watch a movie, while I helped her mother with the dishes. For the most part, we worked steadily and without saying much, except for me asking where certain items were stored.

Just when I thought we might get through the chore without any more discussion about me, she asked if I had ever wanted to have any children of my own.

I stopped in the middle of drying one of the last dishes and looked at her. "I'm not sure how to answer that," I said.

She looked at me with an expression that I could only characterize as confused.

"We talked about it," I said, referring to my former spouse, who she had only met two or three times. "She wanted to. I know that."

"But you didn't?"

"I wouldn't say that," I told her. "Whenever she'd ask whether we should try, I'd tell her that I wanted to wait."

"Wait for what?" she asked.

I looked away. "I guess that depended on whatever I was doing at the time. Whether I was writing a book or developing a new course or applying for tenure. I suppose I thought it would be better to wait until that was done."

"But things are never done, are they? Something else always comes along, doesn't it?"

I looked back at her. "I guess."

"Is that why you guys got divorced?" she asked.

I had to think about that one before I answered. "No," I said finally. "There was more to it than that."

I could see that she wanted to ask the next question. And if she did, I wasn't sure what I would say. In fact, I wasn't sure I could even answer it myself.

"You could now," she said instead. "I mean have a child. It's not that late. It's much harder for a woman your age."

"I suppose," I told her. "But it's not like I've had a lot of options the last few years. It may have passed me by. If so, that's OK. I'm alright with it."

She looked sad at hearing that. I wasn't sure I liked being pitied like that.

"Well, your niece is going to need some male influence now that her father is gone," she said. "Not that he was all that involved lately. She admires you. A lot. She's proud that you're her uncle. If you ever wanted to help out, I know she'd welcome it."

I worked up a smile, not quite sure how to respond. It wasn't that I didn't want to. It was more that I was afraid I might fail at it. That I wouldn't have the first idea how to even begin. I didn't say that, of course. Instead, I thanked her for telling me and let the matter drop. She didn't press it, and went about wiping the counters while I put away the last dish.

When we were done, she asked if I wanted to go into the family room and turn on the basketball games. I was somewhat surprised at the offer, assuming that my brother might have soured her on the sport, but it turned out she was still as big a fan as when they were married. As for me, I had been fully prepared to go without watching them. In light of why I was there, it seemed a rather frivolous activity on my part.

"I never saw him play," she said as we sat down on the couch. "Except on the playground."

"He was good," I told her. "Real good. It's too bad he didn't stick with it in college. He would have been a star there, too."

She nodded and looked like it was just another disappointment that he had racked up in his life.

"Funny how we could be from the same family and be so different," I said. It was an innocuous statement on my part, certainly not one meant to start the conversation that followed.

"Your brother was always jealous of you, you know. For how you are."

I paused for a moment, surprised to hear it verbalized. "Actually I didn't know that," I told her. "Until last week anyway."

She looked at me oddly and I remembered then that I hadn't told her about my trip out to see him.

"You talked to him last week?" she asked.

I was forced to concede that I did, and then proceeded to tell her a very sanitized version of my visiting him after concluding some "business" in Little Rock.

"Why didn't you tell me this before?" she asked.

I lied and told her that I thought I had, over the phone. Then I apologized. She studied me, as if to determine if I was being completely candid.

"With all that's happened, I've been a little spacey," I added.

She seemed to accept that excuse. Then asked how he looked to me and whether he showed any signs of being in poor health.

I told her that he seemed fine, which wasn't a complete lie. I didn't mention the fighting or risk-taking behavior I had observed.

"Well, anyway, he never wanted you to know about it," she said. "But he was jealous. It made it hard on him, especially when he found himself out of work or in some job he didn't like. Which was most of them."

I felt as uncomfortable talking to her about the relationship as I did with my brother, and I hoped to change the subject, but she wouldn't let it go that easily.

"I was intimidated by you myself," she said. "At first anyway. But you never lorded it over me."

I wanted to thank her for saying that, but I thought it might sound disingenuous. Instead, I told her that I hoped I had never done that to anyone, least of all her.

She smiled. "So what are you working on now?" she asked.

I'm sure it was just an innocent question, but something about the whole series of events that led me to be sitting in her house that night caused me to abandon the usual deflection I would employ whenever I was asked that question in recent years. Instead, I confessed openly to how much trouble I was having writing the book and how worried I was that I might never produce anything approximating what I had in the past.

When I finished, she looked at her hands and was quiet for a time. The announcers droned on about the game, while I waited to hear what she might have to say to that.

"Why do you think that is?" she asked finally.

"I wish I knew," I said.

"That's awful," she told me. She sounded like she meant it, which broke my heart, considering the struggle her daughter had obviously been going through her whole life.

"Don't feel too sorry," I told her. "I'm OK. I've got money. And my health. I may just have to get used to the idea and decide how to spend the rest of my life."

"Well, you dry a mean dish," she said with a smile.

I laughed, trying to show that I could take the joke, but I must have failed. I could read it in her face.

"I'm sorry," she said. And I have no doubt she meant that, too. She got up then and told me she'd be right back.

I looked at the TV for the minute or so that she was gone, but I couldn't have told you the score or even who was playing.

When she came back, she was carrying the manila envelope that I had slipped inside the Fed Ex mailer and sent to her from the airport in Saint Louis. She sat down with it still clutched in both hands. From what I could tell, she had followed my instructions and hadn't opened it.

"I haven't had time to go to the bank and rent a safety deposit box like your note said."

"I was going to ask you about that," I told her. "You can give it back to me now. Things have changed since I sent it."

She didn't offer it to me. In fact, she seemed to clutch it a little tighter.

"I feel like there's something in here you should tell me about."

I looked at her, not quite sure how much to say, if anything.

"I think it's better that you don't know," I said finally.

There was a short pause before she spoke again.

"It's why he's dead, isn't it?"

It was a pointed question, one going right to the heart of the matter. As his wife, I probably would have owed it to her to tell her. As his ex-wife, I thought, not so much. Besides, she was right - my brother's knowledge of what was in there was what led to his death, and I didn't want to put her in the same position.

"He died of a heart attack," I told her. "That's the preliminary finding. There's just paper in there."

The first part of that was probably true, although what brought it on might have had some connection. The latter part was definitely a lie. It wasn't just paper. It was a whole lot more than that.

"OK," she said. Then she handed the envelope to me. "I won't ask why you sent it to me for safe-keeping. If it's just papers."

That last word hung in the air as I took the envelope and laid it on my lap. If I was being totally honest with myself, those papers were nearly as big a reason for my being there as was my niece. After my brother died, I was even more determined to find out what that list was all about, and it was always my intention to take them back with me after the visit.

"This has to do with me," I told her. "And a promise I made to someone. That's all."

"Why did you go all the way out there to see him?" she asked, ignoring what I had just said.

"I didn't," I said. She raised her eyebrows. "I told you. I went for something else."

"And you're not going to tell me what that was," she said.

I shook my head. She gestured at the manila envelope.

"It had to do with that," she said.

"That's right," I said.

"So whatever is in there must be pretty serious if you're trying to protect me by keeping me from knowing."

I gave a shrug that more or less told her she was right.

"But you let your brother put himself in danger."

"No," I said, more forcefully than I meant to. "I only went to see him because I was close to Fort Smith and hadn't heard from him in awhile. He did get involved after I got there, that's true. But I never asked him to. In fact, I tried to talk him out of it. But the danger was almost like a drug to him."

That last bit must have hit a nerve somewhere inside her. She sat back and nodded, like she could picture it. Unlike me, she had to have known all about my brother's attraction to danger and risk, having been married to him for so long.

"I'll trust you then," she said. "But if it's that bad, I don't want it or you here for any length of time. No offense, but that girl means too much to me."

I told her of course and that I'd leave first thing in the morning. I half-expected her to tell me that I could at least stay until the afternoon, but she didn't. I realized then that it might have been a mistake to send the papers to her in the first place.

We watched the end of the first of the two games that turned out to be not very close and somewhat of a disappointment. She asked me if I had predicted the winner. Only then did I realize that I couldn't remember which teams I had picked to be in the Final Four, let alone the championship game. Every year before the start of the tournament, I would pore over all of the team records, strength of schedule and just about every other statistic I could get my hands on before finally filling out my bracket. And after each game I'd analyze the outcome and try to commit it to memory in case it might turn out to be a factor in filling out the bracket the following year. Considering how much time I spent watching the sport, you'd think I would have done better than I did, but I can assure you that I was no Rafe Plum when it came to forecasting the tournament.

During the break between contests, she went into the kitchen to get some popcorn and a couple of beers. That was when I got a call on my cell phone.

I looked at the number before answering and, as with the call from my brother, I didn't recognize it. I considered just turning it off when something caused me to re-think it and press "answer."

"Are you enjoying the games?" a voice asked me.

I thought I recognized it, but part of me was hoping I hadn't. I didn't respond.

"That's what you're doing, right?"

It was the older of the two men in suits. Of that there was little doubt. That he knew what I was doing sent a shiver through me, and my first inclination was to look out the window, which I did, using the curtain to shield me from view. I didn't see anyone out there, but by then it was quite dark and they could have easily been hidden among the many trees and bushes.

"Where are you?" I asked.

"Why? Do you want me to stop by?"

"No," I said, and meant it with all my heart.

"Disappointing game, no? I sure hope the next one's better."

I thought that I detected something about his tone of voice, something not quite so all-knowing as before, almost like he was probing instead of gloating over having found me. That's what caused me to rethink my original concern and do what I did next. I let go of the curtain and stepped into plain view.

"It would be unusual to have two blowouts at this stage," I said, staring straight out the window, just as I would if I knew someone was out there watching.

"Seems like a mismatch to me," he said. He didn't say anything about seeing me or change his tone in any way. So I waved my arm in a long slow fashion, as if trying to get someone's attention.

"Nah, I think this one will go down to the wire," I told him.

Again, there was no mention of me or the waving. "I don't know," he said. "Michigan State looks awful strong."

I decided then to up the ante and gave him the finger. Put it right up against the glass so that he couldn't miss it. Once more, there was no response. He wasn't out there. I was sure of that.

"I'm going to go with the upset," I said then.

"That would be something," he said, with a laugh. "Kinda like Villanova-Georgetown all over again, huh?"

I froze at that. Then I hit the "end" button to terminate the call.

I suppose it was possible that he mentioned that famous 1985 contest purely out of coincidence. Then again, it might easily have been his way of letting me know that he had discovered the name I had been using prior to my arrest in Boston. The same last name as the MVP of that game. The name that the new phone was registered under. The phone that I was still holding in my hand.

If he had, then he could run a trace protocol and locate the cell tower through which the call was being routed. Once he determined that it was in Vermont, he'd know who I had come to see. And he'd be coming soon after. I looked at the phone to check the time that had elapsed for the call. It was less than ninety seconds. I had turned off my location services days before and was pretty sure that a minute and a half wasn't enough time for the more complicated network trace to run. Still, the technology for cell call triangulation has improved over the years, and I couldn't be one hundred percent certain.

I didn't have time to think about it for very long, since my sister-in-law walked in then carrying a tray with a bowl of popcorn and two glasses of beer. She noticed the change in my expression right away.

"What's wrong?" she asked.

I told her that she needed to get her daughter back home as soon as possible.

"Why?" she asked. "What's the matter?"

I told her that we needed to leave, and I asked her if there was someplace safe she could stay.

"Now?" she asked. "Tonight?"

"Yes," I told her. "And maybe a few more nights. I'll let you know when you can come back. It's just a precaution."

"Is this some sort of joke?"

I told her it was anything but.

"What happened?" she asked. "You're scaring me."

"I'm sorry," I said, and meant it more than anything. "I don't think you're in any real danger, but it's best to be safe."

"You weren't worried ten minutes ago," she said, growing agitated. "Why now?"

I explained a little about the call I had just received and its relationship to what was in the envelope, again without getting too specific.

She thought about what I said for a few seconds. "This person who called, did he have something to do with your brother's death?"

I told her that he might have.

I can't really describe the expression I saw on her face after I said that. It was somewhere between utter disbelief and intense hatred.

"Why don't you call the police then?" she asked, her tone suddenly icy and distant.

I tried to tell her about the murky ties to the government and the possibility that the police would be warned off the case. She looked at me like I had gone crazy.

"Not ours," she said. "They wouldn't be. I know all of them. From the chief on down."

"And do you think they would post a couple of men here around the clock for two or three days? To watch over you?"

"I think that would depend on what you told them."

"I don't think we can take that chance. Like you said, she's too important."

Off that last, she stared. "Oh, that's rich," she said. "I invite you here. Into my house. Into my daughter's life. After all the times you haven't been here. And you bring me this?"

I told her I was truly sorry and that I would make it up to her somehow.

She didn't respond to that. Instead, she went to get her phone and called whoever's house her daughter was at. I listened to the exchange and it sounded about as incongruous as one would expect under the circumstances.

In no more than ten minutes she had two bags packed and was waiting by the back door for her daughter to return. She hadn't said a word to me in that whole time. When the car finally pulled into the driveway, I asked if she could drop me off at a car rental place.

"This isn't New York City," she said, bitterly. "Nobody here rents cars at ten o'clock at night."

Of course. It was a foolish thing to ask. So I asked instead if there was someplace open near the bus stop where she could drop me. She just frowned and told me to get my things.

The bus stop where I came in was not a true station. It was just a covered bench with three glass walls and a framed schedule hanging on the back one. As we sat in the idling car at the curb in front of it, she told me that I could buy a ticket in the drug store next door when it opened in the morning. I looked around, and there didn't appear to be any place open on either side of the block, save for a small tavern across the street.

"How late are they open?" I asked, indicating the bar.

"Till two," she said.

"What time does the drug store open?"

"Nine," she told me.

"Tomorrow's Sunday," my niece pointed out from the back. "They don't open till eleven on Sundays."

She had been silent up until that point and I had no idea what her mother had said to her when she came home, since I had gone up to the guest room to get my duffel bag. Whatever they discussed, my niece still seemed to have some sympathy toward me. I was grateful for that at least.

My sister-in-law looked out the windshield and neither at her daughter nor me. I could tell she was trying to decide just how badly she wanted to punish me.

"You can't make him wait out here for nine hours," my niece finally said, breaking the silence. "He's doing this to protect us. That's what you told me, right?"

"We're not bringing him with us," her mother said.

I hadn't asked for that and would have turned her down had she offered. I finally suggested a motel that I had seen on the ride into town that afternoon. It was about two miles from where the bus dropped me off and looked like it had been built in the 1960s. It only had about twelve rooms, but the sign indicated that there were vacancies. That seemed to satisfy both my sister-in-law and my niece, and I was relieved not to have to nurse a drink in that tavern for three or four hours until they put me out into the street.

The two of them waited in the car while I went into the tiny motel office to register and get a key, and when I came back out to get my bag and say goodbye, my sister-in-law said she'd be back in the morning to bring me to the bus stop in time for my return to Connecticut. Then she drove off without saying another word.

I never asked her where they were going and who they were staying with. I wouldn't have wanted to know. Still, I couldn't help but wonder if they would be safe and whether I should be doing more to insure that they were. When I sent those papers to her, I was certain that those men would have had no reason to seek out a former relative by marriage who I'd had little contact with in recent years, apart from Christmas cards and the occasional phone call. Hell, they had no reason to suspect that I had sent the papers to anyone, since I paid cash at the Fed Ex store and, therefore, left no credit card transaction for them to find. Nevertheless, it appeared that they had somehow discovered the new phone and, in doing so, I had put my niece and her mother in danger. About the only thing I could to do to protect them, and myself as well, was to register at the motel under a third name, that of a college roommate who I hadn't seen in years. Thankfully, the desk clerk didn't ask for ID and, once again, I paid with cash.

As soon as I got inside my room, I did the only other thing I could think of and took out my phone and called Detective O'Connell. I tried both the main squad number and her cell, but she didn't answer either, the second one going straight to voicemail. So I left a message asking her to call me as soon as possible. Given what happened with the phone call earlier, I knew it was a risk to use the phone again, but I needed to talk to her. She was my only hope.

As the sign out front indicated, the motel offered "free cable," and I tried to pass the time watching the second semifinal game of the night while I waited for the detective to return my call. When the game ended at around eleven thirty, she still hadn't done so, and I concluded that she probably wouldn't before morning. So I turned off the bedside lamp and lay back in the bed to watch the post-game analysis, hoping that all that talk might help me to doze off.

It didn't.

Instead, I tossed around, my thoughts ping-ponging back and forth between worrying about the safety of my only living relatives and wondering what made that list and those papers so important to those men.

Finally, unable to fall asleep, I threw the covers off and got up and took the list out to look at once more. I don't know what I was expecting to find. I had read it more than a couple dozen times in the previous two weeks and the words certainly weren't going to change. Nevertheless, I stood there at the foot of the bed, staring at the page in front of me, the yellowish glow from the television illuminating it from behind and exposing the grainy cellulose fibers that make up simple white paper these days.

And exposing something else as well.

The thing I'd been missing all along.

It's funny how you can look at something over and over and still see the same thing. Until you look at it in a different light.

CHAPTER 24

THE FIRST ONE'S BETTER

AWOKE JUST after six that morning, anxious to get the day started and myself away from that town. I recalled that a sign in the dingy office for the motel cheerily promoted "complimentary coffee", and so I got dressed and walked down the row of rooms toward the entrance. I noticed that there were only two cars in the lot, one a ten-year-old Toyota Camry with New Hampshire plates and the other an even older Ford pickup with a Maine registration. Neither gave me any reason to suspect that they might belong to my pursuers. Still, I took in the surroundings as if expecting someone to jump out from inside one of the rooms at any second. Fortunately, no one did, and I entered the office accompanied only by the ringing of the bell on the door.

The counter where the middle-aged female clerk from the night before had checked me in was now unmanned. I looked around and saw one of those tall urns that restaurants use to hold coffee and keep it warm. It was sitting on a table next to the copy machine, up against the adjacent wall. I hadn't noticed it the night before, so it gave me hope. I went over to look for a cup, but there were none in sight. Worse, I didn't detect the smell of freshly brewed coffee wafting from anywhere nearby, and when I put my hand to the urn it was cold to the touch. I looked up on the wall to make sure I hadn't imagined the sign, and sure enough it was there. Given that it was a Sunday morning and not even six thirty, it occurred to me that it might be a little early in laid-back Vermont for free morning coffee. I was about to return to my room when I noticed a wrinkled newspaper on the desk beneath the counter. My eye caught a story headline that stopped me dead:

"NOTED AUTHOR WANTED FOR QUESTIONING IN CONNECTION WITH MYSTERIOUS DEATH OF RECENTLY WIDOWED WOMAN"

I didn't have to read very far to discover my name in the first paragraph identifying me as the author in question. That the article mentioned my books and former professorship was troubling, but I suppose the editor who okayed it must have thought that my background gave the already curious set of circumstances even more of an air of mystery, like one of those unsolved murder sagas they run on Saturday night TV.

I looked up at the top of the page to learn that it was the previous day's edition of the paper, not that it mattered much. It was fresh enough, and I imagined that the local television station was likely to pick up the story, if they hadn't done so already. The photo that accompanied the story was an old one from back in my teaching days, and having gained some weight and shed my beard, it would take a bit of scrutiny for someone to match my current face to the one in the photo. Judging by the fact that I wasn't yet arrested, the desk clerk had failed to do so. However, my sister-in-law would learn about my troubles soon enough and, if she were still coming by to pick me up after having done so, I would have plenty of explaining to do. Of course, there was also the possibility that she would simply call one of her friends in the local police department to come and get me and turn me over to their counterparts in New York.

With that in mind, I grabbed the paper and headed out the door and down to my room. As soon as I got inside, my cell phone started ringing. I closed the door and pressed the button to answer. It was the detective.

"I saw the paper," I told her, without even saying hello.

"I'm sorry about that," she said. "It wasn't me."

"What's that supposed to mean?" I asked.

"This came down from above," she said. "My boss' boss. They want to bring you in and charge you."

"There's an arrest warrant?"

"Not technically," she said. "But once you're picked up, the only way to keep you in custody is to charge you with something and that's what they intend to do."

"On what evidence?" I asked. "I didn't kill her, so there can't possibly be any."

"Hopefully that's true. But they'll charge you with something other than murder just to hold you. Failure to report. Obstruction. Anything. It doesn't have to stick. It just has to keep you from walking out for awhile."

"What for?" I asked. "Why are they doing this?"

"I really don't know," she said. "They're not sharing their thinking with me." It sounded like she was telling me the truth, but given everything that had happened in the previous two weeks, I wasn't sure how much I could trust my judgment anymore.

"How is that?" I asked. "I thought it was your case?"

"Not anymore. When I went in to see my captain to ask him what was going on, he told me I was no longer running it. Then they took the file from me. End of story."

"Well, what do you think? You must have some idea what they're up to."

"I think your theory about some sort of governmental connection might be starting to make a whole lot more sense."

I thought about that for a second. On the one hand, she was all but admitting that she hadn't believed that part before. It was only slightly more reassuring to hear that she was coming around to my way of thinking.

She asked me if the article was the reason why I called. I told her no, that I didn't see the paper until just a few minutes ago. Then I told her about the phone call I got from the older man and my concerns about my niece and my sister in law.

She thought about it for a bit before answering. "Well, if you don't know where they went and they're not at home, I don't think those men would be able to find them very easily. They can't exactly go door to door. Besides, it's you they're after."

That seemed to make sense, and I hoped she was right.

"What do you think I should do then?" I asked her.

"What do you mean?"

"Do you think I should turn myself in?"

There was another pause before she answered. This one shorter. "You know I can't tell you to run. I'm an officer of the court. My official advice is to give yourself up."

I thought about that for a second and her use of the qualifier. "Are you going to tell your captain I called?" I asked.

"It's not my case anymore, remember?"

"Does that mean you won't?"

"If I'm asked, I will. And then I'll tell them that you refused to take my advice. Assuming you do."

"I don't have anywhere to go," I told her.

"Well, I'm afraid I can't help you there," she said. "I wish I could, but I can't."

I was pained to hear that. I had felt alone before, but this was different. I was now being hunted by more than just those two men in suits, and the one person who I thought was on my side sounded like she no longer wished to be there.

"What if I gave you those papers?" I asked her.

"I thought you told me you didn't have them?"

"I didn't then. I do now. What if we meet somewhere and I give them to you?"

Again, she was silent. I had obviously tempted her.

"You could get them tested," I told her.

"Why would I do that?" she asked.

"Because it's more than just those names on the list," I said. "It's about the paper, too."

"How's that?" she asked.

"There's something on there," I said. Then I told her about holding the list up in front of the light from the television and what I saw when I did.

"What is it?" she asked.

"I don't know," I said. "Maybe a chemical of some kind. That's why we need the test. It could tell us what this is all about. If so, it might get your boss to change his mind."

"That's a lot of ifs," she said, "Besides, even if I wanted to, I'd need authorization. There are procedures to follow."

"What if I take you to a place where they'll test them. I'll pay for it. You just come along to keep the chain of custody."

"If I do that I could get myself fired," she said.

"And if I turn myself in I could get myself killed. You know what they did to my brother. Are you going to let that happen to me?"

Once more, there was silence on the other end, and I realized that this was it. For better or worse, I was casting my lot with her. If she turned me down, I was just a man on the run with no place to go.

"OK," she said finally. "I'll meet you. And we can talk about it. See where it goes."

"With or without your friends in the New York State police?" I asked.

"Without," she said.

"And I can trust you on that?"

"I can only give you my word. That's all I can do."

"Fair enough," I said.

"Alright then, tell me where you are. I can be there later this morning."

"No," I said. "Those guys might already be here looking for me. I'm leaving now. Drive over to Springfield. Get there around noon. Park at the exit off the Pike. I'll call and let you know when and where to meet."

She took a moment to think about it. "Alright. Springfield it is."

I thanked her and we hung up. Then I began packing what little I had taken out of my duffel. When I was done, I locked the door and left the key in the room, with the TV turned up so that anyone approaching the door would think I was still in there. Then I stopped by the office again, but not before peeking inside to make sure it was still vacant. Lucky for me, it was, since I wanted to do couple more things before I left.

One of those was to look through the "lost and found" box I saw in there earlier. On top was a winter hat, one of the ones with the long flaps that not only cover the ears, but also a good bit of the face. To help keep you warm. And maybe keep people from seeing who you really are. I took it out and put it on. There were several pairs of sunglasses in there as well, the kind skiers use on the slopes, and I took one with lenses that wouldn't look too out-of-place on the street.

Fortunately, the weather co-operated and I could wear both without calling any attention to myself since the sun was out in full force with the temperature still close to freezing. Even better, the shoulder of the highway remained relatively dry, allowing me to walk along the road without getting soaked or washed away by any run-off. An occasional car or truck went by, but I must have appeared to be just another Vermonter heading to God-knows-where in a state where minding one's own business is practically a government mandate.

I made it into town in a little less than an hour, but it was still about three hours before the drug store would open and I could buy a ticket for the bus. I decided then that I couldn't just sit at that bus stop and risk being seen and having my destination made so obvious. So instead, I came up with another plan.

I walked a half a mile further up the road to a large gas station with multiple pumps that I had passed coming into town on the bus. There were no vehicles filling up when I got there, and so I went inside and got the coffee I had been craving earlier and then went back outside and stood with my back to the storefront, sipping my drink and acting as if I was expecting someone to come by to get me at any minute. Or at least that's what I hoped it looked like to the shaggy-haired twenty-something who was manning the register inside.

I didn't have to wait very long before two large trucks pulled in, one after the other, and parked at the diesel pumps, one on each side. The drivers didn't seem to know one another and went about removing their gas caps without making any contact. When the first one had the nozzle firmly set in the tank and the diesel flowing, he went inside to use the rest room or buy some coffee or, as I hoped, both. I then walked over to the other one to tell him the story I had come up with in the hopes of persuading him to give me a ride.

He looked me up and down as I explained that my car had died the day before and was in a service station in town and that I needed to get back to Massachusetts in order to meet my girlfriend who was waiting for me down in Springfield. I told him that she had agreed to drive me back to Vermont when the car was ready, which might be in a couple of days, but that I didn't have enough money to stay in a motel until then and also pay for the repairs. I informed him that even the cost of a bus ride would severely cut into my ability to get the car back on the road. I hoped my ruffled appearance would bolster my story.

He listened without saying anything until I finally ran out of things to say. Then he told me that his company didn't allow riders. As quick and curt as that. I considered putting on a full court press, given my desperation, but then decided that it would call more attention to myself than I wanted. Instead, I thanked him and waited for the other truck driver to come back out.

He did so just as the other truck was departing, allowing me to feed him the same story. This guy looked to be in his late thirties and in pretty good shape for someone who drove a truck for long hours. There was something about him and the way he carried himself that suggested to me that there was more to him than his job. I couldn't put a finger on it. Not then anyway. Like the other one, he just listened without looking at me and went about topping off the tank. When he was done, he walked back to the driver's side door, leaving me to think that I had struck out once more. However, he surprised me when he turned around, the door half open, and told me it was my lucky day and that he would be passing right through there.

We were on the interstate about five minutes later without another word having been spoken. That was just as well as far as I was concerned. However, that short period of silence was broken when, out of nowhere, he asked me what kind of trouble I was in.

"Car trouble," I said, even though it was obvious that he hadn't bought my story.

"I don't care personally," he said, ignoring the lie. "I've been in all kinds of trouble myself. I can recognize it easy enough on somebody else."

I thought about remaining quiet and seeing if he would just let it go. But then I decided to at least be civil, and so I took off the hat and sunglasses.

"If I told you, you wouldn't believe me," I said.

He laughed. "That's what we all say."

I turned back to look out the window, hoping that would be the end of it.

"You didn't kill anybody, did you?" he asked.

I turned back and he was looking at me now. It sounded like a joke. I was hoping so anyway.

"No," I said, as convincingly as I could muster.

He turned back to the road. It seemed to me that his expression had changed slightly.

"Well just don't kill me," he said. "It's my kid's birthday tomorrow. That would really suck."

"You don't have to worry about that," I told him. "I've never killed anybody and I don't intend to start now."

"Yeah, well, you never know what's going to happen until it happens," he said. "That's why it's always good to think ahead, right?"

I didn't respond to that, and he looked over at me once more, causing me to wonder whether I might have made the wrong choice about how to get to Springfield.

"I was over in Afghanistan," he said, turning back to the road. "Did two tours there. I saw ten-year-old kids setting off IEDs just a few minutes after kicking a soccer ball around. You learn to see things you might not otherwise."

I was surprised to hear something like that coming from him, although it certainly helped to explain the way he carried himself. Still, I didn't know how to answer, so I didn't.

"I read one of your books," he said then. "The first one."

I looked over at him, even more stunned by that revelation than the previous one. It must have shown.

"What?" he said. "Truck drivers don't read?"

I remained speechless, and he laughed.

"Yeah," he said. "It was pretty popular with the guys over there. All that 'be prepared' shit. I bought the second one, too, but it's been sitting on the shelf since I brought it home. I think I might start it tonight."

"The first one's better," I told him. "At least that's what people tell me."

He nodded. "Well, just so you know, I didn't recognize you till you took off the hat and glasses. In case that matters to you."

I was going to say that it didn't, but I knew that he wouldn't buy it. "It does," I told him, my hands reflexively going to the two items now resting in my lap. "That was my hope anyway."

He looked over at me briefly before turning back to the road again. "Whatever brought you here in my truck today must be one fucked up thing. I mean, if you're so smart, how the hell did you get yourself into whatever mess you've gotten into?"

"I've been asking myself that same thing for the last two weeks," I told him.

He stared ahead at the road. His expression serious. "Well, don't you worry. Anybody ever asks, I've never seen you before. I figure I owe you that much at least."

"How's that?" I asked.

He shrugged. "There's no way for me to know for sure, but I gotta think that some of that stuff I read in your book helped keep me alive over there. And allowed me to come home to my wife and kids in one piece. With my head still on straight."

In all the years since that book came out, I'd had a lot of people tell me how something they read in there had helped them in some aspect of their lives. However, it was always in the context of business, never something as sobering as war. I was humbled. So much so, that I couldn't respond other than to nod.

We drove the rest of the way into Massachusetts without saying another word until he pulled into the parking lot of a McDonalds just outside the city limits.

"Good luck to you," he said, when I opened the door and got out.

I thanked him for the ride.

"Like I said," he told me. "I owe you."

I was about to shut the door, when I paused. Then I asked if he might consider doing me one more favor. A small one. From his end anyway.

"As long as it doesn't involve taking someone's life," he said, with a smile.

"Just the opposite," I assured him.

CHAPTER 26

DOESN'T MATTER TO ME

GAZED AROUND for a few seconds before going into the restaurant to get something to eat and decide on a place to meet the detective.

When I walked in, it occurred to me that I hadn't been inside a McDonalds in at least a decade. I was pretty certain that I had never been in one on a Sunday morning, and it was possible that I had never even eaten breakfast at one before. At least I couldn't recall ever doing so. Which, together with everything else that had happened in the previous two weeks, made me think about the bubble I had been living in my whole adult life. Up until then, my world was almost entirely rooted in academia, whether at the university itself or at conferences and events linked in some way to my teaching and research. I never gave much thought to the notion that I might have missed out on anything due to my profession. However, as I ordered my food and looked around, it was clear to me that there were an infinite number of places I hadn't gone to and countless things I had never done. Even something as simple as eating at a McDonalds.

When I got my tray, I settled into a booth and took off the sunglasses but kept the hat on, raising the suspicion of absolutely no one, save for the little girl in a booth two away from mine who kept looking at me over the back of her seat. With some effort, her mother finally got her to sit down and face the other way. When she did, the mother nodded a sort of apology that I acknowledged with a small wave. She smiled.

It looked to me like they were quite happy to be there. In fact, it looked like it was a treat for the girl, perhaps a reward for some sort of good behavior. They didn't appear to be particularly well off, nor did they seem to be living in poverty. Something in between, most likely. But happy. Happy to be together at that precise moment, doing exactly what they were doing. I don't know why I was giving it so much thought. Perhaps it was because I had just come from the home of my niece and her mother, and what was taking place in that booth in front of me might easily have been a tableau of some earlier scene in their life.

Which got me thinking once more about what my sister-in-law had asked me back at her house. Was the decision to put off having children a reason for my divorce? I had downplayed it to her, but was I being truthful in doing so? As I sat there, the feeling came to me that it was precisely the reason. My wife might never have said it so plainly, but what she did give me as reasons could easily have found their origin in that type of selfish behavior on my part. Looking at that pair in the booth, I then wondered how different my life might have been if we'd had a child. What I might have sacrificed by pursuing my work so single-mindedly. What experiences I might have missed, like the simple pleasure of having breakfast with a son or daughter in a place that gives out toys along with the food. It certainly wasn't something I was expecting to think about when I walked in the door. So I was glad then when the pair eventually departed, the girl clutching the small stuffed animal that came with her meal, and I was able to turn my thoughts to the upcoming meeting with the detective.

Since it wasn't to happen for another couple of hours, I took my time eating, but was only able to extend the meal for so long. When I finished, I got up and got another cup of coffee to avoid having the manager keep eyeing me and wonder if I was going to plant myself there for the better part of the day. I also kept looking at my watch as if to signify that I might be waiting for someone. I figured that the gesture might buy me a little more time and tolerance.

Someone had left a newspaper behind in another one of the other booths, and I snatched it up before one of the employees came by to clean the table. There was nothing on the front page about my predicament. I attributed that to the fact that it was a Massachusetts paper as opposed to the one from Albany that I saw back at the motel. However, my relief turned out to be temporary when I found a small sidebar on page four. Luckily, there was no picture, and I doubted that anyone would associate the man described in the story with anyone in the restaurant, if they even bothered to read it in the first place.

I set the paper aside and once more caught the eye of the manager, who was a middle-aged woman with long loose curls for hair that I thought might have been a wig. Her expression told me that I was probably only minutes from receiving a warning, my having seen the sign near the rest room stating that tables were not to be occupied for more than two hours. I looked away without acknowledging her stare and sought to retrieve my phone from my pocket, acting as if it had just rung, though no sound was made. I tapped the screen as I would have had there actually been a call to answer. I then pantomimed speaking into the phone, although I said nothing at all. I ended the charade with another tap of the screen, pocketing the device as I stood to gather my tray. I then went to the trash bin to discard my cup and napkins and, instead of heading to the exit, I walked over to the manager who was still watching me.

"I wonder if you could give me directions to the nearest mall?" I asked.

I may as well have asked her to recite the Gettysburg Address, she was so startled. However, after gathering herself, she proceeded to give me simple instructions for getting from there to "the nicest one in the area." I responded with a smile and then asked if she could recommend a taxi service.

"I could," she said, "but the bus will take you right up to the front entrance. And for a third of the cost."

She then pointed to the bus stop not three hundred feet from the restaurant and told me that the next one would be coming by in less than fifteen minutes.

I thanked her and told her how pleased I was with the food at her establishment. Then I waved as I walked out, again retrieving my phone as if to call someone who might be waiting for me, though there was probably little reason for me to continue the show at that point.

True to her word, about a half an hour later a city bus deposited me at the front entrance of a mall about four miles away from the McDonalds. I got the idea of the shopping center as a meeting place when I saw an ad for Macy's in the newspaper I read back at the restaurant. On a Sunday in early spring, with weather unsuitable for any extended outdoor activity, I was pretty certain that a mall would be crowded. Not Christmas shopping crowded, but not Tuesday-night-in-February deserted either. I wanted the cover of being surrounded by people moving in all different directions, giving me a number of ways to hide if those men had somehow learned of the meeting. As a last resort, I figured that I could always pull a fire alarm and create some chaos to help camouflage my escape out of one of the multiple exits.

Once inside, I saw that there was a wide variety of retail outlets in the two-level complex, and I selected one of those chain bookstores to wile away the hour or so before calling the detective. I have always felt at home in a bookstore, and so I wandered aimlessly up and down the aisles looking at the new releases for both fiction and non-fiction. I even browsed the bargain bin. Finally, unable to resist the temptation, I walked to the "Business" section where I saw that they had about a half a dozen of my first book in stock. I've found that to be typical of most large booksellers. However, since my other two books didn't sell nearly as well, that was all that I would usually find. Therefore, I was surprised to see that this particular store also had two copies of my third book, the one that sold the fewest copies and the one that the detective told me she had been unable to find in Albany. I took that as a sign that I had been right to trust her, and as I was thinking that, another idea came to me. And so I took a copy off the shelf and brought it up to the register to purchase for her.

When I was done with that, I decided that it was time to call and give her my location. To get some privacy, I went to a deserted corner of the mall and dialed her cell phone.

She answered on the first ring.

"I was starting to think you were fucking with me."

"Where are you?" I asked.

"Parked at the Springfield exit on the Pike. Just like you told me. I was just trying to decide whether I should turn around and head back."

I assured her that I fully intended to keep our meeting and told her where I was.

"I'll be on the main floor at the fountain," I added. "You can't miss it."

"Fountain," she said. "Right."

"You came alone," I said. Not a question.

"I told you I would, didn't I?"

"Just checking," I said. Then I told her I would be waiting for her and hung up.

I had selected the fountain as a meeting place because it gave me a clear vantage point from the second level of the mall. In fact, I could sit behind one of those freestanding advertising boards and see it from all approaches. Anyone looking up would have to stare for quite some time before they might spot me, and with the hat and sunglasses on they shouldn't be able to recognize me. Then again, being indoors I thought that those accessories might also attract attention, so I dumped both in a trashcan and sat down with most of my body behind the board.

I watched for the better part of thirty minutes before I saw the detective walking purposefully toward the fountain from the direction of the main entrance. I surveyed the people walking behind her and saw no one who looked suspicious. I then took in the complete surroundings on the first floor to see if I could spot anybody milling around with no apparent purpose. I didn't see anyone worthy of scrutiny, but just to be safe I waited. Even though I trusted her, I told myself that I had to be sure.

The only seats were around the fountain and they were about half-occupied, most of them by women and children. I watched as the detective wandered over and took one of the empty spots. I gave it another minute or so, during which time I could see the frustration growing on her face. Finally, when I was satisfied that she was alone and hadn't been tailed, I got up and made my way down the stairs.

She stood abruptly when she saw me walking toward her.

"What kind of game are you playing?" she asked.

"Just making sure," I said.

She frowned, and then looked at the duffel bag I was carrying.

"Are they in there?" she asked, meaning the papers.

I told her they were and sat down. I put the bag on the floor between us.

"Do you mind if I see for myself?"

I shrugged and gestured for her to help herself. She bent over and pulled the bag over and unzipped it and rifled through it till she came upon the manila envelope. She opened the flap and looked inside, then back at me. I shrugged once more. She closed it up and put it back in the bag while I looked around to make sure that no one was paying attention. As far as I could tell, we were unwatched. When she zipped the bag closed, I turned back to her.

"Are you ready for this?" I asked.

"Depends on what 'this' is."

"I told you, I'm going to bring you with me to a place that'll test them. You'll be along to establish chain of custody."

"They're open on a Sunday?"

"No," I said. "That's what 'this' means."

"You mean you expect me to stay with you until tomorrow morning?" From the sound of it, she had never considered that possibility.

"There's no other way," I told her.

She looked far more troubled by the notion than I would have liked.

"I'm guessing you didn't pack anything," I said.

"So we're going to share a hotel room or something, is that the plan?" she asked, ignoring my statement.

"Unless you've got some other idea."

She looked around for a moment. Then shook her head.

"Where are we going to do this?" she asked.

"Stamford," I told her. "There's a lab down there I trust. Sterling reputation."

"Do they know we're coming?"

"No, but I know one of the owners. It won't be an issue if we show up unannounced."

She sighed. "I suppose I'm driving as well?"

"Unless you want to take the bus."

"Alright," she said, with a huff. "Let's get going then."

I stood up and grabbed the bag, and then we began walking back in the direction she came from. As we did, she asked if she could see my phone.

"What for?" I asked.

"Never mind," she said. "Do you want me to come or not?"

I did, obviously, so I stopped and handed it to her. She asked me the password to unlock it, which I gave to her, and then she hit a few buttons. Then a few more. When she finished she handed it back to me. I pocketed it, and hurried to follow her as she started walking again.

"What did you just do?" I asked.

Instead of responding, she stared straight ahead, a look of concern on her face.

I followed her gaze and saw two uniformed policemen walking elbow to elbow in our direction some twenty yards away. I wanted to believe that they might be there at the mall for a different purpose, a shoplifter maybe, but my gut was telling me something else. That I might have been wrong. That maybe the detective hadn't been worthy of my trust after all.

"Did you just call them?" I asked her.

She frowned. "I told you. I came alone."

She didn't wait for me to respond and put her arm out for me to stop. I did. She did the same. The policemen kept coming.

"Let me handle this," she said, her voice low.

They quickly closed the distance between us and stopped a few feet away. The larger of the two said my name. Nothing else. I didn't respond.

"What's this all about?" Detective O'Connell asked him, her tone official.

"He needs to come with us," he said, gesturing at me.

She then pulled out her shield and displayed it for them.

"He's wanted in New York," she said. "He's already in my custody."

"It's no longer your case, remember?"

It wasn't either of those cops who said that. The voice came from somewhere behind us, and I turned around to see a middle-aged man in a suit, although not one of the two I had been running from for the previous two weeks. This one I didn't know. However, everything about him told me that he was a cop. He was accompanied by two others dressed in jeans and winter jackets, like most of the people in the mall. I assumed they were cops as well. I looked over at Detective O'Connell and could read the disappointment on her face.

"You followed me here, Warren?" she asked the man.

"Let's just say I had a hunch you wouldn't let go that easily."

"Your boss?" I asked the detective. She kept her eyes on the man and nodded.

"They know we talked this morning," I said to her. "They're monitoring my phone. They told him."

Warren gave me a look, surprised that I knew what had happened. Then he turned and gestured at the two uniformed policemen who then stepped forward, and one grabbed my duffel bag while the other took a firm grip on my elbow.

"Check him first," Warren told one of the plainclothes officers.

He nodded and then stepped forward and patted me down. He found my phone and wallet, which is all I had on me. He showed them to Warren.

"Throw 'em in the bag," he said. And the uniformed cop held up the duffel while the plainclothes guy did as he ordered. If he saw the manila envelope, he didn't let on, and zipped the bag closed.

"You fucked up," Warren said, turning to Detective O'Connell. "You can drive back now and we'll talk about how you're going to pay for it. Tomorrow. In my office. First thing."

He sounded like a father who had just caught his daughter smoking pot with the high school janitor. He then stepped around her, followed by the two detectives who arrived with him, and joined the two uniformed policemen who pushed me forward in the direction in which they had come. I turned to look at Detective O'Connell who watched helplessly. I thought I might have detected some regret in her expression, although I couldn't tell whether it was for allowing me to be taken into custody on her watch or for having gotten mixed up with me in the first place.

In minutes, we were outside a different entrance, where an unmarked van was idling in the fire lane, folks entering and leaving the mall walking around it with only mild curiosity. When the two uniformed cops had me at the curb, the side panel opened and another uniformed policeman stepped out and helped to push me inside. The other two entered after me. The last thing I saw before I got in was Warren and his two plain-clothed associates getting into a dark sedan with New York plates parked right behind the van.

After that, we were on our way. Without a window in the back, and with a metal partition separating the driver from where we were seated, I couldn't see outside and had no idea in what direction we were headed.

"Are we going back to New York?" I asked the uniformed officer who spoke to me in the mall.

He stared straight ahead and acted like he hadn't heard me.

I turned to the other guys back there with us. "Anybody else here in a more talkative mood?"

I saw one of them crack a small smile, but otherwise they all remained expressionless.

My duffel bag was at the feet of the cop furthest from me. I wondered briefly why Warren had chosen to let them take it as opposed to taking it with him. That seemed like a mistake to me, letting it out of his sight. Then again, maybe he knew nothing about the papers inside or their importance.

Even though I was unable to see outside, I had pretty well determined that we had gotten onto the Mass Pike about fifteen minutes later, as indicated by our slowing down and nearly stopping, followed by a slow, sharp ascending turn, followed by a sudden acceleration. Of course, it could have been a different highway, but my gut told me that we were on the Pike, and it was my guess that we were heading west, back toward the New York border, probably to Albany.

However, my thinking changed when, another thirty minutes later, we decelerated and made another slow, sharp turn, this time in a descending manner, before stopping briefly. The fact that we didn't accelerate to the degree we did before told me that we had exited the Pike, which was way too soon for Albany, a destination we wouldn't have reached for another hour at least. Being familiar with that part of the interstate, I determined that we must have been on a state road in some small town or rural location still in Massachusetts. It could have been east or west of Springfield. That I couldn't tell. From there, we drove for another twenty minutes or so before eventually turning right onto a gravel surface and continuing for some distance prior to coming to a stop.

The engine on the van was then turned off, and I was able to hear another vehicle enter the same area and pull up behind us. I assumed that to be Detective O'Connell's captain and his two men. That engine shut off as well and three doors opened and closed, as we all remained seated in the back of the van, me looking from face to face, while they all stared straight ahead. Over the sound of the ticking engine, I could hear footsteps in the gravel moving away from us, although it was unclear whether it was from all of the men or just one or two. Then there was the faint sound of a door opening and closing, followed by complete silence, save for the occasional hum of a car going by on the highway somewhere in the distance. It stayed that way for some time until I once again heard a door far off opening and closing, followed by footsteps coming back toward us.

Even though I had been expecting it, the sudden opening of the sliding door sent a jolt through me, as did the piercing sunlight that temporarily blinded me.

"Bring him out," said the voice belonging to Warren.

My eyes slowly began to adjust as the uniformed men hauled me out of the van and onto what appeared to be a long access road. From what I was able to determine, we were somewhere off the highway, surrounded by tall pines, with about a foot of melting snow on the ground on either side of the drive. It was still late winter here, and judging by the hilly terrain, I thought we must be somewhere in the Berkshires, west of Springfield. If so, we were pretty far from any metropolitan area, with homes and businesses few and far between. I turned to look at Warren who nodded at the two men who had accompanied him, and they nodded back at him and walked to the car behind us. They didn't get in, but rather leaned up against it. Warren watched, and then turned back to us.

"You two come with me," he said, indicating the two officers who had approached Detective O'Connell and me at the mall. "And bring him and the bag," he added, pointing in my general direction. He told the driver of the van and the other uniformed officer to wait there.

Without a word of response, the two policemen each grabbed an elbow, and the one on my right took the bag from the third, and we followed as Warren walked toward what looked like an auto body shop or garage some distance away. Behind me, I heard two doors close once again, but neither vehicle started their engine. I tried to turn to look back to see what they were doing, but one of the officers yanked me hard enough to force me back around.

When we got to the door of the shop, Warren opened it and entered, standing just inside and waving for the other two to escort me in, which they did. Warren then flipped a light switch somewhere, and the room was indeed revealed to be a garage filled with assorted tools and auto parts. The floor was pockmarked concrete, dirty and oil-stained in spots, and there were fluorescent lights hung on chains from the ceiling giving it all a harsh glow. As far as I could see, there were no cars whose bodies needed repair, leaving me to guess that this shop hadn't been operating for some time. A wooden table and three folding chairs were set up at the far end of the room, and it appeared that they might be a recent addition or at least recently arranged there, perhaps by Warren when he or one of his men entered before. Warren indicated to the two officers that they should bring me over to one of the chairs.

"What about this?" one of the cops asked, holding up my duffel.

"Set it over there," Warren said, pointing to a bench on the other side of the room from where I was now planted. The cop did as he was instructed and then both turned and looked at Warren as if awaiting further orders.

"You guys can go now," he said. "We got it from here. Thanks for all your help."

The two cops exchanged a look. One of them seemed as if he was about to object, but instead he just nodded, and they both walked back across the floor and exited. I could hear their footsteps on the gravel fading in the distance, then the sound of doors opening and closing, followed by an engine starting and wheels crunching on the stones. It grew silent for a few seconds and then I heard a single set of footsteps coming toward the shop. The whole time, Warren was checking his phone, as if he were expecting a text or an email or maybe a voice message. He never once looked at me. If he was afraid that I might try to fight my way out of the jam I was in with just the two of us in there alone, it didn't show. He didn't even look up until the door to the shop opened and one of the other two men he came to the mall with entered and walked over to where he was standing.

"Any word?" the man asked.

Warren shook his head and closed the phone. Then he turned to where I was seated and grabbed one of the other chairs and sat across from me.

"She advised me to turn myself in," I told him, referring to Detective O'Connell. "I told her I would if she was the one to take me in. By herself." It was a lie, of course, but I felt an obligation to try and save her job. After all, it looked like she had gone way out on a limb for me.

He just shrugged like it didn't make any difference to him.

"So what're we waiting for?" I asked.

"Not what," he said. "Who."

I didn't like the sound of that and pictured the "who" he might be referring to.

"Why are you doing this?" I asked. "You know I didn't kill her."

"I don't know any such thing," he said.

"What would be my motive? To kill an eighty year old woman I haven't seen in thirty years?"

"Doesn't matter to me," he said.

I thought that was an odd thing to say, but then I remembered that we were waiting for someone who, if I was right, would probably soon be taking me off his hands.

CHAPTER 26

No Doubt Deceased

W|E ALL STAYED in our same positions, saying nothing for another five minutes or so, when I heard the sound of another car pull up outside. Again, doors opened, although not all at once. There were footsteps that started and stopped, and then a single set resumed, sounding as if they were headed in our direction. I was getting pretty good at detecting footsteps by then. As they neared, Warren gestured to the other detective that he should go to the door. When he got there he opened it partially and waited. From where I was sitting I couldn't see outside, but the other cop didn't look back at Warren or appear to be surprised in any fashion.

Finally, he stepped aside to allow the older of the two men in suits to enter the garage. He stopped as soon as he saw me at the table, and broke into a smile that had more than just a hint of smugness behind it. The detective behind him closed the door again and assumed his previous position as the man in the suit looked around and spotted the duffel bag sitting on the adjacent bench. He turned to Warren.

"That his?" he asked, meaning me.

"It is," Warren said.

The man nodded, and then walked across the floor to where it was. He unzipped it and rifled through it until he found the manila envelope. He pulled it out, unclasped the flap and took a quick look inside. He looked back up at me and smiled again. Then he re-sealed it and put it back in the bag, zipping it up again.

"Good job," he said to Warren.

Warren nodded, but didn't say anything.

The man then walked over to the table. "It's just the three of you, right?" he asked, looking around.

For a moment, Warren seemed surprised and maybe a little uneasy, as if he might have missed something. "Now, yeah," he said. "I had the local police help out at the mall. It's their jurisdiction. I didn't want to get into a pissing contest over this."

The older man made an odd gesture with his lips.

"Where are they now?" he asked the detective.

"I told them they could go," Warren said. "I didn't want them here when you got here. I didn't think you'd want that either."

The man in the suit looked at him and then at the other detective before answering.

"You're right," he said, turning back to Warren. "I didn't want them here. In fact, I didn't want them at all. I didn't want anyone but you and your men. I thought I made that clear."

Warren pushed his chair back reflexively, but didn't stand.

"I don't recall you saying anything like that," he said. "All you said was to handle it discreetly."

"And you took that to mean it was okay to bring in the local police?"

"Yeah," Warren said. "Like I told you, this isn't our jurisdiction. You're lucky they were as cooperative as they were."

"Am I?" asked the man. Then he reached into his coat pocket. I looked back and forth at the two men from New York and could see that they were on edge, unsure of what he was going to come out with. I know I was.

The man in the suit then slowly removed the lighter that he had with him back at the rest stop. I saw Warren's eyes go to it, confusion registering on his face.

"And what do you think those locals are going to go back and tell their bosses now?" the older man asked him.

"How the fuck should I know?" Warren said, his eyes still on the lighter.

The man in the suit shook his head, clearly disapproving of whatever was going on. He then flipped open the cap on the lighter, but snapped it closed again, making a surprisingly loud click when he did. I remember thinking at that moment that his using it back at the rest stop may not have been a message to us after all. That maybe it was a tic. Or some sort of ploy. A way of distracting an opponent.

"Forget all that," Warren said. "What do we do now?"

"*We* don't do anything," the man said, opening the lighter once more. This time he sparked a light.

"What's that supposed to mean?" Warren asked, trying to ignore the distraction.

"It means you're all done here," the man said, closing the cap on the lighter and making another loud click.

I looked over at the other detective. His arms were crossed, but he was looking anything but relaxed. Warren glanced over at him, as well, and then turned back to the man in the suit.

"I told you I'd help you pick him up. And I did that. But this is our case. You want to talk to him first, fine. Have at it. But we got a murder to close and he looks like our guy."

"What are you trying to say?" the man in the suit asked. Of the three, he was the one who appeared the most in control. I didn't like that.

"I'm saying we'll wait around while you ask him whatever the fuck you want, and when you're done, we're going to put him in the car and drive him back to New York."

The older man opened the lighter again and put his thumb on the little wheel, but kept it that way for several seconds. He didn't spark it. It was just a small gesture, but somehow it managed to increase the tension in the room.

"That won't be necessary," he said, finally. "We'll just take it from here."

Warren stood up and stepped aside then, attempting to assert his dominance, I suppose, in a situation that appeared to be slipping out of his control.

"You know," he said to the man, "I called that number you gave me and you checked out like you said you would, but they wouldn't tell me what agency you're with. They said I wasn't cleared for that. But I think it's high time I found out."

"Is that right?" the man asked.

"Yeah," said Warren. "You know, maybe I should have listened to my detective after all. She's pretty fucking smart. Maybe the best I got. She told me quite a story the other day." He looked over at me then. "I thought it was all bullshit from him, but now I'm not so sure."

The older man didn't respond. Not with words anyway. Instead, he closed the lighter, again making the clicking noise.

"In fact, I think maybe you ought to show me your credentials before we decide who gets to take it from here," Warren said, his annoyance growing.

"You want to see my credentials?" the older man asked. When he did, he put his thumb to the lighter again, as if poised to open it once more.

"That's right, I do," Warren said. "And cut the shit with that fucking thing."

As we all waited to see what he would do, the man in the suit stared. Then he shrugged and pocketed the lighter. Just as he did with the waitress back at the rest stop. Then he put his hand back in his jacket again, the breast pocket this time, only he kept it there longer than it should take to remove something. The air became even more charged as the seconds ticked by.

Finally, he slid out a leather wallet that he held up, clutched between his thumb and first two fingers. However, instead of holding it out for the cop to take, he tossed it to him. Except he missed. It hit the edge of the table and fell to the floor. If I had to guess, I'd have to say it was intentional.

Warren gave him a look, like he was dealing with a petulant child. Then he shook his head and bent down to pick it up.

When he did, the man in the suit snatched a gun out of his other pocket and spun around and shot the cop at the door. He then turned back to Warren who rose up just in time to take a bullet to the forehead. The back of his head exploded, and I managed to duck and avoid the brain matter that was sent flying. Right after that, I heard a single crack outside, followed by hurried footsteps heading in our direction. The entire sequence took less than ten seconds.

When I finally sat back up, I saw the detective who was at the door now lying in a heap on the floor. Motionless. No doubt deceased. The footsteps outside grew louder, but the man in the suit seemed unconcerned and simply stood there with the gun still in his hand. He paid no attention to me. The door then swung open and the younger of the two men in suits stormed in, his gun held out in front of him. He stopped when he saw his partner standing there. His eyes then went to the two dead cops on the floor.

"Everything OK in here?" he asked, looking back up at the older man.

"Fine," he said, showing absolutely no ill effects from having just killed two men in rapid succession.

The young one looked around for a couple more seconds before turning back to the older man. "Want me to bring the other one in here?"

I assumed he meant the other detective outside who I had to believe was now as dead as his two colleagues.

"No," the older man said. "Leave him out there. They'll straighten it all out later."

The younger man nodded.

"Just go back out and keep your eyes open," the older one told him. "I'm going to call someone to clean this up."

The young one did as he was told, closing the door behind him. Then the older man turned to me and pocketed the gun and sat down in the chair where Warren had been just moments before.

"This didn't turn out like I planned," he said, setting his hands on the table in front of him.

"I imagine not," I told him, my heart still racing.

"We're going to have to find someplace else to talk," he said with a frown.

He then pulled out his phone and hit a couple of buttons. After a few seconds, he got up and went to the other side of the room and spoke into the phone, his back to me. I was unable to hear what he said. I assumed he was talking to whoever was being assigned the task of sorting out the mess he had just made.

In that moment, I considered searching for a gun on Warren, thinking it might be my only way out. He was only a few feet away from me, but I decided that I'd never make it out of the chair and find it without alerting the man across the room, who seemed to have some pretty fast reflexes for a guy his age. Besides, something was telling me that I might be better off waiting to see what was going to happen next. After all, if he had intended to kill me, he'd had plenty of opportunity to do so at that point.

After a few more seconds, he closed the phone and came back to the table. Then he knelt down and rummaged through Warren's clothes until he found the gun that I had considered searching for. He looked it over and then flipped the safety off. Then he turned and fired a shot into the wall to the right of the door. He let loose another round to the left. Then he turned back to me and, for a moment, I thought I was about to take the next bullet. Instead, he pulled out a handkerchief and wiped down the gun. When he was done, he placed it in Warren's hand, holding the barrel with the cloth and pressing Warren's fingers around the grip. He stood up then and surveyed the scene before turning back to the door through which his younger associate once again entered. He looked at me as if he was surprised to find me still breathing.

"Ready to roll?" he asked, turning to his older associate.

"Yeah," the older man said. "I'll take the bag. You bring him."

The younger one nodded and started walking toward me.

"Cuff him first," the older one said. "Just in case."

We drove out of there in the car that they must have arrived in. It was a nondescript brown Ford Taurus with West Virginia plates. I half expected to see those distinctive blue government tags on it, but then realized that if those guys really were with the feds and wanted to stay below the radar, they wouldn't have had anything so obvious pointing to their employer.

As the older one had instructed, I was cuffed and riding in the back by myself, my duffel bag on the seat next to me. Unlike the typical police cruiser, there was no partition separating me from the front. In fact, the interior of the car looked much like the exterior, which is to say that it resembled your typical rental. Not Hertz or Avis, but one of the lower tier brands. I'm sure that was intentional. The younger one was driving and the older one sat in front next to him. They didn't tell me where we were going, but remained silent. I suppose they expected me to do the same, but I had no such intention.

"There's something on the paper," I said. "Some sort of substance."

The younger one glanced up at me in the rearview mirror, but didn't respond. Instead, he looked over at his older associate.

"How long did it take you to figure that out?" the older man asked, without turning around.

"Longer than it should have," I admitted.

He didn't say anything to that.

"It's something you gave those people," I said. "An experiment maybe. It's making them sick. They're all going to die."

"We're all going to die," he said.

"Doctor Condon worked for you guys. Before he came to my town. Right?"

"I wouldn't exactly call it an employer-employee relationship," he said.

"So what would you call it?"

He turned around to look at me then. "We'll have plenty to talk about when we get where we're going. I'm all through answering questions for now."

He turned back around and gestured at the younger one, who flipped on the radio, tuned it to a rap station, and put the volume up loud enough to make conversation all but impossible.

Unlike in the van ride from the mall, they didn't do anything to keep me from watching where we were going. I could see that we were on a state highway, headed east, as indicated by the setting sun behind us, until we made our way onto interstate 91 and headed south. I didn't try to talk to them again, and so they eventually turned down the radio to an acceptable volume. The mood didn't improve.

The older one's statement about continuing the conversation once we got to our destination told me that they wanted something from me, and it couldn't have just been the list and the other papers that the doctor's widow gave to me, for they already had them in my bag. That caused me to wonder what they could possibly be seeking and, more to the point, what I could possibly provide. And it had to be something important or they would have left me back there with Warren and his two men, with a bullet between my eyes.

Pretty soon, we crossed the border into Connecticut and continued to drive south on the route that one would take from Springfield to get back to my town, and I couldn't help but conclude that that's what they had in mind. It made little sense to me why they would want to go back there, but that seemed to be the most probable destination.

However, an hour later we turned west onto interstate 95 and passed the exit one would ordinarily take to bring me home. Some sixty minutes after that, with the signs for New York City appearing more frequently, I began to think that we must be headed to one of that city's five boroughs.

It turned out I was right, and I watched as we entered Queens and made several turns, taking us further from the interstate and more deeply into what seemed to be an abandoned industrial section. Empty warehouses dominated the neighborhood. Few had windows intact. None had lights on. Of course, it was Sunday evening, but I suspected that on a weeknight they'd be just as dark.

Eventually, we pulled in front of one of those warehouses on a completely deserted street, and the younger man shut off the ignition. He then looked over at the older man next to him who took in our surroundings in quick fashion, then nodded. They both exited then, and the younger one opened the back door and pulled me from the car. The older one opened the back door on the other side and retrieved the duffel bag.

He then followed his younger associate and me as we walked up the five steps to an entrance that was to the left of a large garage door. There was a padlock on the side of it near the bottom, securing it to the metal frame. Unlike the rest of the building, the padlock and hinge looked new, as if only recently added. There was a matching set on the rusted door in front of us. The younger man stepped aside as the older man took out a key chain bearing at least a dozen keys and tried three of them before finding the one that opened the padlock.

We then entered, and the older man flipped a nearby switch and the place was lit up by several rows of fluorescent lights. Unlike the body shop, this wasn't a garage of any kind. There were no benches or tools. In fact, it was just one large room, probably meant for storage in its previous iteration. The floor consisted of thick wide wooden planks, coated with what I took to be creosote judging by the smell, with space enough between them to easily drop a half dollar through on its edge.

The older man looked around until he spotted another door a good fifty feet across from where we were standing. He then turned to the younger man and gestured that we should all head in that direction.

And so we did.

CHAPTER 27

IS THAT YOUR IDEA OF A JOKE

THIS DOOR WASN'T locked, and the older man simply turned the handle and pushed it open. This time, the lights came on automatically, presumably on a sensor. Again, there was nothing but a wooden table waiting for us, this time with only two chairs, causing me to wonder if there was an instruction manual somewhere for off-the-book government agencies that recommended the use of a simple table and chairs when conducting interrogations.

The older man told the younger one to put me in the seat on the far side of the table, facing the door through which we had just entered.

"Un-cuff him first," he added.

The younger man did as he was told, and then pushed me into the chair where I was happy to unkink my arms and try to rub some circulation back into my hands.

The older man gestured for the younger man to stand behind me, which he did. The older one then set the duffel bag on the table between us.

"Before we start, where's your phone?" he asked.

"Those cops took it," I told him. Which was true, partially anyway.

He frowned, and then waved toward his younger colleague who went about searching me. When he was done, he looked up at the older man and shook his head.

I thought for a moment that might be it, that they'd leave it at that, and if I got lucky, I might somehow retrieve it and call for help, though I'd have trouble telling anyone where I was.

Almost like he was reading my mind, the older man suddenly pulled the duffel bag toward him and went through it again. This time he came out with the phone, causing me to wonder how he had missed it back at the body shop. He held it up for me to see.

"Very clever with the new name. Call forwarding. If my friend over there hadn't thought to match calls to your secretary's cell with ones to your sister-in-law's, we might have never found out."

I realized then what a big mistake I had made. It never occurred to me that they might monitor both of their numbers. Gloria's for sure. Right from the get-go. But not my sister-in-law's. Not until her former husband died anyway. Making it logical to assume that I might call her. And that they might look for that. I fucked up. And it looked like it might cost me.

I watched as he opened the back of the phone and removed the SIM card, and then dropped the latter on the floor, edging it with his toe into one of those cracks where it disappeared, unlikely ever to be found. That done, he put the phone back in the duffel and took out the envelope. He opened the clasps like he did back at that body shop and this time pulled out the three sheets of paper inside. He set them down next to the bag where I could see them.

"All this could have been avoided if you'd just given us these back at the doctor's house," he said, tapping the top sheet.

"I suppose," I said. "But then I'd probably be as dead as Plum."

He laughed.

"Killing people is funny?" I asked.

"Hardly," he said. "What's funnier is not killing them."

I gave him a look to indicate that he was making little sense.

"Plum's alive," he said. "Though with a new name. Social security. The whole works."

I was confused. He nodded, like he was reading my thoughts again.

"That wasn't him in the motel," he said. "We saw the story in the news about an unidentified body in the fire and we thought we'd use it. Like I said at the rest stop, we wanted to get your attention."

"But the cops came to see his sister..." Even as the words were coming out, I knew it was a foolish thing for me to say.

"It's not that hard to find a couple of police uniforms," he said. "Or the men to wear them."

"In fact, you met them," said the younger one behind me. "Out in Arkansas."

He was obviously referring to the Samoan and his cohort. I looked over at the older one. "You had them kill my brother, didn't you?"

"No," he said, with a frown that I suspected wasn't quite as genuine as he hoped. "They did that on their own. And went well beyond their authority in doing so. Apparently they weren't very happy with how your brother treated them the first time they met."

"If I get the chance I'm going to treat you the same way," I said.

"I understand your feelings," he said. "There's a lot you don't know."

"I know that whatever you gave those people on that list is killing them."

He stared at me for a few seconds, his expression giving nothing away. He then removed the duffel bag from the table and took a seat opposite me.

"How did you get to be so fucking smart?" he asked.

"Is that your idea of a joke?"

"No," he said. "I'm serious. Did you ever think about what made you so fucking smart? You know, compared to the average guy. Like your brother, for example."

I ignored his attempt to poke a finger in my wound and decided to play along.

"Genetics," I said. "I won the gene lottery. Like LeBron James. Only not basketball."

He smiled. "Again with the basketball."

"Education helped, I suppose," I said, ignoring him. "Ten thousand hours. All that shit."

Now he laughed. Apparently, I was quite amusing.

"You have another theory?" I asked.

"Theory is the wrong word," he said. "It implies that the matter is still under debate. Unproven. Which, in your case, it most certainly is not."

Suddenly, I started to feel uneasy, although I wasn't quite sure why.

"Let me ask you," he said. "When did you first think of yourself as smart?"

I drew back a bit, hardly expecting the question. "What difference does that make?" I asked. "I was a kid. Second grade? Third? Who cares?"

"You're close," he said. "Your test scores blew up in the fall of the fourth grade. Or don't you remember?"

Actually, once he said that, I did. I had always tested well in school, placing near the top of my class, but it was around that time that my grades went off the charts, causing everyone to sit up and take notice.

"What's your point?" I asked him.

"Remember when you got sick and landed in the hospital?"

"Yeah, so?" I said. Despite my defiant tone, my unease was beginning to grow.

"How did you get better? Do you remember?"

I tried to think back to that time. As I've said, I don't recall much of my stay there, but I did remember that part. "They gave me some medicine," I said. "Antibiotics or something. Radical, huh?"

"In fact, it was," he said. "An anti-viral actually. A type of steroid. Your doctor gave you a series of injections and your infection got better in about a week and you were allowed to go home. And eventually back to school."

Suddenly, I felt like I was on the deck of a ship rolling in the waves, a thought just starting to form in the back of my mind.

"And you went back to him once a month for a year to get additional treatment," he continued. "Just in case. Do you recall that?"

Of course I did. Injections. 'Shots' as we called them. Every kid remembers getting shots. In my case, I would enter the doctor's office, the one in the former stable in the back of his home, and each time he'd be waiting there for me with a syringe on his desk. Before injecting me, he'd ask how I was feeling and if anything was different. I don't recall ever telling him anything other than I felt fine and nothing was different. Except that it was.

"It was an experimental drug," he said. "And it worked well. Except that it had a side effect. One that wasn't known at the time."

I didn't say anything. I was too busy trying to sort out what he was telling me.

"That's right," he said, with a nod. "It worked even better at increasing brain function than it did at killing the bug. For most anyway. They're still not quite sure how. But it did."

He paused then, I suppose, to let me catch up.

"So wait a minute," I said, looking down at the list in front of me. "You're saying I was given the same thing as those people on that…"

I didn't finish the question. There was no need to. I already knew the answer.

CHAPTER 28

SOME PEOPLE LIKE BEING SMART

SAT BACK then, my breath caught in my throat, stunned by the all-consuming feeling that everything I had believed about myself up to that moment was a lie.

In a matter of seconds, my whole world was upended. And yet, at the same time, fully explained. All of it. My long list of achievements. One after another. Seemingly without effort. Month after month. Year after year. From the age of ten all the way through college and grad school. And beyond. Right up until I left my teaching position a few years ago. It all made sense. Try as I might, there was no denying what he had just told me.

Then, almost as quickly as it came on, a wave of revulsion replaced it, and I was struck with the notion that I was somehow at fault for everything that had happened. For the wide disparity in accomplishment between my brother and me. For the wedge it drove between us. For the distance and separation I felt between me and everyone else around me for almost my entire life. For the decision to postpone having a child, choosing work over family and bringing on the divorce that followed. Even worse, for the "inability to connect on a real level with another human being," as my ex-wife always used to tell me. All of it, a sin of my own making. My fault for swimming in that pond and getting sick in the first place. Crazy, I know, but without having done so, none of this would have ever happened.

Without thinking, I launched myself across the table and managed to get both hands around the older man's neck, hoping to choke the life out of him and erase the previous few minutes of my life. Whatever advantage I might have had only lasted for a couple of seconds. By then, his younger associate was on me and had his own arm around my neck, easily pulling me off him and onto the floor where we wrestled for a time. Actually, he wrestled while I mostly threw wild punches and clawed at his face, like a wounded animal facing its imminent demise.

It wasn't long before he had me face down in a headlock with a knee planted firmly in my back. I struggled to get free, but he exerted even more pressure to my spine and neck, in opposing directions, causing me to scream out, although it may have been more rage than pain that made me to do so.

"You're going to break his back," the older man finally said to the younger one.

He was seated now, rubbing his neck with one hand, the red marks from my fingers clearly visible on each side. After hesitating for a second or two, his associate removed his knee and straddled me, although he kept a hand on the back of my head.

"I understand your anger," the older man said, looking down at me. "I know this must be hard for you to hear. But you're going to have to face it now. You have the good doctor to thank for that."

Instead of responding, I flung back my right hand, hoping to strike the younger man's head. I missed, of course. But I wasn't quite ready to surrender.

"If you promise to behave, I'll have him let you go and we can discuss this," the older one said. "And if you listen to what I have to say, you'll see that there might be a silver lining in this."

I considered trying to break loose, but I knew it would be futile. That even if I got free, it wasn't going to change anything I had just heard. Nor was it going to bring back the person I used to be. Or at least thought I was. And so I finally nodded once at the older man, and after I did, he told the younger one to release me. Which he did.

I got back on my feet slowly and rolled my neck, both of the men watching me warily, as if I might explode once more. Instead, I simply walked over and pulled the chair back to the table and sat down.

"Tell me more," I said to the older one. "About this drug."

He nodded, apparently satisfied that peace had been restored. Then he took the three sheets of paper and put them back in the envelope and handed them to the younger man, who put them back in the duffel. When he had done so, the older man turned back to me.

"It took them awhile to gather all the data," he said. "They were looking for negative side effects at first. That's the usual focus. But then they began to hear about the other thing. All anecdotal, of course, but every instance they investigated was verified. Unlike adults, children's intelligence is tested routinely. Measured at least four times a year. A vital part of the education process. And all that data is there, just waiting to be examined. Only a fool could miss a jump like yours. Of course, they wouldn't be able to explain it. Not without knowing more."

"But Condon knew," I said.

He nodded. "Eventually. As did most of the others. Doctors, that is. They're smart too. The people I work for had to do some fancy footwork to get them all on board and continue the use of the drug for its side effect rather than its original intent. We held a big meeting down in Washington. Very secret, of course. They all came. And those who voiced the greatest objections were permitted to stop. Like your Doctor Condon."

271

"Except they had to keep him quiet," I said.

"Oh yes," he said.

"So you threatened him."

"Not me personally. But yes."

That explained why he waited until his death to say anything. And why he didn't want his wife to know. It was all beginning to make sense.

"How did he find out about the others on the list?" I asked. "They weren't from our town. None of them were patients of his."

"No," he said, sounding disappointed. "But somehow he managed to contact a few of the other doctors who had administered the drug. Of course, they were forbidden from talking to one another, but then people are forbidden from cheating on their taxes as well, aren't they?"

"It didn't work out the way you hoped, did it?" I asked, already knowing the answer.

He shook his head. "It never does."

"People got sick," I said.

"Some, yes. Unfortunately."

"And died."

He nodded.

"So that's why he gave me the list. To figure it out. Make it all public."

"Something like that, I imagine. Yes."

"And he put some of the drug on the paper. To help me prove it."

The older man shrugged. "We were tipped off a couple of days after he died by one of those doctors he had contacted for the names. We were late getting to the widow's house. Otherwise, none of this would have ever happened."

It was suddenly not so far-fetched to picture the government involved in something like this. The import of what they had stumbled upon had to be too great for them not to try and protect it.

"How many people took the drug?" I asked. "More than those on the list?"

"Oh yes," he said. "It's a big country."

I paused before asking the next question, but was unable to resist.

"Would I recognize some of those names?"

He smiled, as if he knew where I might be heading. "You would, no doubt."

I paused again before asking the next. "So are you saying that some of the greatest achievements of the past thirty years are attributable to a side effect from that drug?"

He lost the smile. "Some, yes. But not all. After all, some people are naturally smart."

I took a moment to consider the impact of what he had just told me. It was almost unfathomable.

"And all of us who took it are going to die," I said. Not a question.

"Oh, you'll die alright. Though not necessarily from that drug."

"You mean it doesn't kill everyone?" I asked, somewhat surprised.

He shook his head. "Only about thirty-five percent. Nothing the FDA would ever approve, of course."

"What about the other sixty-five? They're all OK?"

He gave me that fake frown again. "See that's the thing."

"What's that?" I asked.

"The effects of the drug wear off over time. For some it's a shorter time than others, but eventually it wears off for everyone."

"That's it? It wears off? No other side effects?"

"Yes and no," he said.

"What's that supposed to mean?"

"Some people like being smart," he said. "And when they no longer are, that's a form of side effect too, wouldn't you say?"

I didn't answer. Once more, there was no need to. I could hardly challenge what he'd just said. After all, I was living proof. It was all right there in my recent past. My loss of focus as a professor. My decision to resign rather than admit I was failing. My agreeing to write that book, but not being able to. Hell, it even explained my poor driving skills. I'm sure if I looked harder, I'd find countless more examples. I stared at him, trying to figure out where this was heading.

"So where's that silver lining you were talking about?" I asked.

He smiled once more. "We've discovered over the years that if we give those with diminishing skills another dose of the stuff, they ramp right back up again. Smart as ever."

"Plum," I said, suddenly knowing.

"Yes," he said.

"So he wasn't running from you guys."

"Oh, hardly."

"So why did he leave in such a hurry then?" I asked.

"You threw quite a scare into him. Showing up out of the blue like you did. He thought it might be coming to an end. He called and asked us what to do."

"He likes what it's doing to him," I said.

He nodded.

I looked down at the scratched and dented surface of the table, as if it might somehow hold the answers to all my questions.

"We hear you've been having trouble writing that book."

I looked up. Surprised. Though I shouldn't have been.

"Feeling a bit of a fraud?"

I watched then as he removed from his pocket a vial, the kind that might hold a drug that you would administer by syringe. He set it on the table in front of him.

I stared at it for a few seconds. Then, almost reflexively, I reached for it.

He pulled it away, like you would with a child and a forbidden treat.

"That's what you were going to tell me back at the rest stop," I said, looking up at him.

"What's that?"

"I agree to keep quiet and you give me another dose of that." I nodded at the vial.

"There'd be a few other details we'd have to work out first," he said.

"Like what?" I asked.

"Like assuring that you don't change your mind later on."

"And how would you do that?"

He smiled. It was an oily one. "You have a lovely niece."

The younger man grabbed the back of my collar, anticipating another assault by me. But I had no such intention. I was immune to shock at that point.

"And what if I don't accept your offer?" I asked. "Just tell you to go fuck yourself?"

"I think you know the answer to that," he said.

"You could've killed me back in Massachusetts," I said. "Solved all of your problems right there."

He shrugged. "Despite what you might think, we're not barbarians. As you said, some of the greatest advancements of the last thirty years have come out of this. Society has benefited from your work. Just like Archer."

"What about Plum? Seems to me he's not benefiting anybody but himself."

"Actually, we've all managed to profit off him a little bit," said the younger one.

The older man looked up at him, frowning once more. Then he turned back to me. "We consider Plum to be our little jab at organized crime."

I laughed, though none of it was funny. We sat there for a few more seconds staring at one another. Sizing each other up.

"So you want me to decide right now?" I asked finally.

"Why?" he asked. "How much time do you need?"

"A couple of years," I said.

He laughed. Then he looked at his watch. "You can have ten minutes," he said.

"What about those New York cops?" I asked. "That was quite a mess you left up there. And the other ones who drove me there. Won't they start asking questions?"

He frowned, like he was disappointed in me. "About what? Nothing happened up there. Surely you've come to realize how we do things."

I did indeed. I sat back then to mull over my options. Which seemed to be rather limited. After all, I was seated across the table from someone who'd already killed four people that I knew of. And another - my brother - by proxy. I had little doubt that he'd kill me, as well, if I didn't take the offer. It looked to me like he was holding all the cards.

"Can I do it myself?" I asked him.

"What do you mean?"

"Inject it," I said. "I don't see a doctor here. And I sure as hell don't trust him." I gestured at the man standing behind me. "Or you, for that matter."

He seemed to consider that for a bit as he regarded me. Then he finally shrugged. "I don't see why not. We've found that a big muscle works best. Shoulder or thigh. Though there's usually some soreness afterward."

I remembered. The pain lasted for days back then. I nodded.

He turned to his cohort. "Go ahead. Give it to him."

The younger one paused for a second, then came around from behind me, but just stood there, expressing his silent objection, I suppose. The older one gave him a look, a command of sorts. The younger one frowned. Then he withdrew from his pocket a syringe, still in its wrapper. He handed it to the older one who set it on the table, along with the vial.

"It's very valuable," he said, indicating the medicine. "I wouldn't waste a drop."

"You're really going to give me ten minutes?" I asked.

He looked around the room that had no windows or doors other than the one we had just entered through. There was nowhere for me to go. He stood up and smiled. "Why not?" he said.

"And just so I'm clear, if I take it, you'll leave my niece alone?"

"So long as you stay mum," he said.

I stared at him, wondering just how much I could trust him.

"Ten minutes," I said finally.

He repeated those words back to me.

Then he picked up the duffel and he and his companion walked out, closing the door behind them.

BACK WHERE WE STARTED

CHAPTER 29

I Hope You Have a Lot To Tell Me

A S THE HANDLE on the door turned, I buttoned the bottom of my sleeve and sat back in the chair. The syringe was on the table in front of me, a tiny drop of the drug hanging off the tip of the needle. The crumpled wrapper lay next to it.

I remained silent as first the younger, then the older of the two men walked in, stopping across the table from me. They both looked at the syringe at the same time and each of their faces seemed to relax as they drew the same conclusion.

"Wise choice," the older one said, setting the duffel on the floor next to the table.

"I haven't gotten completely stupid yet," I said.

He smiled. When he did, I picked up the syringe and held it up for him to see, my thumb on the plunger.

"So that's it?" I asked. "Just the one dose?"

"For now," he said. "We can talk again later. If the need arises. But for the time being you should be all set."

"So what's next?" I asked. "Do you at least give me a ride home?"

"Sure," he said. "We can do that."

The younger one stared at the table as his colleague spoke. Suddenly, he shifted his eyes to me. "Hey, where's the vial?" he asked, accusingly.

"I thought you'd let me keep it," I said, with a shrug. "Seeing as I've done what you asked. It's empty anyway."

"Doesn't matter," said the older one, sounding like we were old friends now. "We need it back. There'll be traces in there. We wouldn't want you to get any ideas."

I nodded, but didn't say anything. Instead, I reached into my pants pocket and retrieved it. Then I set it on the table in front of me, closer to me than to them.

After a pause in which the younger one must have realized I wasn't going to make it any easier for him to reach it, he frowned and bent over to grab it.

Before he could, I leapt forward and stabbed him with the empty syringe, hitting him just below the left ear and pushing in the plunger as I did.

He immediately sprang upright and grabbed for the syringe sticking out of his neck, his eyes wide with fear. He then staggered back a step and made a sound that wasn't quite a scream, although it clearly conveyed both his surprise and displeasure.

I looked over at the older one who simply sat there watching, frozen, almost like a spectator. I then backed away from the table, waiting to see what would happen next.

The younger one took a couple of steps to go around the table toward me before putting a hand to his chest. His other hand went to the table to keep him from falling. It didn't. He simply collapsed on the floor, just to my right, and lay motionless.

It all went about as well as I'd hoped. I knew that I couldn't take the younger man in any kind of fight. Not by myself anyway. I knew also that I probably couldn't take the older one either, but at least I might put forth a decent effort. Maybe land a lucky blow or two.

I watched warily as his eyes drifted from his colleague on the floor and then back to me. Then, displaying the same calm demeanor that he showed with those cops back at the body shop, he stood slowly and took a step to his right, away from the body on the floor. I took a step in the opposite direction, making sure to keep the table between us when he did.

"This is quite an unfortunate change in circumstances," he said. "Not that I liked that smug bastard even a little bit."

He took a look around the room, for what reason I couldn't say, before his eyes seemed to go past, but then return to the tiny puddle of liquid just under the table on my side. He looked up at me, surprised.

"Is that what I think it is?"

"I know," I said. "It's very valuable. Shame to waste it."

He shook his head. "Looks like you did get stupid after all."

Just as I was thinking that it might be time to flip the table and make a rush at him, he slid the same gun he used to kill Warren out from his breast pocket and leveled it at me.

"So you're going to kill me now?" I asked, backing up a step.

"You made the choice," he said, with a shrug. "Besides, I have everything I need." He nodded toward the duffel on the floor.

I fixed him a cold stare. "Do you?"

The question caught him by surprise. I could tell by the way he stiffened.

His eyes narrowed. "What's that supposed to mean?" he asked.

It was my turn to look down at the duffel. "How do you know those are the originals in there?"

He looked down at the bag again. Then back at me once more. Chewing on the thought.

"I've had plenty of time to make copies," I told him. "You've never seen them before today. You don't know what they're supposed to look like."

He met my stare with one of his own. "Bullshit," he said.

"You didn't really think I was going trust those cops, did you?" I asked.

He didn't answer right away. I could see his mind working then.

"If those aren't them, then where are they?" he asked.

"Right about now?" I said. "On their way to Albany. State police headquarters. To a detective you haven't met yet. She ought to have them by Tuesday. Along with a few instructions."

I could see that he was rattled now, although he was trying his best not to show it.

"What kind of instructions?" he asked.

"Dig up the bodies of the first three that died," I said. "And test Toyland before he does. Then match what they find in those tissue samples with what's on those papers." I smiled. "Oh yeah, I told her to have them tested, too."

He stared at me, working it all over in his mind. "I thought you just said you didn't trust the cops?"

"I don't," I told him. "Not all of them anyway. But this one earned it. And she knows the whole story. Archer. Plum. Everything."

"Well, I can stop her," he said. "I'll just go over her head. As high up as I have to. How do you think I got them to give you up in the first place?"

"You really think that's going to work now?" I asked. "Because I imagine they might be a little harder to persuade after they find out what you did to their colleagues."

He continued to stare. Clearly, he didn't have an answer ready for that.

"Like I said before," I told him. "I haven't gotten completely stupid."

His eyes narrowed once more. "You're lying," he said, almost spitting it out.

"You think so?" I asked.

He looked down at the duffel again, then back up at me. And in that moment, I thought I could detect a change in him. His old confidence seemed to be returning. He gave me a big smile. Then he bent down and unzipped the bag with his free hand and reached in and slid the envelope out. He then stood up and set it on the table in front of him. He undid the flap with that same free hand and shook the envelope until the tops of the sheets appeared. Then he pulled them all out and held them up.

"Let's see who's telling the truth here," he said.

He set the gun down on the table, just an arm's length away - his, not mine. Then he reached into his jacket pocket and took out that lighter he liked to play with so much.

He uncapped it and sparked a flame with his thumb, smiling once more. Then he moved it just under the papers. Close, but not quite close enough to set them ablaze.

"If these are the real ones, then they're all you've got," he said. "And you can't afford to lose them, can you?"

He inched the flame a little closer. When he did, I could see the bottom of the lowest page just starting to brown. I worked to keep my breathing steady and held his stare.

He cocked his head. In control once more. "Real or fake?" he asked. "What do you say?"

Now I was the one without a ready answer. The seconds ticked on as the bottom of the lowest sheet began to smoke, but not yet flame.

"I say you should drop it."

It wasn't me who said that. The voice came from somewhere behind him. Which is where I looked to see Detective O'Connell in a shooter's stance just inside the open door, her department-issued handgun in both hands.

The older man spun around to face her. As he did, his arms spread wide, separating the papers from the flame and causing it to go out. He stared at her for a second or two.

"Is this who I think it is?" he asked me, without looking back.

"Drop it," she told him once more. Her was voice steady and strong.

"It's nice to finally meet you detective," he said, ignoring the command. "We were just talking about you."

"Shut up and do what I said," she told him. Then she took another step forward, bringing her fully into the room, her weapon still trained on him.

He looked down at the lighter, open but with no flame now. I saw his thumb inch up to the little wheel, poised to spark it once more.

"If you light that thing I might have to shoot you," she said.

"I'm afraid you might have to do that anyway," he told her.

She looked confused.

"I can't let you bring me in," he said, with a shrug. "I'm under strict orders."

I saw him turn his head then, ever so slightly toward the spot on the table where his gun was. I saw the detective's eyes go there as well, before looking back up at him.

"Don't," was all she said.

A couple more seconds went by. Then the man let the lighter drop to the floor, making a sharp noise when it hit. But he kept his hand open after he did. His gun hand. Which was now inches closer to the table.

Time froze as we all waited to see what would happen next. I could hear the soft ticking of the clock on the wall behind me. Feel the cool air wafting in through the open door behind the detective. Smell the carbon aroma from the flame that had gone out moments before.

Then, just when I thought it couldn't go on like that for another second, the younger man sprang up from the floor next to me.

Turns out, my mother's doctor was wrong - injecting air into a human being isn't a sure bet to cause death, even if you should hit an artery or vein. As I learned later, an embolism might, at best, cause a brief loss of consciousness. Which turned out to be the case with him. And quite fortunate for me. Because the older man chose to use his partner's revival to reach for the gun.

And when he did, the detective fired two quick shots.

The first opened a hole in the forehead of the younger man whose own gun was already out of his jacket and rising in her direction.

The second hit the older man in the chest, on his left side, most likely piercing his heart. He had just managed to get his hand on the gun, but failed to get his fingers around it before he was hit. And his hand slid away from it as he fell. I suspect that both men were dead seconds after they hit the floor.

The detective and I stood there staring at them for a time after that, the air in the room feeling electric. As did my heart. Like someone had just put the paddles to it.

The detective finally turned to me, her gun still pointed in their direction.

"I hope you have a lot to tell me," she said.

CHAPTER 30

NOT EXACTLY LIKE THIS

As it turned out, I did.

We were back on interstate 95 about ninety minutes later, in Connecticut and headed for my home, Detective O'Connell at the wheel of her unmarked cruiser. I had just finished telling her everything that had happened since we left that mall in Springfield, and she was answering my question about how she came to find me down in Queens.

"We put a track on your phone," she said.

I asked her when they did that.

"Right after we saw that you had called the widow the day of the funeral."

"That was my old phone," I said.

She nodded. "We wondered why it kept showing up in the airport in Philadelphia. For days, in fact."

"I put it behind some toilet paper in a storage closet there," I told her.

"Yeah, we figured it was something like that," she said.

"But then you got my new number."

Again she nodded. "Eventually. When you called me after your brother died."

"But you couldn't track it," I said, a bit confused. "I had the GPS turned off."

"You did," she said. "Very clever."

Then it dawned on me.

"That's what you did back at the mall," I said. "You turned it back on."

"Correct," she said.

"You thought something like this might happen," I said.

"Well, not exactly like this. I certainly didn't expect Warren to show up, if that's what you mean."

"So why did you check it?" I asked. "I mean, after he sent you home?"

"I don't know," she said. "A hunch, I guess. I was on the Pike on my way back when I decided to look. I assumed that they were bringing you back to Albany, but the GPS showed them going in the opposite direction."

"So you turned around," I said.

She nodded. "It didn't seem right. Unfortunately, I had to drive to the next exit to do it. Which is why I was so late getting to that garage."

I asked her if she was there when the shots were fired.

She shook her head. "I had just driven past the turn-off when I saw a car pull out and drive away."

"You didn't follow us?" I asked.

"I didn't know who it was," she said. "I didn't even know you were in there. Not then anyway."

She then went on to tell me that she pulled into the driveway to see why Warren's car was still there and that's when she saw her colleague on the ground outside.

I asked if she went inside, already knowing the answer.

She nodded. "I shot video of the whole thing inside and out. Then I called it in to the locals."

"But you didn't wait for them," I said.

She looked over at me. "Would you have wanted me to?"

The question didn't require an answer. Had she decided to wait, I would've been dead down in that warehouse. I had no doubt that the older man would've killed me even if he had burned those papers. He just hadn't realized it yet. First he needed to know if I was telling the truth. And if he would have to go after the detective. And I knew he needed to know. That's what saved my life. Well, that and the detective.

We sat in silence for a few seconds. "You know we're going to have to go up against some powerful people now," I said. "Do you think that video is going to be enough?"

"It won't have to be," she said, "We've got that, too, remember." She motioned with her head at the back seat where a plastic bag contained the two guns from those men in suits, along with the syringe, the vial and my cell phone, minus the SIM card. I had watched her bag them back at the warehouse.

"Fingerprints and ballistics," she said. "Better than an eyewitness. And I've already sent the footage to my work email. My personal one too. And just to be safe, to my former roommate. She's a computer jockey. They'll never find it unless we want them to. And we will."

I smiled. Impressed, if not completely sold.

"What about the cops down in Queens? Shouldn't we have called them?"

She shook her head. "I thought it would be better if I lined up things on my end first. Which I'm going to start doing right after I drop you off."

We drove the last few miles in silence, each of us sorting out what we had just gone through, and we eventually arrived at my condominium just as the sky was beginning to darken. As she put the car in park, I took my duffel bag from the floor and put it on my lap, but didn't open the door. She gave me a look, curious.

I unzipped it and took out the manila envelope with the papers inside.

"Don't you want these?" I asked.

She looked confused. "I thought you told me they were copies?"

I smiled and watched as her expression slowly changed.

"You lied," she said, looking surprised.

"Yeah," I told her. "Well, partially anyway."

The confusion returned.

"Only one is original," I told her. "The other two are copies."

Her confusion gradually gave way to a smile. "You separated them?"

"I did," I said.

"What the hell made you think of doing that?" she asked.

I pulled the pages from the envelope and fanned them out for her. "I'd always wondered why the doctor gave me three separate sheets of paper. Everything he wrote on them could have fit on one page, with room to spare. I tried to figure out why the hell he would do that. What reason he might have had."

I saw it dawn on her. "He put the drug on all three. Not just the list."

I nodded.

"He didn't want to limit you to having just one chance to nail those guys," she said.

"Pretty smart," I said. "Three bites at the apple."

I could almost see her brain working now. "So you were thinking that when we met at the mall we'd have the one sheet to get tested if Warren hadn't shown up. And if those other guys somehow found us and got their hands on the envelope before we could test it, the other two sheets would be waiting for me back at my office."

"Something like that," I said.

She didn't ask me where or when I made the copies. If she had, I would have told her about using the copy machine back in that empty office in the motel in Vermont. Before I left for Springfield.

She shook her head like she was still sorting it out. "So when did you send them to me?"

"Back at the mall," I told her. "Right before we met."

Once again she looked confused. "There's a post office at the mall?"

It was my turn to shake my head. "I bought you a present."

She gave me a look like she wasn't following.

"I got you that book of mine," I said. "The one you couldn't find."

I unzipped the side pocket of the duffel and pulled out the business card she gave me back in Boston. In addition to her name and the main phone number for the detective unit, it had the address of the New York State police headquarters. Where her office was.

"It was in a bookstore there," I said, referring to the book. "I asked them to mail it to you. Told them the sheet of paper I put inside was an inside joke. You should have it by Tuesday."

"Wow," was all she said. Until the realization hit. "Wait a minute. Did you say 'sheet'?"

I nodded.

She laughed. Incredulous. "Where's the other one?"

I turned the card over and handed it to her.

"I gave it to someone else to hold," I said. "Told him if he didn't hear from me in a week to give you a call."

She read the back of the card that bore the name and phone number of that truck driver who gave me the ride. I told her about Afghanistan and how grateful he was for my book.

"You thought something like this might happen," she said, repeating my line.

"Well, not exactly like this," I said, repeating hers.

She smiled. "Three bites," she said.

I shrugged. Then she took the papers from me and reached around and put them with the evidence on the back seat. I got out of the car then, but didn't close the door.

"So I guess you'll be in touch?" I asked, bending over to look at her.

"Oh yes," she told me. I nodded, and then closed the door. She powered the window down. "I'm looking forward to reading that book," she said.

I laughed and then watched as she powered the window back up and drove off.

Out of reflex, I turned around to survey the neighborhood, half expecting those men to be sitting in a car watching me, instead of turning cold in that warehouse down in Queens.

I didn't stay out there very long. Instead, I went straight up to my unit and poured myself the last of that bottle of Bushmills. Then I sat down in my favorite chair and turned on the television. It was tuned to ESPN where the hosts were going on about the Final Four. Which prompted me to sift through the items on my coffee table to try and find the bracket that I had filled out just eighteen days before. When I finally found it, I discovered that I had correctly picked all four of the teams that made the semi-finals. In more than twenty years of following the tournament, I'd never done that. Ever. Even better, I had correctly picked the two teams that would be playing for the championship the next night. I sat back and had a big laugh about that.

Not long after, I fell asleep in that same chair, the TV still on, wondering whether I would even bother to watch the title game, let alone care who won.

CHAPTER 31

SMART

A MERE TEN days later, thanks almost exclusively to Detective O'Connell's video footage, along with those guns used by the men in suits, we were able to reach a form of detente with the group that employed my two pursuers. More specifically, with the man who told us that he was representing the government on their behalf. We found him by calling the phone number that the older of the two men in suits had given to Warren to vouch for his credentials. Once Detective O'Connell laid out the full story to him, he immediately agreed to meet with us.

He told us his name was "Tom Jones." We got a big chuckle out of that, his using the name of the famous Welsh singer and sex symbol from the 1960s to hide his real identity. Detective O'Connell reminded me that it was also the name of the protagonist in one of the earliest English novels and that he could have had that in mind when he chose it. Whatever his inspiration, he never told us who he really was or who he represented or what part of the government direct-deposited his checks. However, a video call with the U.S. Attorney for the District of Columbia confirmed that "Mr. Jones" was indeed empowered to make a deal on behalf of the federal government.

To avoid any possible surprises, we insisted that the meeting take place at state police headquarters in Albany, a building that housed more than a hundred law enforcement officials. Mr. Jones agreed without objection. His only stipulation was that we limit attendance at the get-together to the three of us, along with the superintendent of the state police, so that we could all be assured that we were negotiating at the highest levels, while at the same time limiting who was privy to what had taken place in the previous four weeks.

Within a minute of the meeting starting, Jones admitted that the two men who had been assigned the task of recovering the list and those papers had "greatly overstepped their authority." While they were permitted to access multiple federal and state databases to find me, and were definitely tasked with purchasing my silence with another dose of that drug, they were never cleared to use deadly force on me or anyone else. He then informed us that the Samoan was currently under arrest out in Arkansas for my brother's death. It was being described as an armed robbery gone bad, felony murder being the charge, since the "heart attack" occurred in the course of the felony, making it murder in the eyes of the law as much as if he had been shot. Apparently, they never found the injection site or failed to even look. However, after an anonymous tip, they found the Samoan's fingerprints both on the baton and elsewhere in the house, thereby placing him at the scene. And since he was strictly a subcontractor and had no idea who he was working for, he was no threat to reveal anything about the drug program to the police out there or anywhere else for that matter.

Because of the gunning down of three members of the New York State Police, all verified by the video and the ballistics and fingerprints, there was little that Jones could say in response to our demand that the program be discontinued. We also insisted that the remaining people on the list, as well as others like them, be left in peace. Unfortunately, that also meant that they were to be left in the dark. After some debate, it was agreed that it would serve no useful purpose to inform them of what had happened to them as children.

And while it was understood that they might continue to suffer an erosion of their skills, that was deemed to be a far better option than to try and explain why it was happening to them in the first place.

On that note, Jones agreed with us that all of the drug should be destroyed, as soon as it could be reasonably arranged, with the detective and superintendent invited to witness it at some agreed-upon time and place. Along with all the other evidence, the original papers and however much of the drug that was still in that vial would remain in the custody of the state police, stored in a secured location, while the videos that the detective shot would continue to be held by both the state police and the detective's former roommate. All of it would immediately be released to the public if the agreement was in any way breached by Mr. Jones or whomever he was working for, said breach to include any harm coming to me and/or the detective.

"Which will never happen," Jones told us. "This has already gone too far. We believe it's best that this never come to the attention of those in the world who we don't consider to be our friends." That no doubt meant the Russians, the Chinese and God-knows-who in the Middle East. As much as my instinct told me I shouldn't trust him or anyone he was associated with, the threat to national security seemed sufficiently real, leading me to believe that the order to shut down the program had to have originated from an even higher place than the U.S. Attorney for the District of Columbia. Probably the highest.

The superintendent and Jones also agreed to concoct a story that Warren and the two New York State detectives had accidentally stumbled upon the site of a drug lab operated by a gang out in western Massachusetts where "a shoot-out had occurred." This fable allowed them to be buried with honors befitting their heroic status. As to why they were there in the first place, it was decided that they were going to meet with some Massachusetts authorities about a joint training exercise and that a "communication error" had led them to the wrong location. I found that all a bit hard to swallow, but the story was never to appear in any public record, only in police files that would be sealed due to "an undercover investigation" into that fictional gang's enterprise.

Finally, I was cleared of all suspicion regarding the widow's death, an autopsy report revealing that she had died of a "sudden heart attack," with no foul play involved. At my request, the state police released a statement to that effect, which appeared everywhere in the print, broadcast and on-line media. That all of those law enforcement agencies could lie so effortlessly was troubling to me, and I wondered how much more fiction like that I might have accepted from them and others like them over the years.

Once our meeting was concluded and the agreement finalized, I said my goodbyes to the detective, thanking her in the most sincere manner for both believing in me and saving my life. I then made the three-hour drive back to Connecticut, where I planned to spend some considerable time trying to figure out what to do with the rest of my life.

The first thing on my agenda was to settle the matter of that book that had been hanging over my head for so long. That turned out to be the easiest decision of all: I simply returned the advance to the publisher, every penny of it, along with the sincerest of apologies. They seemed happy to receive both, and I was relieved to finally be free of the obligation. When I informed Gloria of that decision over a lunch at the college a few days later, she was disappointed, no doubt wishing that I would go back to my earlier work. However, I told her that it was my intention to take up something new, something even better perhaps. Of course, I never told her what had happened to me or all that I discovered about myself in those weeks I was away but, as always, she didn't pry. She simply wished me the best, and offered to help me out on weekends, should I ever need her. I thanked her and told her that I'd keep it in mind. I don't think either of us believed it would ever happen, but I know that it felt good for me to hear it. And probably for her to say, as well.

After several nights of restless sleep, struggling to come up with some new plan for my life, it finally dawned on me that I actually had something far more important to do than settle on another line of work. It was something offered to me near the end of my journey, before I was told the secret of my past. Something that I hoped would help me atone for all the arrogant ways of my past. And at the same time, it was something I never thought I'd have a chance at again after my divorce: to be part of a family once more. If anything positive had come out of those three weeks, it was my coming to learn that I have a niece who looks up to me and is in need of a male influence in her life, particularly after the loss of her father. It's humbling to think that I could actually be the one to help guide her as she moves forward on the path from childhood to adult. Fortunately for both of us, I have the time and money to do that, and I intend to work as diligently at that as anything I have ever done in the past.

I was worried at first that her mother would refuse to allow me take on that role after what happened that night in Vermont, and I wasn't certain that she'd ever believe me when I told her that the threat to them was gone for good, particularly since I couldn't go into any details as to why that was. However, after I shared those concerns with Detective O'Connell over the phone one night, she offered to pay her a visit. And I gratefully accepted the offer, even though I wasn't sure what the detective could say that might convince her. Nevertheless, whatever she said, it must have worked, seeing as my sister-in-law called me the very next day and invited me to come up and stay with them for a while.

"A little longer than the last time," she added.

I plan to make my first trip up there sometime in the next week. I imagine that when I get there, we'll have more than one discussion about things like intelligence and ability and aptitude. I'll probably be asked a lot of questions that I won't know the answer to. Hell, after what I was told by that man down in that abandoned warehouse a month ago, I'm still struggling with the simplest of questions: who am I? Am I still that person who wrote all those books and accomplished all that I did over the years? Obviously, on some level I must be. But then, was that the "me" that originally came into this world or was I some early form of artificial intelligence, modified like one of those ordinary Toyota sedans that automobile enthusiasts often soup up to race-level performance?

Which raises an even simpler question: what is thing we call "smart?" Where does it come from? Is it like curly hair or blue eyes, purely the product of the DNA passed down from our parents? Something precise and permanent? Or is it a thing that can be honed over the years by lots of study and hard work?

All I know is that I have worn the label of "smart" my whole life. In truth, I've grown as accustomed to it as I have to my own face in the mirror every day. So I wonder what it will be like should it turn out that the man in the suit was right and my skills continue to erode.

I suppose I'll eventually find out. And, when I do, I'm confident that I'll be able to live with whatever the consequences might be. Until then, I'm comforted by the fact that, despite whatever decline may have already taken place, I did exactly what Doctor Condon had asked me to do when he assigned me that task. And in doing so, I've come to believe that there might have been something else he wanted me to discover along the way. Something that I have indeed learned in these past few weeks.

That like my niece and my brother and my sister-in-law and that truck driver and just about everyone else on this planet...

I'm smart enough.

Acknowledgements

The author would like to thank the following: Kate Flora for a terrific edit and much-needed "nit-picking;" John Clark for a great read and helpful suggestions; my beta readers Gary Tanguay and Jeff Ritchie for finding things I never would have and offering much-needed advice; fellow writers Alan Glynn and Eric Rickstad for their generous support (buy their books and read them - you'll thank me); and, finally, but most importantly, my wife for being the very model of what a supportive partner is and should be.

Reading Group Suggested Questions

1. Why do you think the author chose not to give the main character a name?
2. What other characters did he also not name? Why do you think he did that?
3. Which characters did he chose to name and what do you think was the reason for each of those?
4. Would you have made the same decision as the main character in that abandoned warehouse down in Queens?
5. Would you have made the same decisions as the main character with respect to everything that happened after the events that took place in that warehouse?
6. Do you believe that what was revealed to the main character down in that abandoned warehouse in Queens is something that could have really happened?
7. Who is your favorite character and why?
8. Do you agree with the main character's statement in the final line of the book?
9. What was the biggest surprise to you in the book?
10. Would you have made the same decision as the main character did after returning to the widow's house the second time?

About the Author

Drew Yanno was born and raised in upstate New York and received both his undergraduate and law degrees at Syracuse University.

After serving a clerkship in Albany, NY, Drew joined a large law firm in Boston where he worked for several years before founding his own firm. Throughout that time, he also taught law in the Carroll School of Management at Boston College.

In 1993, Drew began writing screenplays. Two years later, his screenplay *No Safe Haven* was purchased by Universal Studios after an eight hour bidding war. Drew went on to write a number of screenplays, both on spec and for hire. In 2000, he founded the screenwriting program in the Film Department at Boston College where he taught for eleven years.

His first novel, **In the Matter of Michael Vogel** was published in 2013 and was named one of the best books of 2013 by Digital Books Today.

If you would like to share your thoughts about **The Smart One**, feel free to write Drew at drew@drewyanno.com. You can also follow him on Twitter at @drewyanno.

62152340R00191

Made in the USA
Lexington, KY
30 March 2017